Starring Me

Krista McGee

Thomas Nelson
Since 1798

NASHVILLE DALLAS MEXICO CITY RIO DE JANEIRO

To my grandmother, Marie Brush,
thank you for your constant love and support.
And to my daughter, Emma Marie,
the most amazing birthday present ever.

Published in Nashville, Tennessee, by Thomas Nelson. Thomas Nelson is a registered trademark of Thomas Nelson, Inc.

Published in association with literary agent Jenni Burke of D.C. Jacobson & Associates, an Author Management Company, www.DCJacobson.com.

Thomas Nelson, Inc., titles may be purchased in bulk for educational, business, fund-raising, or sales promotional use. For information, please e-mail SpecialMarkets@ThomasNelson.com.

Publisher's Note: This novel is a work of fiction. Names, characters, places, and incidents are either products of the author's imagination or used fictitiously. All characters are fictional, and any similarity to people living or dead is purely coincidental.

Library of Congress Cataloging-in-Publication Data

McGee, Krista, 1975–
Starring me / by Krista McGee.
p. cm.
Summary: Will seventeen-year-old Kara have to give up her acting dream when she learns that her audition for a television variety show starring a big-time teen celebrity hinges on her relationship with God?
ISBN 978-1-4016-8489-1 (pbk.)
[1. Auditions—Fiction. 2. Acting—Fiction. 3. Television—Production and direction—Fiction. 4. Christian life—Fiction.] I. Title.
PZ7.M4784628St 2012
[Fic]—dc23 2012006508

Printed in the United States of America

12 13 14 15 16 17 QG 6 5 4 3 2 1

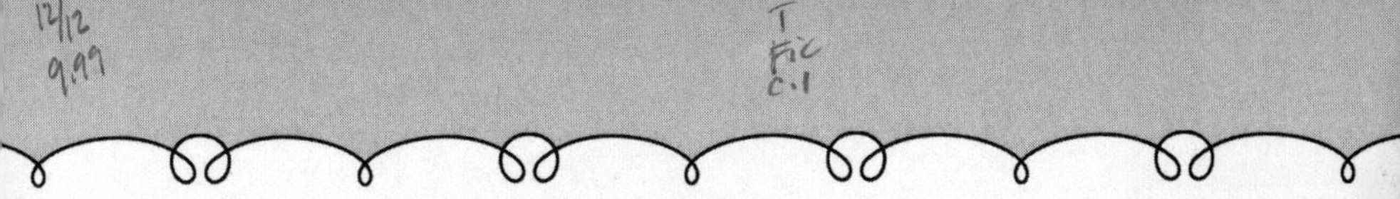

Chapter 1

"I want my parents to pick my costar." Chad Beacon, current pop sensation, sank back in the leather chair.

Chad watched as the eight network executives sitting at the conference table stopped everything—stopped taking notes, stopped texting, stopped moving.

"Excuse me?" Samuel Dillard, the head of the new teen network, leaned closer to the table, his eyes tiny slits.

Dad folded his arms. "If our son is going to be spending several hours every day with a young woman, we want to decide who she'll be. We want to make sure she shares our faith and our values."

Dillard placed his palms flat on the mahogany table. "Mr. Beacon. We appreciate that you want to be involved in your son's career. We applaud that."

The others nodded their agreement before Dillard continued. "But this is a brand-new show on a brand-new network. We want Chad because he already has a fan base, but—"

"Quite a large one," Mom interrupted. "After winning *America's Next Star,* Chad's popularity has been growing. More than we know how to handle, to be honest."

"That's for sure." Chad thought back to his time on the popular TV show. Two years before, he had competed against hundreds of other young people to be chosen by millions of viewers as *America's Next Star.*

"You wouldn't believe how many shirts I've had ripped off—not that I wanted that. I tried to stop them, but holding one side of my T-shirt while a Hulk-sized girl is on the other, well . . ." Chad looked at his parents, both sending him "Shut your big mouth" stares. "Not the time for this conversation, right. Sorry. Go on."

"Actually, this is exactly why we're willing to discuss this show in the first place," Dad said. "Chad is being pulled in directions we don't want him pulled in. He's just seventeen. We don't want him to give up his childhood yet."

"But we do want him to be able to do what he loves." Mom placed a hand on her husband's arm.

Dillard relaxed back in his seat. "Then we want the same thing. Chad is a talented young man—we've seen that. And I know his albums have sold well."

"Quite well," Dad affirmed. "But he wants to explore his other gifts as well."

"That's where we agree wholeheartedly. Those of us here at Teens Rock want him to be able to use all of his talents. Not just singing, but acting, comedy; we're even willing to give him creative license when we begin writing the episodes."

"Now that's what I'm talking about." Chad spoke

directly to Mr. Dillard. "Singing is fun, don't get me wrong. But I don't want to be *just* a singer."

"And we don't want that either, Chad." Mr. Dillard's broad smile made him look like the Joker from *Batman*.

"We appreciate that," Mom said. "But Chad is still a teenage boy. The wrong kind of girl playing opposite him in this show could create more temptation than we want him to have to face."

"Perhaps." Dillard shrugged. "But we are interested in putting together a show that will be successful. You'll be around the set. You can help him if his costar is too . . . tempting."

"This is nonnegotiable." Dad shook his head. "We choose his costar or Chad will not do the show."

"This network may be new"—Dillard's voice echoed in the cavernous conference room—"but we're financed by one of the largest networks in the country. We've already got producers and actors lined up at our door. Advertisers are battling each other for sponsorship privileges."

"We've done our homework." Dad placed his elbows on the table, hands clasped. "We know all about Teens Rock. We like the idea of it. But we also know you need a popular young teen star to help get this show off the ground."

"Look." Dillard seemed like a deflated balloon. "We always do a thorough background check on the girls who audition."

Another executive turned toward the Beacons. "And we have a zero-tolerance policy for drugs and alcohol already in place."

"That's wonderful," Dad said. "But we want more than

a young woman without a criminal background who isn't addicted to drugs or alcohol."

"That's not what she was implying."

"We're not trying to be difficult, Mr. Dillard." Mom looked at him and smiled. "But we take our responsibility as parents very seriously."

"That's an understatement." Chad winked at his mom.

"Enough." Dillard lifted his hand. "We understand your position. I think we need a few minutes to discuss it. Privately."

Samuel Dillard stood and walked to the large door, ushering Chad and his parents out of the room. They walked back to the lobby of the Teens Rock office.

"So, what do you think they'll decide?" Chad asked. The lobby was decorated to look like what he imagined the overpriced designers believed was the bedroom of an American teenager: splatter paint on the walls, retro furniture, and gumball machines sitting on a lime green shag rug.

Dad eased himself into an oversized beanbag chair and groaned. "I hope they'll decide to get real furniture in here. Beanbags and sixty-eight-year-old bones do not mix."

Mom held her husband's hand as he helped her into another of the beanbag chairs.

Chad looked at his parents. When Bill Beacon met and married Maria over forty years before, they became Christians and committed to raise a large family that loved their Savior. But that dream faded as years went by and Maria couldn't conceive. Finally, when the couple thought their chances were gone, God gave them a son.

"We have prayed over this decision," Mom said. "If God wants you on that show, you know he'll work it out."

Chad leaned against the wall beside them. "And what if he doesn't?"

"Sweetie." Mom reached for his hand. "Do you want it if God doesn't?"

"But this show sounds so perfect. I mean, come on, a teen version of *Saturday Night Live*? Me and the mystery girl hosting, with teen stars joining the cast every week for different sketches? I'd get to sing, act, even write some of my own stuff. I can't think of anything that would be more fun than that."

"You didn't answer my question."

"Mom." Chad groaned. "I want God to want this."

"I know." Mom gave him a sympathetic smile. "And God knows your heart. Even better than you do. And if this doesn't work out, that just means he has something even greater planned for you."

"So you don't think it's going to work out?"

"I don't know what's going to happen." Mom squeezed his hand before releasing it. "But if they come back and insist on their own choice for your costar, then we'll have to walk away."

"I'm not a kid." Chad ran a hand through his blond hair. "I was with tons of girls on *America's Next Star,* and hardly any of them were Christians. I handled that all right."

"Yes." Dad joined the conversation. "But we've discussed that before. That show was just for a couple months. And you were competing against them, not working with them every day."

"And you were only fifteen." Mom leveled her hazel eyes at her son.

"So I had fewer hormones at fifteen?"

"You better watch the way you speak to your mother, Chad." Dad frowned.

"Sorry." Chad closed his eyes. "I know you think this girl and I may end up dating."

"We didn't say that," Mom said.

"But you think it, right?"

"Well." Mom looked to Dad. "It's only natural that you might be attracted to one another."

"But even if you don't date her," Dad said, "she will influence you, and you her."

Having spent the last two years adjusting to fame—not being able to hang out at the mall with friends or even walk into a restaurant without being accosted—the thought of having a friend to be with every day and a place where he could be himself was exciting. *Oh, God, I really want to do this show.*

Mom's cell phone chimed Beethoven's Fifth, interrupting their conversation.

"Hello . . . Flora? Slow down . . . You ran over a squirrel? Okay . . . okay . . . No, it's fine . . . No, I don't think you should call 911 . . . *No,* do not try to pick it up." Mom stifled a laugh. "Flora, it happens to all of us. It's fine, really . . . His tail is twitching?"

Dad grabbed the phone from his wife's hand. "Get back in the car and run over it again . . . Of course you can. It's going to die anyway. Flora, it's no big deal. It's a squirrel . . . No, I can't come over there. We're at a meeting downtown." Dad rolled his eyes. "You're where? . . . No, I don't know anyone in Winter Park. What are you doing there? Are you sitting on the side of the road? . . . You're in the middle of the road? . . . Get back in your car . . . Flora, get in the car. If you keep standing there, you're going to get run over yourself. It'll be fine."

Dad pulled the phone away from his ear as Flora let out a scream that sounded like a bad opera singer's high C. "Someone just ran over it? Well then, all's well that ends well . . . I thought you said anytime is a good time for Shakespeare? . . . Yes, go get a smoothie. That's a great idea. Bye."

Chad looked at his father and laughed. "So Flora ran over a squirrel in Winter Park?"

"That she did." Dad leaned back in the beanbag chair.

"And why did she go out to Winter Park?" Chad asked.

"Because a store there sells organic wheatgrass."

"Of course."

If the dictionary had pictures, Flora Lopez's head shot would be right beside the word *eccentric*. With ever-changing hair and retro-hippy fashions, the funky fifty-year-old was a walking contradiction. She was a mature Christian with an unparalleled work ethic. She didn't even need a planner. Flora's photographic memory kept the entire Beacon family on time and on schedule. Her quirks kept them in stitches.

"Twenty years with us, and that woman can still surprise me." Dad shook his head.

Chad laughed. "That's why we love her."

"Mr. and Mrs. Beacon, Chad." Samuel Dillard stepped into the lobby. He looked like he had just eaten an entire lemon—peel and all. "You may come back in."

Chad held a hand out, first to his mother, then to his

father, as they fought their way out of the beanbag chairs. Mr. Dillard walked away.

"He didn't look happy," Chad whispered to his mother.

"That may bode well for us." Mom smiled.

The threesome walked into the conference room, and Mr. Dillard returned to his seat at the head of the table.

No one is looking at us. Every spoonful of Chad's corn chowder from lunch inched its way up his esophagus. *Why aren't they looking at us?*

"Chad," Mr. Dillard said, making a one-syllable name impossibly long. "Before we tell you our decision, we want to know what *you* really want. Not what your parents want."

Chad looked from Mr. Dillard to the other executives. "Excuse me?"

"You'll be eighteen in, what, six months?"

"November 25th, sir. That's six months, twenty-one days." Chad looked at his watch. "And seven hours. But who's counting?"

Chad's laughter echoed in the room. No one else joined in.

"We're counting." Mr. Dillard pressed his wide lips together. "When you're eighteen, you will no longer be bound by the restrictions of your parents. You will be an adult. We are willing to wait until then to begin the show. We can start taping after the New Year and have a summer start date. How does that sound?"

Chad looked from the network executives to his parents. "It sounds like you don't like what my parents had to say. Which I understand. I feel the same way sometimes."

"I'm sure you do." Mr. Dillard's Joker smile made another appearance.

"I may be fairly new to the business, but I do know that, no matter what, someone is going to be around telling me what to do. Parents, agents, producers, sponsors." Chad watched Dillard's smile melt. "And everybody says they want what's best for me. But only my parents have the track record to prove it."

Samuel Dillard cleared his throat. "Chad, I certainly respect your parents. And I believe they believe they have your best interests at heart, but—"

"You believe we *believe* we have Chad's best interests at heart? What is that supposed to mean?" Dad leaned forward in his seat.

"It means that we believe you think being overprotective is what's best for him."

"Overprotective?" Mom frowned at Mr. Dillard. "He's just spent the last two years on television and in recording studios, mingling with all sorts of people."

"With you right by his side." Mr. Dillard folded his arms. "You homeschool him, right? You don't let him out of your sight, don't let him make his own decisions?"

Chad had heard enough. He stood. "I'll make my own decision right now. I'm out of here. You think you can belittle my parents—and me—and I'd still want to work with you?"

The female executive next to Chad put her hand on his arm. "We're on your side, Chad. We want you to grow as an artist. We want to give you wings. You are a good son. I applaud your loyalty. But you've got to do what's right for you now."

Chad glared at the group of executives. "And you think what's right for me is waiting so you can pick my costar instead of my parents? So you can have the final say in what's going on? How is that what's right for me?"

Mr. Dillard motioned for Chad to sit. He glanced around the room. An unspoken message was sent from the other seven executives to Mr. Dillard. That man sat up, his hands emphasizing his words. "Fine. You win."

The disappointment Chad had felt at Dillard's behavior was replaced with excitement. He was really going to get to do this.

"But the costar has to be talented. This is a sketch comedy show, and this young woman will be one of the two main stars. She has to be able to play different roles, speak in different accents. Sing. She needs to have had some experience. I'm not going to allow you to bring some little choir girl in here. We're investing too much in this show for that."

"I never said we wanted a choir girl," Dad said. "But we do want a Christian girl."

Mr. Dillard sighed. "All right, how about this? We have our casting agency hold auditions and narrow the pool down to ten. We're not concerned with what religion those ten are, just that they're talented enough to star in this show."

"All right." His father nodded.

"Those ten come down here to Orlando for a few weeks of intense auditions." Dillard made air quotes on the words *intense auditions*.

"And . . . ?" Mom asked.

"And you guys watch those auditions. You can watch the tapes of their screen tests, see which ones you like."

"Why can't we just talk to them personally?" Dad asked.

"We don't want anyone knowing Chad is starring in

this show yet. He's a hot commodity." Dillard arched his eyebrows. "We don't want this news to leak out. We want to make a huge announcement, get it to the big magazines and talk shows at the same time, right before we're ready to launch the show."

"I don't know . . ."

"Actually, Mom." Chad touched her arm. "I like it."

"Really? Why?"

"We get a chance to see the girls for who they really are. You know how some girls act when they know I'm around."

Dad nodded. "Good point. If these girls know they're not just competing for a role on a show, but a role costarring with you on a show, that's going to be big news. They'll be acting all the time, trying to get the part."

"But how much can we really learn about the girls by watching their screen tests?" Mom asked.

Mr. Dillard scratched his head. "How about this: We tape the audition process. All of it—the screen tests, the girls sitting around together, getting to know each other, working on sketches of their own. You could see more of them and we could turn that into a TV show that could be aired in the weeks leading up to the first show."

The woman next to Chad jumped in. "That's a great idea. You could build up the suspense, give the girl a fan base before we even start."

"And if we keep our October start date, we can get the shots of the auditions edited and ready to go in September. One show a week, leading up to the big reveal at the end. That, alongside the media blitz we have planned—" Dillard slapped his hand on the table, causing sheets of paper to fly upward. "I love it. This is brilliant. We'll start out with an audience of millions."

Dad lifted a hand to halt the merriment. "But I still don't see how watching girls audition allows us to really get to know their characters."

"Come on, work with me, Beacon," Dillard growled.

"Flora." Chad grinned.

The network executives and Chad's parents all looked at him like he had grown a second head.

"Sorry," Chad said. "Flora is our assistant. She's like family. But she's never been on TV with us."

"Absolutely refuses to even have her picture taken," Dad said.

"Exactly." Chad's voice rose as he continued. "None of the girls would know she's connected with us. She could hang around and get to know them, and then she could give us her firsthand impressions."

"That's a great idea," Mom said.

"How do you expect to explain her presence with the girls?" Mr. Dillard asked. "Just have some random woman walking around behind them? That won't work."

Mom leaned forward. "The girls will be in a house together, right? While they're auditioning?"

"Yes, I suppose," Mr. Dillard muttered.

"Then Flora could be the housemother. You'll need an adult supervising them anyway. I can vouch for Flora. She's been working for us for more than twenty years."

Mr. Dillard looked around the table. "I guess that could work. But are you sure she'll want to do it?"

Chad smiled. "Flora loves trying new things."

"That she does." Dad laughed.

"Well, all right. We'll get the auditions under way. Give us a month or so to narrow down our top ten, then we'll bring your Flora in."

"Okay, Mr. Dillard." Chad shook the executive's large hand. "I think this is the beginning of a beautiful friendship."

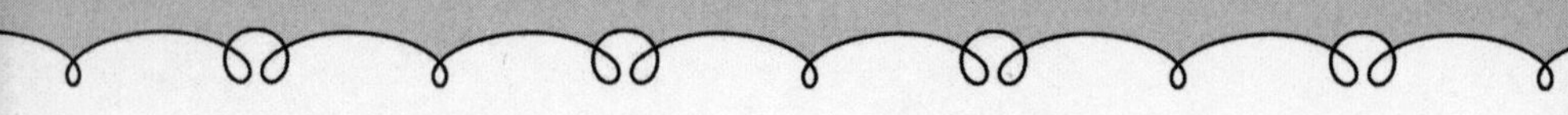

Chapter 2

Seventeen-year-old Kara McKormick hung up the phone and screamed. And screamed. Her mother came in from the backyard, screaming.

"Kara." She panted, slamming the back door as she rushed to her daughter. "What's the matter? What happened? Are you all right?"

"Yes, I—" Kara screamed again, hugging her mother and dancing around the kitchen. "Ma, you'll never believe this." Kara started to scream again, and her mother placed a firm hand over her mouth.

"Kara, my ears are bleeding, you're so loud. Take a deep breath and tell me what's got you so excited."

She removed her hand from Kara's mouth with a warning look. Kara bit her tongue and jumped up and down. "Okay, Ma," she said, still jumping. "I have been chosen to . . ." Kara stopped midsentence, her mouth frozen.

"Kara Elaine McKormick." Hands on her hips, she stared

at her daughter. "Do not scream. What are you, five? Just tell me. Quickly, before you explode."

"I get to audition for a TV show that's just for teens on a network that lets its stars help write the scripts and the songs and plan the publicity. And this show is going to be the first one, the big one, and they're investing lots of money into it, so it'll be huge and they want me to audition. Me, Ma." Kara stopped to breathe—something she hadn't done the entire time she had been explaining the phone call to her mother.

"You're auditioning for a show?"

"Not just any show, Ma," Kara said, still catching her breath. "A huge show. Major."

"That's great, sweetie." Her mother opened the fridge and pulled out a can of soda. "So when are the auditions?"

"I don't know."

"Where are they?"

"I don't know." Kara grabbed the countertop to keep herself steady. "I was so excited, I didn't ask. Oh no. This is terrible. It's all over. Why didn't I ask?"

Ma opened the soda and handed it to Kara. "Think back to the phone call. Who called?"

"Okay, it was, um, it was a man . . ."

"All right, a man called and he said . . . ?"

"He saw me on *The Book of Love* and thought I had spunk."

"He's right about that." Ma rubbed Kara's back. "Then what did he say?"

"He asked if I was interested in auditioning. I said yes. He asked if I could come into the city for auditions. I said yes."

"Did he say when to come in or where?" Ma continued rubbing Kara's back and Kara took a deep breath. "He said he'd call with more information in the next few days."

"All right, then." Her mother squeezed Kara's shoulders. "I knew we'd figure it out. So we'll wait for the phone call and get you into the city. You'll audition, they'll love you, and you'll be on TV."

"Ma." Kara shook her head, her long auburn ponytail swaying. "It's not that easy."

"People already love you." Ma reached up to push a stray lock of hair from Kara's cheek. "How could they not?"

"I need to call Addy."

Addy Davidson and Kara had been roommates on a reality TV show just a few months before. Neither had won the competition to be the president's son's prom date, but they had come away from the experience close friends. Addy, while not winning the date, had won the boy, and Kara enjoyed teasing her friend about the budding romance. Addy denied any such thing, saying that she and Jonathon were still "praying" about their relationship. But Kara knew better. She also knew that Addy would be thrilled about this audition. Kara picked up her cell phone and punched in Addy's number.

"What do I want more than anything in the world?" Kara asked as soon as Addy finished her "Hello."

"Nice to talk to you too, Kara." Addy laughed. "And yes, I'm doing just fine, thanks for asking."

"No time for chitchat. Careers are being forged. Lives are being changed. Destinies are unfolding."

"What was the question again?"

Kara could imagine Addy's sideways smile as she spoke. "What do I want more than anything else in the world?"

"To come visit me in Florida."

"Addy Davidson. This is no time for sarcasm."

"All right, fine." Addy cleared her throat. "My friend Kara McKormick wants, more than anything in the world, to be an actress."

"You are correct, madam. And your friend is getting that opportunity because she has been chosen to audition for a new teen variety show on a brand-new teen network."

"And my friend is talking in third person because . . . ?" Addy asked.

"Did you hear me? I'm auditioning for a TV show. A teen show. Me." Kara jumped up and down again. Her mother, rolling out pizza dough on the counter, shook her head, smiling.

"That is fantastic, Kara," Addy said. "I'm happy for you."

She walked to the alcove beside the kitchen and sat in front of the computer, typing *New Teen Television Network* into the search engine.

"It's a variety show, Addy. Comedy—which you know is my specialty."

"Definitely."

"Also some music and dancing and . . ." Kara stopped and screamed.

"Ouch."

"Sorry, but I just typed in information about the network. And guess what I found?"

"They're looking for a tall redhead to star on its variety show?"

"Well, that, of course, goes without saying." Kara laughed. "But guess where this new network is located?"

"Kalamazoo?"

"Addy." Kara's "mom" voice took over. "Don't make me put you in time-out. A real guess."

"Tampa."

"Close."

"Really?"

"Really," Kara said. "Orlando. The network is in Orlando. How far is that from you?"

"About an hour. I could see you all the time."

"If I make it." Kara's voice returned to its normal decibel level. "There are probably a million girls trying out."

"But there's only one Kara McKormick."

"That's true. I really want this. I mean really, really want it."

"I'll be praying it works out," Addy said.

"You know I don't believe in that." Kara walked to her bedroom.

"That's all right. I do."

"Positive thoughts are always good," Kara said. "You form yours into prayers, and mine will be directed toward the gods of television."

"Does the McKormick clan know yet?"

"Just Ma." Kara lay down on her bed. "But it won't take long. As soon as she tells Pop, the rest of my family will know within an hour."

Kara's large, blended family consisted of five older

siblings, four of whom were married with kids. They all lived on Long Island, and when they were all together—which occurred at least once a month—the house shook with noise and laughter.

"Well, I better let you go enjoy the silence. It won't last long."

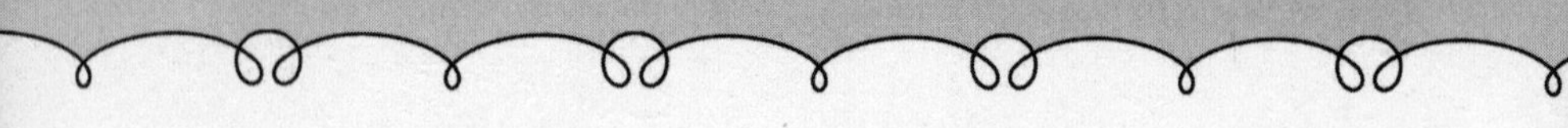

Chapter 3

"Mwuah, mwuah."

"Bbbbbbbbb, bbbbbbbbb."

"To sit in solemn silence in a dull, dark box . . ."

Ma looked at the throng of girls packed into the soundstage, then she looked at her daughter. "What are they doing, Kara?"

"Warming up. We learned this in acting class. You have to get all your facial muscles limber. It helps with enunciation and expression."

"It looks pretty silly to me."

Kara surveyed the mass of girls. *There must be five hundred girls here. They all look like they could star in a TV show. These girls have probably been acting since they were in diapers.*

"Kara, you're nervous." Ma looked at her with a frown. "I don't think I've ever seen you nervous."

"No, I'm fine. Don't worry about me. I've got this."

"Look over there." Ma pointed to a table with a Line 1 sign taped on its side. A dozen girls waited as two women scanned through sheaves of paper, handed out stickers, and pointed them to Line 2. "I guess that's where we start."

Kara and Ma stood behind a girl about Kara's age. *That can't be her mother.* Kara eyed the stunning twentysomething woman standing beside the girl.

"The audition starts right now," the woman whispered to the girl. "You've got to own it right from the start. Show them you aren't intimidated. Stand up straight, look them in the eye, and shake their hands. Make sure you thank them for the opportunity. But don't grovel."

An agent? Kara panicked. *She has an agent?*

Kara looked around the soundstage. *Am I the only loser who came with her mother? Everyone else has an agent or manager or, what is that, a whole entourage?*

Kara watched as the girls in front of her gave their names to the ladies at the table and received a number. A few girls were turned away.

"This is not a cattle call," one of the ladies at the table said. "You have to have been invited to this audition. You weren't."

The girl who had brought her agent along—or vice versa—walked away in tears.

"Go ahead, dear," Ma said when it was Kara's turn at the front table. "This is my daughter, Kara. She's the best. You're gonna love her."

"Ma." Kara's face burned. Her mother meant well, but she looked like an old lady, with her gray hair and her sensible shoes. All the other girls were with "power women." *And I'm with "super granny."*

She turned to the lady in front of her. "Kara McKormick. Kara with a *K*."

The lady flipped through a stack of papers with her perfectly manicured acrylics. "From *The Book of Love*, right?"

"Yes, ma'am." Kara smiled.

"I loved the monologue you performed during the talent competition. It was very funny." The woman highlighted Kara's name on the list and gave her a sticker with the number 414 on it. "I've got you down. Now go over to line two and get your script. Good luck."

Kara and Ma once again stood behind a young woman and her beautiful agent. The agent turned around. Her hair was brown with reddish highlights, and her makeup appeared professionally applied.

"I knew you looked familiar." She extended her hand to Kara. "Sharon Sanders. I followed *The Book of Love* closely. I assumed some other agent already snatched you up." The agent looked at Ma with a frown. "Obviously, I was wrong."

"My daughter doesn't need an agent. She's a teenager. All she needs is me and her father. That's what I told the other folks that called up, and that's what I'm telling you."

Kara turned to her mother. "What other folks, Ma?"

"Folks like her—agents who want you to make money for them. I've read about them in the magazines. Poor girls get sucked in by their lies and then leave their parents and end up on drugs." Ma glared at the agent. "You're not getting your hands on my Kara."

Kara looked from her mother to the agent, stunned. The agent smiled and pulled a card from her purse. "I understand your concern, Mrs. McKormick. There are some agents like that. But I believe in family. I hope to have many children someday. My agency involves parents in every aspect of the decision-making process. So if you change your mind, please give me a call."

Ma looked at the card as if it were a poisonous snake. The girl standing beside the agent looked at Kara as if *she* were the poisonous snake. Kara took the card, put it in her back pocket, and thanked the agent.

When they left the second line, Ma put a protective arm around Kara. "I want you to throw that card out. I don't care what she said. Those agents are bad news. I don't want you turning out like those girls in the magazines."

"But, Ma, she just wanted to help." Kara looked back at the agent. She was coaching her client, giving her hints, showing her how to stand and move her hands. "If I'm going to be an actress, I'll eventually have to get an agent."

"Who says?" Ma stood up straight.

"Everybody." Kara motioned around the room. "If I don't get a part on this show, will you let me get an agent?"

"You are too young to have an agent."

"I'm seventeen, Ma." Kara rolled her eyes. "And it's an agent, not a pimp."

"Kara McKormick." Ma lowered her voice. "Don't you say words like that. See, this is what I was talking about. You just have an agent's card and your mouth is already filthy."

"I've got to look over this script." Kara sighed, pointing to the black folder the man at the second table had given her. "And since I don't have an agent, you have to read with me."

The soundstage was packed, so Kara guided her mother to a corner where they could have a semblance of privacy while still being able to hear the loudspeaker announcing the numbers.

"I'm not good at the drama," Ma said. "Your pop should have come. He's better at that."

Kara laughed. "That's for sure. But Pop's at work, so you'll have to stand in." Kara opened the folder. "Sit next to me so we can read together. You're And and I'm But."

Ma looked over at her. "Excuse me?"

"Ma." Kara pointed to the first page. "The script. We're at Conjunction Malfunction, see? I'm the conjunction But."

"I don't know if I'm going to like this." Ma's gray curls shook.

Kara and her mother read through the script.

"That was perfect, sweetie." Ma pulled a pack of cheese crackers from her purse. "Want one? I brought some juice too." Ma reached back into her purse, dubbed "the corner market" by Kara's siblings.

"No, Ma." Kara pushed the crackers away. "That was just a read-through, so I'll know what the skit is about. Now I need to practice really saying the lines."

"What are you talking about?" Ma closed the magnetic latch on her purse. "You just said the lines."

"Yes, but I need to get into character. You know, try some different accents, choose which words to emphasize."

"You can't just say the words?"

"Where's the fun in that?" Kara looked over her lines again, trying to commit them to memory. "I love being able to create a character."

"But this is so silly." Ma glanced over Kara's shoulders.

"I love silly!" Kara said. "And I want to show the casting

directors I can play a character that's very different from who I am. You know, show that I'm versatile. This is a variety show. I'm thinking of maybe using a southern accent. What do you think?"

"Southern? You can do southern?"

"Why sure I can," Kara drawled, a perfect southern belle. "I just spent two months in Tennessee. I listened to those folks down there. I practiced talkin' like them. What do you think?"

Ma clapped. "I think you're perfect."

"Thanks, Ma." Kara looked at the script again. "But there's more than that. I need to be upset at the beginning. But I don't want to overdo it. The comedy is in making it believable. I need to really look like I'm upset. But I can't look too upset because it's a comedy."

"This is all very confusing." Ma waved her hands.

"Just keep reading the other lines."

"But I can't do the accent and the crying."

"That's all right, Ma. I'll do the acting. I just need to practice hearing the lines before mine so I know my cues."

"This is a lot of pressure, Kara. Maybe your father shoulda come."

Kara pulled the agent's card from her pocket. "I could always call Ms. Sanders."

Ma snatched the card from Kara's hand and threw it in her purse. "Fine. I'll read."

After reading through the script several times, Kara felt prepared. She had been able to memorize her lines and perfect her accent.

"Number 414?" a man with a bullhorn announced,

stepping out from behind a metal door at the back of the large room. "Number 414. You're up."

Kara hugged her mother and walked toward the door. *Look out, folks. Kara McKormick is in the house!*

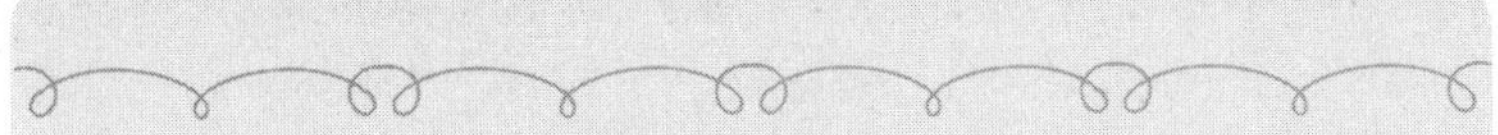

Conjunction Malfunction

(AND is standing by herself. BUT enters, crying.)

BUT: Why do I even bother?

AND: (Overly cheerful) Good morning. Beautiful day.

BUT: No.

AND: What?

BUT: (Crosses to stage left) No, it's not a beautiful day. It's never a beautiful day. Sometimes it starts out as a beautiful day, but . . .

AND: (Follows BUT) But what?

BUT: That's me. I'm BUT. My job is to ruin people's days.

AND: I don't understand.

BUT: (Still crying) Of course you don't. I know you. You're AND. Everybody loves you. You make people happy. It's a beautiful day AND the sun is shining. Her boyfriend gave her flowers AND candy.

AND: Let's go the store AND get some new clothes. You're right. I do make people happy. But . . .

BUT: Exactly.

AND: I didn't even finish my sentence.

BUT: You didn't have to. It always ends with something negative. I'd like to go shopping, BUT I can't. I'd like to go out with you, BUT you're too ugly. I'd like to give you an A on the math test, BUT you missed

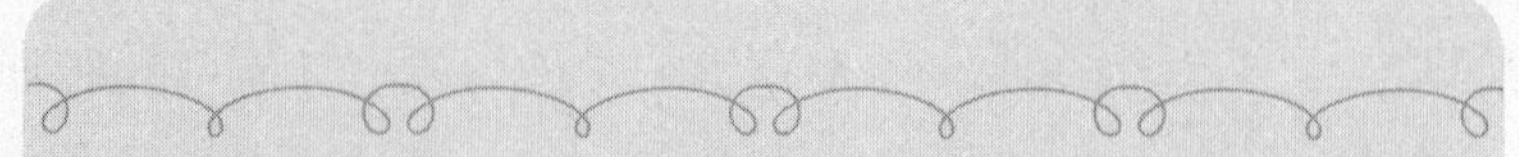

every question. People hear my name and they cringe. I'm like a disease. (Sits)

AND: I never thought of it that way.

BUT: Of course you didn't. You're AND. People hear your name and they get excited. They know they're getting more.

AND: That's true. People do love me. You know, just this morning, a man used me to tell his kids they were going to Disney World AND on a cruise.

BUT: Do you know what I was used for this morning? "I just graded your final exam. I'm sorry, BUT you got an F."

AND: That's terrible.

BUT: I know.

AND: Don't you ever get to say anything nice?

BUT: No.

AND: Wow. That must be terrible.

BUT: Thanks.

AND: No, really. I'd hate that. To be hated and dreaded. How awful.

BUT: (Stands) What did you just say?

AND: I said I'd hate that.

BUT: After that.

AND: To be hated and dreaded. How awful.

BUT: (Grabs AND's shoulders) You said "and."

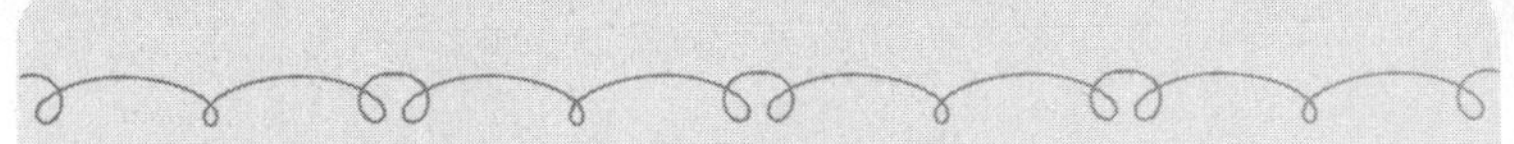

AND: So?

BUT: It was bad. To be hated AND dreaded. You made it worse by using "and."

AND: (Crosses to stage right) Wait, no—I make people happy.

BUT: (Follows AND) AND sad.

AND: But—

BUT: Yes!

AND: What?

BUT: You were about to use me for something positive.

AND: What?

BUT: I said you make people sad, and you said "but." BUT I also make people happy. You failed the test, BUT I can give you extra credit. I wanted to break up with you, BUT I couldn't because I love you too much.

AND: AND you are my soul mate AND you complete me . . .

BUT: AND you have bad breath, AND this test is worth half your grade, AND you'll never be able to play basketball again, AND—

AND: (Screams) Stop it! Stop it! You made your point. (AND cries) Why do I even bother? I'm leaving.

BUT: Good-bye, then. (AND leaves) It really is a beautiful day.

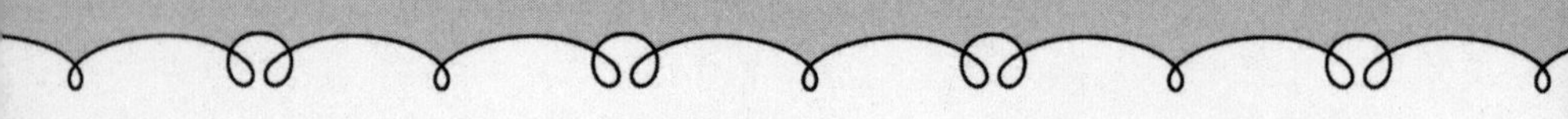

Chapter 4

Sit down and tell me all about it." Pop motioned for Kara to join him at the table. "Ruthie, got some more of those meatballs? I could use a second helping."

"Pop." Kara watched as her mother spooned several meatballs onto her father's plate. "You know the doctor said you need to be careful with your cholesterol. Why don't you have some salad? Or some fruit? We picked up a huge watermelon today at the market."

"Let me see. Watermelon or meatballs?" Pop scratched his head. "I think I'll take meatballs."

"And your cholesterol?"

"I'll have the watermelon for dessert," Pop said. "Then it'll all be even."

"All right, Pop. Whatever you say."

"That's more like it. Now, tell me about the auditions."

"They were long." Ma sat down with her plate of pasta.

"That, I know," Pop said. "You two didn't come in until, what, midnight?"

"We didn't pull out of that studio until ten o'clock," Ma

said. "And even then, the traffic coming back into Long Island was awful. I hate driving in the city."

Kara leaned forward. "I told you I'd drive, Ma."

"You were asleep before we even crossed the Brooklyn Bridge." She shook a plump finger in Kara's direction.

"I would have stayed awake if you'd let me drive." Kara smiled.

"All right, ladies. The auditions?"

"They were so fun, Pop." Kara stood up from the table. "I got to read a script with another girl. There were so many girls there. I was able to memorize all my lines before my turn came."

"I think I had the whole thing memorized too." Ma laughed. "The And and the But and the crying. It was all pretty silly. But our Kara was great. She even cried real tears. Real tears, Ralph."

"I thought this was a comedy show," Pop said between bites of meatballs.

"It is." Kara sat back down. "The crying was supposed to be funny."

"It was too," Ma said. "Kara stuffed her whole sleeve with tissues, and she kept pulling them out and blowing her nose, then throwing them behind her."

"The directors were even laughing, and you know they saw that same skit dozens of times."

"Of course they liked it." Pop patted Kara's head. "You're the best actress in the world."

"She really is, Ralph. I had lotsa those agents coming up, wanting Kara." Ma said the word *agent* like it was a communicable disease.

"I don't see what the problem is, Ruthie. We got a girl with loads of talent—she should have someone helping her. What do we know about show business? Nuttin'. I know how to teach math and you know how to make meatballs. So why not get some help from someone who knows this stuff?"

"Thank you, Pop." Kara hugged her father. "See, Ma?"

Her mother grabbed her plate and slammed it into the sink. "I know more than meatballs, Ralph McKormick. I know agents want to make money off talented little girls, and I won't let them get their paws on my Kara."

"All right, Ruthie." Pop joined his wife at the sink, hands on her hips. "There's no better mama in the world than you. If you think Kara doesn't need an agent, then Kara doesn't need an agent."

"Thank you." She accepted his embrace.

"Don't I get a say in this?" Kara asked, her heart sinking.

Pop shot Kara a sly grin. "You want to go against your mother's wishes? Break her fragile little heart?"

Kara opened her mouth to answer right as the phone rang. "I'll get that. Hello?"

"Kara, it's Addy. I wanted to find out how the auditions went. Is this a good time?"

"Perfect." Kara walked into her room and shut the door. "They were amazing. I think the directors liked me."

"So, how soon until you're in Florida?"

"Awhile," Kara said. "I'll find out this week if I made callbacks, but I don't know how long after that until they make the decision."

"They would be crazy not to pick you, Kara."

"Crazy in show business is not uncommon."

Addy laughed. "True. Maybe I should rephrase. You are so incredibly talented that the directors will have no choice but to pick you."

Her laugh made Kara smile. "Yes, much better. Go on."

"Seriously, Kara, don't worry. It'll all work out."

She looked around her room. Pictures of her in various school and community theater productions filled her shelves. Reminders of how much she loved acting and how desperately she wanted to get this part. "Oh, Addy. I wish you were here. I'm so nervous. You always make me feel calm."

"I wish I could be there too. Not even for you. I just want some more of your mom's sweet rolls."

"Thanks, Addy." Kara threw herself down on her bed. "I feel so loved. Come on, we're talking about me here."

"Forgive me for interrupting." Addy laughed again.

"I really would like you to come up if I make callbacks. Ma won't let me get an agent, and there's no way she's going to want to go to another audition with me."

"Actually, Jonathon invited me to the White House for a few days," Addy said. "Uncle Mike said it was fine for me to go. But I'm nervous about going there alone."

"You're nervous about seeing a boy who is head over heels in love with you?"

"Kara," Addy groaned.

"Oh, don't get all 'but we're just friends' on me. I watched this romance from the beginning, remember?"

"I am not having this conversation."

"You don't need to." Kara rolled over to her stomach. "Because we both know it's true. Besides, he invited you to the White House. I'd like to think Jonathon and I are friends too. But I didn't get an invite."

"You know how much it scares me to be around a lot of people, and the White House is crawling with people." Addy made a squeaking sound, and Kara could hear her clap. "I have a great idea. How about if I ask Uncle Mike if I could come to New York first? That way I could come with you to the auditions?"

"Keep talking."

"And then you ask your parents if you could come to the White House with me? You could be like my conversational bodyguard."

Kara laughed loudly into the phone. "I love it. Conversing with White House staff so you can have time with Jonathon. It's a deal. I just need to make sure Ma and Pop are okay with it."

"All right, then. I'll check with Uncle Mike about coming up to New York."

"But I don't even know if I'll make callbacks yet."

"You'll make it."

Kara pressed the End button on her phone. "I hope you're right, Addy."

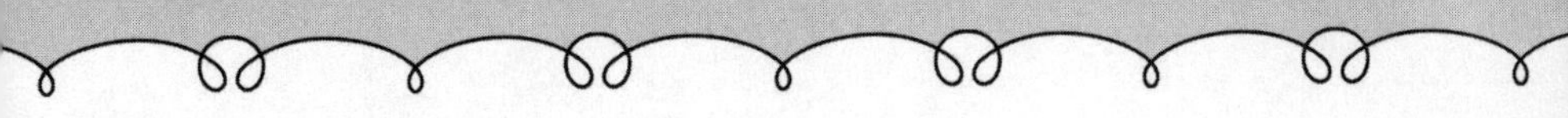

Chapter 5

"Dude!" Chad's longtime friend Will Payne threw a basketball at Chad's chest. "It's been awhile."

"Yeah, well, you know." Chad dribbled a few times before taking a shot from the free throw line. The ball hit the rim and bounced backward. "My schedule."

"Good thing you've got a career in music." Will's shot went right through the hoop. "'Cause you're sure losing your touch in basketball, dude."

"Just need to warm up." Chad bounced the ball out of Will's reach and ran for a layup.

Will grabbed the ball as it, once again, bounced off the rim. "Let me know when you're warmed up, then, all right?"

"Game on." Chad got in front of Will and took control of the ball. After thirty minutes of one-on-one, the game was tied.

"Time." Chad put his hands on his knees, breathing hard. "I need some water."

"But we're tied up." Will held the ball on his hip. "Come on, man. Tiebreaker shot. Then we'll head in."

Chad straightened. "I don't know. I'm tired."

"What are they doing to you?" Will tossed the ball into the air. "You're turning into a—"

Chad jumped up, grabbed the ball in midair, dribbled over to the hoop, and tossed it in.

"Hey." Will caught the ball Chad threw at him. "What was that?"

"That was me winning." Chad grinned.

"No way does that count. I demand a rematch."

Chad walked up the steps to his friend's house. "After we get some water."

The boys sat at the table just as Beth, Will's nine-year-old sister, walked in. "Hi, Chad." She sat at the table, head in her hands, and stared at Chad.

"Give me a break." Will splashed water on Beth's face. "This is Chad. You spit up on him when you were three months old. Stop looking at him like that."

Beth grabbed a napkin and wiped her face, tears welling up in her eyes. "Will, that was mean." She ran off and Chad watched the door from the kitchen swinging in her wake.

"I'm sorry," Will said.

"No, it's all right."

"I know you want things to be normal when you're home."

"I'm starting to realize that I have to adjust to a new normal."

"A new normal, huh?" Will walked to the pantry and pulled out a bag of potato chips. "That's pretty deep."

"You know what I mean."

"Dude, the highlight of my days is when I beat my little

brother in Wii baseball." Will sat down and dug into the chips. "So, no, I do not know what you mean."

Chad laughed.

"So what's next for you? Shooting a commercial with a model? Going to Hawaii for a concert?"

"Not even close." Chad poured some chips onto a paper plate. "Driving up the East Coast in the RV."

"Normal kid stuff, huh?"

"Yep." Chad nodded. "Although I do get to stay at the White House for a couple days."

"Oh, just that." Will wiped his hands on his shirt.

"I'm going to hang out with Jonathon before he starts college."

Jonathon Jackson, the president's son, and Chad had become friends the year before. After Chad won *America's Next Star*, he had been thrown into the spotlight. Because of his age and his looks, he had often been put together with Disney's teen girl stars. At the time, Jonathon had been dating Disney star Janie Smart. While that relationship didn't last, Chad's and Jonathon's did. They talked often and got together whenever their mutual schedules permitted.

"That's part of your new normal?"

Chad could hear an edge of jealousy to his friend's voice. He couldn't blame him. Will was a great friend, but Chad imagined it would be hard on anyone to watch someone he'd known from childhood become famous. *At least Will still treats me the same*. Many of Chad's friends had changed since he had become famous. They either treated him like he was from a different planet or constantly asked him for things. Like the phone numbers of some of the girls he'd worked with.

"All right, superstar." Will stood from the table. "You owe me a rematch."

The boys played for another twenty minutes, until Flora's shrill voice interrupted the game.

"There you are. Playtime's over, Chadster. You've got schoolwork to do."

"Aw, Flora." Chad threw the ball to Will. "I'm the only kid in central Florida doing schoolwork in June."

"That's a bit of hyperbolic rhetoric," Flora said. "And what have I taught you about that?"

"Big words too?" Chad laughed. "This really isn't fair."

Along with assisting his parents with their personal business, Flora had helped educate Chad. Both his parents were involved in his homeschooling. But where their expertise waned, Flora took over. English was her specialty. Literature was her passion.

"*Hyperbole*, from the Greek, means 'exaggeration.'" Flora wrapped her thin arm around Chad's and pulled him back toward the house. The fact that she was a full foot shorter than her student didn't bother her in the least. "And to say that you were the only young man in central Florida having to engage in schoolwork is a grand hyperbole. Will has summer reading for his school, don't you, young man?"

"Thanks for reminding me. See ya, Chad." Will waved good-bye and walked inside.

"But he doesn't have to read *Pride and Prejudice*." Chad looked down at Flora, a wide grin on his face.

"Do not speak unflatteringly of Jane," Flora said, walking beside Chad. "She is the greatest writer to have ever lived."

"I thought that was Shakespeare."

"William was, of course, quite good," Flora said. "But no one can compare to Jane Austen."

"It's all manners and balls and, 'Oh, Miss Bennet, I daresay you have such fine eyes.'"

Flora stopped and stood on her tiptoes, making her eyes reach Chad's shoulders rather than his chest. "There is no such line in the book. And if you persist in mocking Jane Austen, I'll make you read *Persuasion* next."

Chad laughed and patted Flora on the head. "Not that, please. Anything but more Jane Austen."

Flora turned to say something else but tripped over a root and fell to the ground. Her tie-dyed jumper bunched up around her knees, revealing socks with yellow smiley faces.

Chad put his hand out to help her up. "Nice socks." He smiled.

"I know." Flora fluffed her orange hair and wiped the dirt off her socks. "I've named the faces, you know. Poor Geoffrey Chaucer has a stain right by his right eye. We'll have to fix that up. Emily Dickinson is fine, though. So is Walt Whitman."

"How about Jane Austen?"

"Jane Austen?" Flora stood and put her hands on her hips. "I would never name one of my sock faces Jane Austen. That would be crazy."

Chad looked up at his house. Modeled after the turn-of-the-century Florida estates, it was a sprawling two-story wood home with a wraparound porch. The house was painted white—every year. That was one of Chad's chores. Flora always worked with him, giving each of the two dozen shutters a new coat of red paint. The front door was painted red also, and the porch housed two large swings, rockers, and hanging plants.

The red door opened and Mom came out, wiping her hands on her apron.

"All finished with your pottery, Mom?"

"Almost," she answered with a smile. "I just need you to load it into the kiln for me."

"You got it."

"Then it's time for US history," Mom said.

"Where's Dad?"

"On his way. He said to read the next chapter in your textbook and be ready for a quiz."

Flora released Chad's arm. "And after that, Maria, I think he needs a little more time with literature. He said some shocking things about my Jane just now."

Mom laughed. "Chad, you know better than to speak disrespectfully against the great Jane Austen."

"Thank you," Flora said. "And we're just about to find out something scandalous concerning Wickham and Lydia. But that's all I'm going to say. You're just going to have to keep reading to find out what it is."

"I can hardly wait," Chad sighed.

"I know." Flora clapped her hands. "No matter how many times I read Jane, I always experience a thrill. That's what makes her the best."

"Flora." His mother stopped her assistant before she

walked into the house. "I got a call from the executives this morning. They plan to have the top ten girls for Chad's show chosen in the next couple weeks. Would you be ready to be 'housemother' on July first?"

"Of course. I have been praying every day that God will show me just the right girl. In fact, I believe he's going to show me the one the very first day. I'm praying for a sign, like a spotlight on the right girl, showing me who she is. We won't even need a whole month."

"I appreciate that, Flora," Mom said. "But it takes more than one day to know a girl's character."

"Perhaps," Flora said. "But it doesn't take long to see her true heart."

"As long as you're ready. A houseful of teenage girls will be quite a challenge."

Flora smiled. "I am already reading up on teenage girls and their habits. I am even watching some of their shows so I can understand their language. I will be beast."

Chad laughed.

"That means 'really great,'" Flora said. "It's being used as an adjective now. Which is quite humorous since that word has only been used as a noun since its first appearance in Middle English almost a thousand years ago."

"Those girls are going to be in for a shock," Chad said as Flora walked into the house.

Mom smiled. "Yes, but we both know Flora is an excellent judge of character."

"True." Chad nodded. "She knew right away that roofing contractor last year was a scam artist."

"I just wish we'd listened to her then," Mom said. "This

time, we will. She'll be able to spot the good girls from the fakes."

"I just hope the girl she chooses is fun. And pretty."

"And a Christian." Mom patted Chad's back.

"Of course, Mom." Chad smiled. "That goes without saying. But a pretty, fun Christian. Who, preferably, does not want to sit around discussing Jane Austen."

"We'll see, honey. Now go down to my studio and put my pottery in the kiln."

"Yes, ma'am." Chad kissed his mother's cheek and jogged inside, still thinking about his costar.

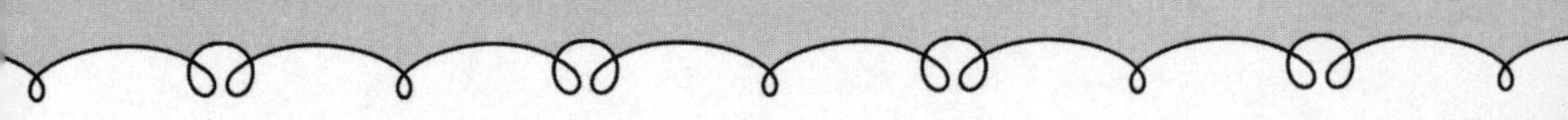

Chapter 6

"Where do we go next?" Addy looked at the subway map, trying to decipher the myriad colors and lines.

Kara snatched the map away from her friend. "Addy, just follow me. I know where we're going."

Ten minutes later, the girls came aboveground.

"You know where you're going?" Addy looked down the dirty street lined with shops advertising items Kara knew Addy's uncle wouldn't want her seeing.

"I thought I did." Kara put her hand to her nose to avoid breathing in the foul stench of the neighboring sewer. "The auditions are on Fifty-Third and Seventh. We should be right there."

Addy looked up at a street sign. "That says Eleventh Avenue, Kara."

"Great." Kara smiled. "So we're close."

Addy groaned, and the two made their way down Fifty-Third Street.

"Aren't you worried we'll be late?" Addy asked. "The auditions start at ten o'clock. It's nine thirty. We won't make it."

"Sure we will." Kara pulled Addy into a faster walk.

"Hey, long legs," Addy groaned, "I can't walk as fast as you. Slow down."

"I thought you said you didn't want me to be late."

"Why don't we just hail a cab?" Addy said.

"For four blocks? We'd look like tourists."

"I am a tourist."

"Well, I'm not." Kara stepped over a huge crack in the sidewalk. "Now, let's go."

"Maybe you should have let your mom come."

"No way. She hated the last auditions. Besides, this is why you came to New York, Addy. To be my good luck charm."

Two women stopped Addy and Kara before they could cross the street. "You two are from *The Book of Love*, aren't you?"

Kara beamed. "Yes, we are. I'm Kara."

"Could we have your autograph? My daughter just loved that show. I'm sorry you didn't win."

Kara signed the woman's Playbill from a Broadway show. "We may not have won the show, but my friend Addy here won the boy."

"Really?" The second woman leaned in. "Are you two an item? What about Lila? Did he dump her after he took her to prom?"

Addy didn't speak so Kara jumped in. "We don't kiss and tell, ladies . . . Oops, I guess we just did. Gotta run now."

"Kara," Addy said once the two crossed Ninth Street. "Why did you say that? I'm so embarrassed."

"They are going to tell that story to everyone they know. We just made their day."

"But you said I kissed Jonathon."

"No, I said we don't kiss and tell," Kara said.

"Implying that there was kissing to tell about."

"Addy, relax. So what if people think you kissed him. What's wrong with that?"

"But I didn't."

"You want to." Kara smiled.

"Kara McKormick." Addy walked faster, forcing Kara to lengthen her stride. "I should just leave you to go into those auditions by yourself."

"Right." Kara laughed. "And how do you think you'd get yourself home?"

"You brought me all the way out here to hold me hostage?" Addy laughed.

"Hey, I can't help it if you have a bad sense of direction."

"Hey, what 'New York City expert' got us lost?"

"Who's lost?" Kara pointed to a building the next street over. "The Holt. And we've even got three minutes to spare."

Addy shoved Kara with her shoulder. "That was just dumb luck."

"I thought you didn't believe in luck." Kara pushed Addy back. "And who are you calling dumb?"

Addy stepped off the curb just as a car was speeding through the red light, heading right toward the spot where Addy was standing. Kara grabbed Addy's arm and pulled as hard as she could. Addy fell backward, crying out in pain and pulling her legs back just as the car sped past. The driver stuck a fist out the window and yelled something.

"Addy, are you all right?" Kara bent down. "Can you stand?"

"I don't know." Addy's face was white, and Kara worried she was going to pass out.

"Deep breath." Kara looked up and saw a crowd had gathered.

"I got his license plate numba," a woman with big hair and bright red lips said. "You wants to sue him, I'll testify for ya. He was a maniac. And then he yells at you for crossing the road when you had the green light."

"No, no." Addy pushed herself up. "I'm fine, really." Kara knew from the grimace on Addy's face that she was not fine. But Addy hated for people to feel sorry for her.

"Give her some space, folks." Kara shooed the crowd away with her hands. "Let me help you up."

"I'm fine."

"Addy." Kara grabbed her friend's hands. "I am going to help you up, all right?"

Addy sighed and stood slowly. "Are my pants ripped?"

Kara turned Addy around. "No, just some dirt. And you got a piece of asphalt in your hair." She pulled the gravel out of Addy's long brown hair. "You sure you're okay? I pulled you pretty hard."

"You are surprisingly strong for someone so thin." Addy gave a half smile.

"And you're even lighter than you look." Relief flooded through Kara when she saw Addy's smile. "I thought I was going to fling you up into the air."

"I wish you had." Addy rubbed her bottom. "I'm going to have one nasty bruise."

"Sorry." Kara patted Addy's shoulder. "Next time I'll just pick you up."

"Next time?" Addy's eyes widened. "I'm triple checking before I cross the street from now on."

"Smart girl."

"We better go." Addy looked at her phone. "One minute until auditions."

The girls were still talking about the near accident when they entered the building, but they were quickly silenced. Kara's last experience—a noisy soundstage full of girls—was the exact opposite of this. The carpet in the century-old building was plush and red, the furniture was very high end—mahogany wood and chocolate brown, butter-soft leather. A receptionist sat behind a formidable desk and eyed the young women with an unhappy glare. No one else was around.

"May I help you?" the receptionist asked.

"Yes, I'm here for auditions," Kara said.

"Speak up, please." The receptionist drummed her fingers on the desk.

"I'm here for the auditions." Kara stepped closer to the woman. "The auditions for the Teens Rock show."

"And what is your name?"

"Kara McKormick. Kara with a *K*."

"And who are you here with?" The receptionist looked at Addy and frowned.

"M-my friend Addy."

"Where is your agent?" The woman took her time gazing down the list of names on the sheet in front of her.

"I don't have one."

After highlighting Kara's name, the receptionist looked up. "All the other girls have agents."

"Good." Kara stood up straighter, refusing to let this woman intimidate her. "Then I'll stand out."

"You certainly will." The receptionist gave Kara the slightest of smiles. "Go through the door to your left and find a seat in the waiting room. When your name is called, give these to Ashley." The woman gave Kara a clipboard with several sheets of paper. Before handing them over, she marked the top with a small star.

"Did you see that?" Kara asked as she and Addy sat in the waiting room. "She put a star on my paper. I think that means she liked me."

"She was awful." Addy shook her head.

"I think she's supposed to be." Kara looked at the other girls' clipboards. "I don't see any other stars."

"I don't see any other friends," Addy said. "I feel so out of place."

Kara glanced around the cramped room. Beautiful teenage girls sat next to equally beautiful women and men, all of whom seemed to be coaching their protégés. "You're right."

"Thanks."

"No, I don't mean that you're out of place." Kara placed a hand on Addy's knee. "But I do wish I had an agent. I'm the only one here without one."

The door to the inner room opened and a petite Asian woman walked out. "Good morning, girls. My name is Ashley Win, and my company is casting the show you are auditioning for. First, let me congratulate you on making it this far. Almost five hundred girls auditioned here in New York. We narrowed our pool down to fifty. We have had similar auditions in Los Angeles and Chicago. Those have been completed. This is our final callback audition. We will choose ten girls from the three audition locations, and those ten will be sent to Orlando."

Several of the girls clapped, but Ashley Win silenced them with a glare.

"Once in Orlando, the auditions will be taped. You'll live with the other girls in a house outside of the city, and you'll have cold readings, perform in front of a live audience, and more. It will be a busy month."

Kara grabbed Addy's arm and squeezed so tightly Addy screamed. Ashley Win shot Addy a death glare before continuing. "Today we'll give you a script just ten minutes before your audition. If we like you, we'll ask you to stay. If we don't like what we see, you'll be sent home. No second chances. So be prepared to give the audition of your life. Got it?"

The girls, too afraid of the tiny woman to speak, simply nodded.

"Excellent." Ashley looked at her clipboard. "Chelsea Stockton and Elise Hart? You're up first. Give me your papers, take your scripts, and be ready to perform in ten minutes."

Chelsea and Elise jumped up from their seats and did as they were told, exiting with their agents to rehearse the scene.

"This is so scary," Addy said.

"But amazing," Kara sang. "This is it, Addy. My dream. It's so close I can almost taste it!"

The girl next to Addy spoke to her agent, loud enough for Kara and Addy to hear. "So only ten are chosen out of all the auditions?"

"Yes, Deb," the agent said. "But I know Ashley. We go way back. And believe me, in this business, it's all about who you know."

"Good." Deb threw a smug glance in Kara's direction.

Kara felt like she had been punched. *I'm never going to make the top ten. All I have is a few weeks on a reality TV show. These girls have training and help and "connections."* Kara tried to breathe deeply, but she couldn't suck enough oxygen into her lungs.

"Kara, you okay?"

"Sure. Just auditioning for the role of a lifetime with little to no chance of getting picked. No biggie."

"Take a deep breath," Addy instructed. Kara obeyed. "Let's think about something else."

"Like what?"

"I don't know. Maybe we could play a game."

"Seriously? A game?"

"I just downloaded this great word game on my phone."

"Only you would think a word game would be fun." Kara rolled her eyes.

"Come on, it would give you something to think about other than the auditions."

At the word *auditions*, Kara's tongue felt like it swelled up in her mouth.

"Okay. Mind off of the you-know-whats."

After forty-five excruciating minutes playing Addy's word game, Kara's name was finally called. She was paired with Deb, whose agent pulled her into a huddle as soon as they received the script.

"Don't you want to practice?" Kara called.

"She is, my dear." The agent glared at Kara. "With me."

Kara looked at Addy. "She wants to make me look bad. That is ridiculous. We'd get a lot further if we worked together."

"It's all right. I'll help."

"I'm just so nervous," Kara said as they walked outside. "They've hardly called anyone back. All these girls keep leaving, crying."

"Or having their agents yell at the receptionist."

"True. What makes me think I can compete? What am I doing here?"

"Kara, take a deep breath. Focus on the audition. You only have ten minutes. Spend them rehearsing."

"You're right. Okay. Let's go."

Kara read over the script quickly. "This is cute." She laughed, having finished reading. "I'm the fan, though. That part is tougher."

"Why?" Addy took the script to look it over.

"Not as much fun as the other part." Kara tried to think of a creative way to play a less-than-thrilling role. "I wonder if Deb's agent got her the cheerleader part because of her 'connections'?"

"Stop worrying and practice." Addy shook her finger at Kara.

"You're right. I need to be fairly serious. Normal. Deb's character is the one that's crazy." Kara stopped pacing and looked at Addy. "And no matter what Deb does, I'll be serious. That'll show the directors that I won't break character, no matter what happens."

"What could happen?"

"I bet you anything Deb's agent is in there with her right now, telling her tons of ways she can be ridiculous in this scene and make me laugh. I'm sure that's why she didn't want to practice with me."

"That sounds terrible."

"Hello." Kara took the script back from Addy so she could try to memorize her lines. "Only ten girls are chosen. She wants to do all she can to make sure Deb is one of those ten."

"So what are you going to do?"

"I'm going to be the best fan you've ever seen." Kara handed the script back to Addy. "Ready to practice?"

"Yes, ma'am." Addy winked.

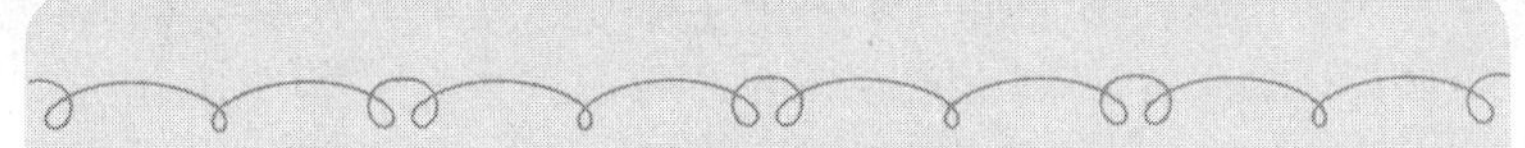

Cheers to You

CHEERLEADER: (Cheering) G-o-o-o-o Team Panther. P-A-N-T—

FAN: (Grabs Cheerleader's pom-poms) Excuse me?

CHEERLEADER: I'm in the middle of a cheer. Do you mind? (Pulls the pom-poms back) G-o-o-o-o Team Panther. P-A-N-T—

FAN: But why are you cheering?

CHEERLEADER: (With her pom-poms on her hips) Because . . . (Cheering again) Team Panther is red hot. R-E-D H-O-T. Red hot!

FAN: I agree. I'm a huge Team Panther fan.

CHEERLEADER: Then join in. I've got more pom-poms. (Picks some up and hands them to Fan)

FAN: (Laying the pom-poms down) Thanks, but don't you think it's kind of weird? Cheering for Team Panther?

CHEERLEADER: Why would it be weird?

FAN: Because Team Panther is a cheer squad.

CHEERLEADER: So?

FAN: So no one cheers for a cheer squad.

CHEERLEADER: Exactly. (Cheering again) I say Team, you say Panther. Team. (Waits, but Fan refuses to speak) (Louder) I say Team, you say Panther. Team . . .

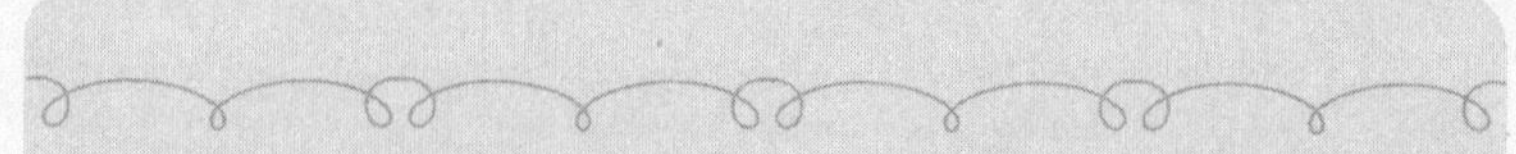

FAN: No, I'm not cheering for a cheer squad.

CHEERLEADER: Some fan you are.

FAN: Seriously. Team Panther is the best in the state. Cheering for them is like . . . like cooking a meal for a great chef.

CHEERLEADER: Everybody needs a cheerleader. Even cheer squads.

FAN: No, I'm pretty sure they don't need a cheerleader.

CHEERLEADER: (Grabs Fan) Look, they're about to go on! (Cheering) Russian, Herky, Basket Toss. Go, Team Panther, show 'em who's boss!

FAN: Great. You just made them mess up.

CHEERLEADER: (Shouts) That's okay, Amber. (To Fan) Obviously, I need to be louder. They need more spirit.

FAN: (Fighting with Cheerleader over the pom-poms) No, you need to be quiet. Can't you see they're trying to concentrate? This is their big move.

CHEERLEADER: The Fountain. Their signature. Don't worry. I've got this. (Cheers) Way up high in the air. Go Team Panther. Catch them if you dare. Go Team Panther. Up into the sky. Watch those Panthers fly. No one can compare. Team Panther!

FAN: Great. They just dropped their flier. You've got to stop. They're going to lose the competition.

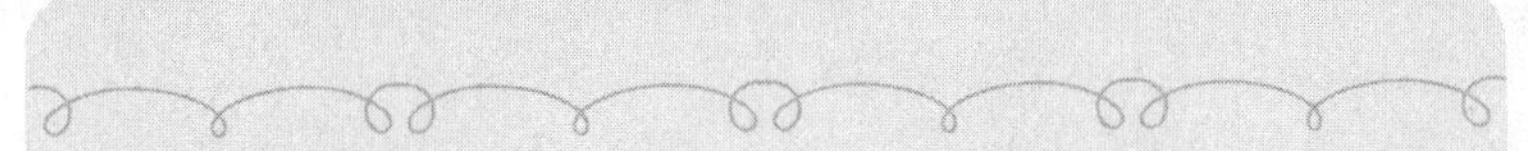

CHEERLEADER: Look at them; they're waving at me. Begging me to cheer them on to victory. (Shouts) Don't worry, Team Panther. I'm here for you.

FAN: Those aren't waves. Those are their fists. They're going to come over here and beat you if you don't stop.

CHEERLEADER: I'm beginning to think you are anti-cheer.

FAN: (Getting angry) No, actually, I am very pro-cheer. I drove all the way up here—left at three o'clock this morning—just to see this.

CHEERLEADER: And yet, instead of cheering Team Panther on with me, you're silencing their biggest fan. If they lose, it's all your fault.

FAN: My fault? You're yelling as they cheer, disrupting their concentration, and it's my fault?

CHEERLEADER: (Cheering) Team Panther. T-E-A-M—

(Fan tackles Cheerleader, but Cheerleader keeps cheering, despite the attack. Cheerleader hits Fan with her pom-poms, knocking Fan out. Cheerleader gets back up and looks out.)

CHEERLEADER: Oh no! Team Panther lost. (Looks down at unconscious Fan) It's all your fault. (Shouts) It's all her fault. I should have stopped her earlier. I'm

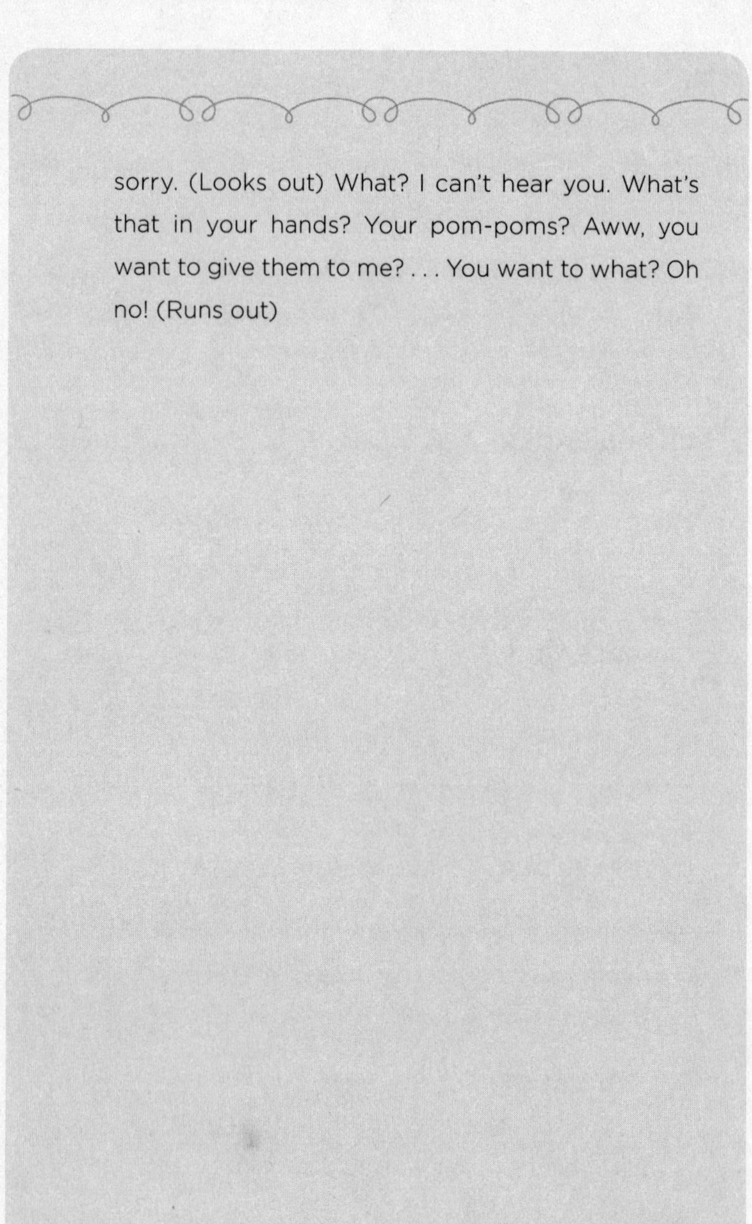

sorry. (Looks out) What? I can't hear you. What's that in your hands? Your pom-poms? Aww, you want to give them to me? . . . You want to what? Oh no! (Runs out)

Chapter 7

"I can't believe I am sleeping in the White House." Kara jumped up out of bed. "Four days ago, I was auditioning to star in a TV show, and today I am waking up in the White House. My life is amazing. Can you believe it?"

"I can't believe you can be that loud this early." Addy pushed herself up on one elbow.

"But we're at the White House." Kara shook Addy. "And Mrs. Jackson is going to give us a grand tour. The First Lady is giving us a tour!" Kara's voice got louder as she spoke, and Addy grabbed Kara's hands and pried them off her shoulders.

"Kara, it's seven thirty. We should still be sleeping."

"We can sleep later—when we're not at the White House."

Addy threw her pillow at her friend and reluctantly walked to the bathroom for a shower.

"I'm at the White House," Kara belted out. *"Three days at*

the White House. Gonna get a tour of the White House. The White House, the White—"

A knock on the door interrupted her solo. Kara opened it to find Jonathon Jackson, First Son, smiling at her. Beside him stood an incredibly good-looking boy who looked very familiar.

"Chad Beacon?" Kara said, trying to smooth back her long red hair and look somewhat presentable. Chad, at a few inches over six feet tall, tan, muscular, with blond hair and hazel eyes, reminded Kara of the pictures of the Greek gods she had seen.

Jonathon smiled. "We were afraid you'd be sleeping, but we heard the singing, and . . ."

Kara's face burned. "You heard the singing?"

Chad spoke up. "Yes. Very nice. Did you make that up yourself?"

Greek god stands outside my door and what does he hear? Me singing the White House song. Kill me now.

"Let me shut the door so I can die of embarrassment in private, okay?" Kara hid behind the bedroom door.

The boys laughed and pushed the door open.

"We won't stay long," Jonathon said, his brown eyes scanning the room for Addy. "I forgot to mention Chad was coming in today."

"Forgot, huh?" Chad laughed again. "You've got him so wrapped around your finger, he can't even think straight."

Now it was Jonathon's turn to have a red face. He ran a hand through his light brown hair. "Chad, this is Kara, Addy's friend. And, Kara, that does not go further than us, all right?"

"Jonathon." Kara put her hands on her hips. "That girl is

as crazy about you as you are about her. I don't know why you guys are acting all shy about it."

"We're waiting on God's timing," Jonathon said.

"You are?" Chad wrapped a muscular arm around his friend's shoulder. "You didn't tell me that. That's awesome."

"And how can you not know who Addy is?" Jonathon pulled himself away from Chad's arm. "Didn't you watch the show?"

"You know my parents don't let me watch much TV." Chad shrugged.

"Not even my show?" Jonathon asked.

"Nope. When I wasn't doing a concert, I was working on my science project. I built a telescope and charted the stars."

"Wow," Kara said. "I want to go to your school."

"He's homeschooled," Jonathon said. "And we all want to go there. Right now, he's on a field trip. For a month."

"During the summer?" Kara asked.

"My parents own an orange grove, so we take our big break at harvesttime, November through January. The summer is the middle of my school year."

"Oh yeah. I remember you talking about that on *America's Next Star*."

"You watched it?"

"I voted for you," Kara said. "A lot. I'm pretty sure I'm the reason you won."

Chad laughed. "Well, thanks then."

Addy came out of the bathroom, a towel on her head and a White House robe wrapped around her thin frame.

"Jonathon!" Addy pulled her robe closed at the top.

"I'm sorry, Addy," Jonathon said. "I was just introducing Chad to Kara."

"Chad Beacon." Kara pointed to the handsome boy standing at her door. "He won *America's Next Star* the year before last. Not that you'd know. Addy watches about as much TV as you do, Chad."

Addy stuck her hand out. "Nice to meet you. And excuse my friend."

"Nice to meet you too. And you, Kara." Chad put his hand in Kara's and she thought her heart would explode.

"Yes, nice to meet you too . . . Chad. Nice to meet you, Chad."

Jonathon winked at Addy. "We were on our way to work out. How about if we meet in the living room at nine? Mom's on a pretty tight schedule."

Kara leaned against the door frame and looked at Chad. "Nine o'clock, sure. We'll be in the . . . the living room. Right. At nine."

The door shut and Addy burst out laughing. "I think that's the first time I've ever seen you tongue-tied. You think he's cute."

"Me and every other teenage girl in the world." Kara sighed, looking at her hand. The hand Chad Beacon touched just moments before. "Why do you think those two boys are such good friends?"

"They have a lot in common. Jonathon told me they met last year and hit it off. They do a lot of things together—"

"Wrong," Kara said. "They are friends because they are both beautiful specimens of maledom."

"Beautiful specimens of maledom?"

"That's right. And there are very few of those species in existence presently, so they need to stick together in order to survive."

"Or they could just be friends who have a lot in common." Addy rubbed her wet hair with the towel.

"I have less than an hour to get myself presentable enough to spend a day with Chad Beacon."

"What about me?" Addy asked, hands on her hips.

"No offense, Addy"—Kara grinned—"but Chad is *way* prettier than you are."

Kara ran to the bathroom before the tip of Addy's towel could reach her behind.

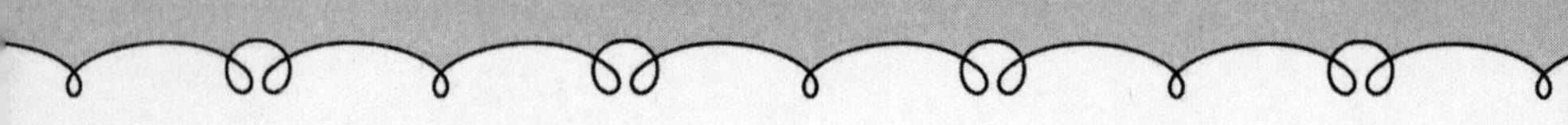

Chapter 8

"She's cute," Chad said as the pair made their way to the White House gym.

"I know." Jonathon smiled. "And smart too. She wants to go to an Ivy League school. She's thinking of Yale."

"Kara?"

"No, Addy."

Chad laughed. "She's pretty too. But I was talking about Kara."

"Oh." Jonathon's face turned red. "Kara is hysterical."

"And pretty." Chad smiled, thinking of Kara's shining auburn hair, her green eyes and creamy skin. "And tall. I like that."

"That's true." Jonathon nodded. "In heels, she might just be your height."

"That's awesome." Chad allowed his mind to linger for a moment on the thought of the beautiful redhead in heels, standing beside him. "But what's this about waiting on God's timing with Addy?"

"Don't laugh."

"Who's laughing?" Chad gave Jonathon a playful punch. "I've been praying for my future wife since I was thirteen."

"Wow. So you don't think I'm crazy."

"No way. But whenever I've talked to you about my faith, you've always blown me off."

"That was before Addy."

"I like this girl." Chad raised his eyebrows.

"So do I. But we're not in a hurry. We decided to just take things slowly, get to know each other, and keep praying about where God wants us to go in our relationship."

"I want a girl like that."

"You can't have mine." Jonathon shot him a mock glare.

Chad put his hands up in mock surrender. "Don't worry. I don't go for brunettes. Redheads are more my speed. Tall redheads."

"Does it matter to you whether she's a Christian or not?"

"She's not a Christian?" Chad opened the door to the gym, trying not to act like that was the worst news he'd heard in a while.

"No." Jonathon added some more weight to the dumbbells. "But she's a great person."

"I hate this." Chad hit the speed bag with more force than necessary.

"What?"

"Every time I meet a girl I like, I find out she's not a Christian. Why doesn't God let me meet Christian girls?"

"So you have to date Christians?"

"If I'm going to get married, it needs to be to a Christian."

"Who said you have to marry her?"

"I think the point of dating is to find your future spouse."

"Whoa." Jonathon put the dumbbell back on the rack. "So you're only going to date one girl?"

"I don't know about that." Chad found his rhythm punching the bag. "Maybe. But I'm not going to date just to date."

"Why not?" Jonathon asked.

"My parents always taught me to treat girls like someone's future wife."

"No offense, man, but your parents were around when dinosaurs roamed the earth."

Chad turned to his friend. "With age comes wisdom. At least that's what they tell me."

"So you don't want Kara's number?"

"I want a whole lot more than her number." Chad put on gloves and moved to the heavy bag. "But I can't. I have to wait."

"You sound thrilled about that."

"I obey what I believe God is asking me to do." Chad threw a left hook. "But I don't always like it."

"So what are you going to do?"

"I'm going to start praying for Kara." Chad held the bag, stopping to catch his breath. "God didn't put her around all these Christians for nothing. He's after her."

"That's exactly what Addy says." Jonathon pressed the weights again.

"Let's hope we're right."

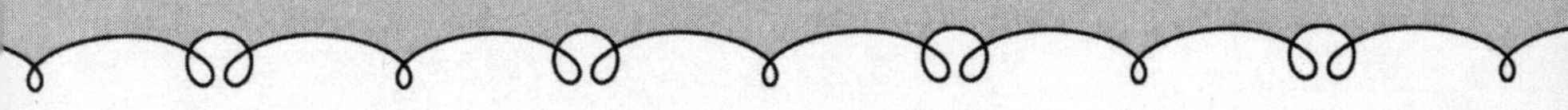

Chapter 9

"And now we're back in the living quarters." Jonathon's mother completed her tour of the White House.

"I love what you've done," Kara said. "I watched the television special where you talked about how you redid all the rooms. But seeing them in person. Wow."

"I'm glad you like it." Mrs. Jackson smiled. "But I'm afraid I have to go now. I have another meeting in a few minutes. Jonathon, you take good care of your guests."

"Of course, Mother."

"Now you can take us to all the secret passages," Kara said after Mrs. Jackson left the room.

"Secret passages?"

"Don't act like you don't know what I'm talking about." Kara folded her arms. "Tunnels going from here to a safe house miles away. Bookcases that are doors."

"You watch *way* too much TV." Jonathon shook his

head. "We do have a movie theater, though. And we get the stuff that isn't even in theaters yet."

"Ooh." Kara jumped up. "Do you have *Mission to Atlantis*? I am dying to see that."

"I'll call and find out." Jonathon pulled out his cell phone and walked away.

"While you're doing that, I need to run to the room," Addy said. "Be right back."

"Looks like it's just you and me." Chad smiled at Kara.

Greek god is smiling at me. At the White House. Oh yes. I could die happy right now.

"So you like movies?" Chad sat on the couch and Kara joined him.

"Love them." Kara's heart raced as Chad's knee brushed hers.

"What's your favorite?"

"I can't pick just one." Kara tried desperately to focus on the conversation and not on how incredibly good-looking Chad Beacon was. "It would be like asking you to pick your favorite song."

"I see your point."

Kara looked over at Chad to find his eyes on her. *He's looking at me! Chad Beacon is looking at me. I should say something. Something funny. Or smart.*

"So where are your parents?" *Seriously, Kara? That's the best you could come up with?*

"Hagerstown, Maryland." Chad stretched out his legs.

"Hagerstown?"

"They love museums and Hagerstown has several."

"Ah." Kara looked from Chad's perfect face to his

arms. Also perfect. *Focus, girl.* "And you didn't want to go along?"

"They like to have little getaways without me every once in a while." Chad smiled.

"Romantic getaway in Hagerstown?" Kara said.

"Well, there are lots of museums there."

"Good for them," Kara said. "So what do you do after this?"

"Finish up history for school. Do some more traveling, then I start on my next big project."

Kara's eyes widened. "And what's that?"

Jonathon walked over before Chad could speak. "We are on for an eleven o'clock viewing of *Mission to Atlantis*."

"Yes." Kara stood. "I'd hug you, but I guess I'll leave that to Addy."

Jonathon's face turned several shades of red right as Addy came back into the living room.

"What's going on here?" she asked.

"*Mission to Atlantis* in"—Kara looked at her watch—"forty-five minutes. I think Jonathon deserves a thank-you."

"Thank you, Jonathon." Addy looked confused. Jonathon cleared his throat.

"Hey, Kara." Chad motioned with his head toward the door. "I think I left something in the gym. Want to come with me to pick it up?"

"I'll go, Chad."

"No, no." Chad smiled at his friend. "You stay here. Relax. I know my way around. I just got the grand tour, after all."

Kara followed Chad. "Nice plan. Very subtle."

"You think?" Chad laughed, walking down the hallway toward the stairs. "I thought they might like some time alone together."

"So you didn't really leave anything in here?" Kara pointed to the gym—a state-of-the-art room filled with every kind of exercise equipment imaginable.

"No, I did." Chad walked to a weight machine and picked up a towel lying on the cushioned seat. "I left this towel just sitting here. My mother would be very upset about that." Chad headed to a wicker hamper in the corner of the room and threw the towel inside.

"We should probably give them a little more time than that." Kara smiled at Chad.

Chad sat on a stationary bike. "You're right. So tell me how you and Addy met. You were on a TV show?"

"Yes, a competition to win a date to prom with Jonathon."

"I remember talking to Jonathon while that was going on. He wasn't crazy about the idea."

"Addy told me he did it to help boost his dad's approval ratings," Kara said. "And it worked."

"Did you like being on the show?"

"I liked parts of it." Kara thought back to her two months in Nashville. "I loved when we got to perform. That was fun. I didn't love golf. I didn't love the catty girls. I did love getting to room with Addy."

"She seems very nice." Chad began cycling.

"Addy is terrific." Kara walked to an elliptical machine and began walking. "She's one of the nicest people I've ever met."

"You guys seem very different."

"Totally different." Kara laughed. "Addy is very reserved. She hated being on the show. I am definitely not reserved. That's probably why we get along so well."

"Interesting." Chad slowed. "Jonathon is reserved too. He knows how to work the crowd—having the president for your father forces that on him—but he doesn't seek out the spotlight."

"What about you? Are you Jonathon's opposite? Is that why you get along so well?"

Chad stopped cycling. "I don't know if I'm his opposite. We actually have a lot in common."

"How did you meet?"

"I was at a party a few months after I won *America's Next Star,* and he was there with Janie Smart."

"The Disney channel diva? He dated her for a while, right?"

"Too long." Chad shook his head.

"You didn't approve?"

Chad paused. "She was very . . . fake. Pretty, talented, all that. But she only ever talked about herself. Not the kind of girl I'd want to see Jonathon end up with."

"You don't have to worry about that with Addy. She's as real as they come."

"Glad to hear it."

"So, anyway, you were at the party, and Jonathon was there with Janie and . . . ?"

Chad smiled. "Right. We ended up at the same table. Janie spent most of the night talking to one of the Disney Channel producers, so Jonathon and I just started talking.

We found out we both like sports, and we hate chemistry, and we really dislike all the hype that goes into being a celebrity."

"Yes, all that money and attention. It must be so difficult for you both." Kara arched an eyebrow at Chad. Then she froze. *I can't mock Chad Beacon. What am I thinking? Now he's going to hate me. Why didn't I just ask about sports? That would have been safe. But no, open foot, insert mouth.* "Sorry. I didn't mean that."

"Sure you did." Chad's perfect smile widened. "And it's a good reminder. I am lucky. Sometimes I forget that."

Kara sighed, relieved that Chad wasn't angry at her. "I plan to be famous someday. Tell me what's terrible about it so I'm prepared."

Chad's laugh was deep and Kara thought it fit him perfectly—a manly, honest laugh. "Don't let anyone make you someone you're not."

"Have you had to be someone you're not?"

"No." His smile faded. "But lots of people have tried. Thankfully, I have great parents. They make sure I don't get too full of myself."

"Well, that's something we have in common." Kara heard her phone ping and pulled it out of her pocket. "I have great parents too. The best."

"I don't know about that." Chad stood.

"Addy says to come back." Kara showed him her phone. "The movie is going to start soon."

"Too bad." Chad held the door open. "I wanted to give them more time."

Kara thought her legs would give way underneath her

when she saw the way Chad was looking at her. *I think he's flirting with me. The most beautiful boy on the planet, and he's flirting with* me.

The two made their way back upstairs and were quickly ushered into the movie room—complete with stadium seating and plush leather chairs. White House staff members brought the foursome fresh caramel popcorn and the soft drink of their choice. Kara sat with Addy on one side and Chad on the other. As the lights dimmed, Kara sat back and prepared herself to enjoy this blockbuster, trying to remember everything about it so she could tell all her siblings about getting to see it two weeks before it was scheduled to release in theaters.

Mission to Atlantis was just as good as Kara hoped, but she had a hard time focusing on the screen because Chad was sitting next to her. She let her own script play in her mind.

Chad: I think you're beautiful, Kara.

Kara: I think you're beautiful too, Chad.

Chad: Not as beautiful as you.

Kara: Oh, stop, you're embarrassing me.

Chad: I'm sure you have boys lined up at your door. And I'm just a lowly superstar whose first album just went platinum. But would you consider, I don't know, going out with me?

Kara: Oh, Chad. You're right. I do have boys lined up at my door. But you can come to the front of the line.

And then he leans over, brushes my hair from my face, and—

"What did you do that for?" Kara shielded her eyes from the bright lights.

"Movie's over," Jonathon said.

Addy rubbed her eyes.

"Did you fall asleep?" Kara looked at her friend.

"Someone woke me up at the crack of dawn this morning."

"I'm sorry," Jonathon said.

"Oh no." Addy stood. "Not you. *Her.*"

Chad stood and Kara looked up. Way up, watching as Chad rolled his neck. "The White House song. I'd like to hear more of that. Maybe I could record it."

A duet. Kara McKormick and the Greek god. Oh yes. It could be the theme song of our first movie. The first of many. He'll have to rescue me from dangerous situations in each one. He is a god, after all. But he'll give up his immortality in the end to be with me. It'll be beautiful. We'll walk down the red carpet together, hand in hand. The interviewers will ask how we manage to have such great chemistry together week after week and he'll say—

"Mr. Beacon?" Bull, Jonathon's large but friendly Secret Service agent, opened the heavy mahogany door, Kara's fantasies once again interrupted. "Mommy's on the phone. You left it in the sitting room."

Chad took the phone from Bull's massive hand. "Thanks, man."

"That's what babysitters are for." Giving Chad a playful punch, Bull walked back to his post outside the theater.

Chad spoke to his parents briefly. *He's so respectful.* Kara listened to Chad on the phone. *Of course. He* is *perfect, after all.*

"They're on their way," Chad said. "Dad insists I get over to one of the museums tonight. They're reenacting a battle from the Civil War, and he thinks it'll go perfectly with what we're studying right now. I get to write a paper on it."

"Slave drivers," Kara said, sad to see Chad go. *I just need a little more time. At least ask for my number. Something.*

"No." Chad walked toward the door. "I told you my parents are great. Really. But they're also quite passionate about my education. And my dad thinks there is no more important subject than history."

Jonathon slapped his friend on the back. "My dad says the same thing."

Chad agreed to meet his parents outside the city so they wouldn't have to drive in rush-hour traffic. One of the White House chauffeurs was enlisted to take Chad to the meeting point. Kara hoped that Chad would invite them along, but Jonathon informed the girls they were invited to dinner with one of the senators from Florida.

Disappointed, Kara said good-bye to Chad.

"I hope to see you again," Chad said.

"Me too." Kara watched as Chad walked away, willing him to turn around, ask for her number, kiss her, lift her in his arms, and carry her away with him.

All she got was a wave.

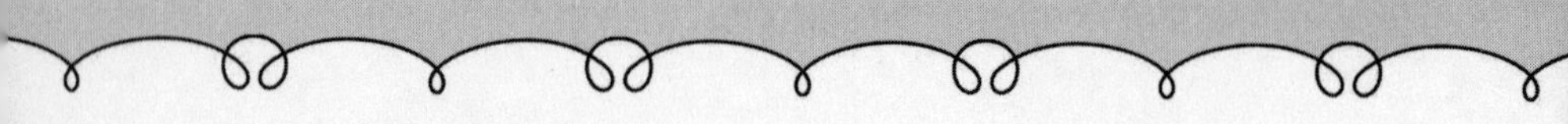

Chapter 10

"This was an amazing trip," Kara said to Addy as they sat at the terminal waiting for the planes to take them home. "I'm glad you forced me to come with you to the White House."

Addy looked at her. "You're welcome."

"I can't believe I got to meet Chad Beacon." Kara smiled. "Wait until I tell everybody back home."

"You guys really hit it off."

"You think?" Kara turned to face Addy. "I mean, I know I thought he was great. But do you think he really liked me?"

"I do, but . . ."

"But?"

"He's a Christian." Addy pulled out her phone to respond to a text.

"I know. But I can live with that. *We're* friends, right?"

"Dating is different." Addy put her phone away.

"I know I felt sparks flying. When we watched the

movie in the media room, Chad's knee kept bumping against mine. Coincidence? I don't think so."

"I'm not saying he's not attracted to you. Of course he is. You're beautiful and funny and quite charming when you want to be."

"I know." Kara laughed. "Go on."

"But Jonathon told me Chad has never dated. He's waiting for the one God has chosen for him."

"What?" Kara sat up straight. "Never dated?"

"Never."

"But you need to date a lot," Kara said. "My brother says it's like buying a car. You need to test-drive several models before you settle on one."

"Dating is not like buying a car."

"Why not?"

"Because you don't buy a car for life. And you don't let a car inside your heart. You don't kiss a car . . ."

"Actually," Kara said, "when my brother Joey finally got his Mercedes, he kissed it. I've got the picture on my phone. Want to see?"

"He would." Addy looked at Kara's phone and laughed. "But you know what I'm saying. You've seen girls whose hearts have been broken by the wrong guy."

"But that teaches them not to make the same mistake again."

"Does it?"

Kara thought of a friend back home who needed to have a boyfriend all the time. One would break up with her, she'd be devastated, but then she'd be with a new guy within a week or two.

"I guess not," Kara said. "But still. To marry the first guy you date? That seems a little scary."

"That's where God comes in."

"God?"

"Yes. I believe he is in control of every aspect of my life. I can trust him to choose my future husband. He loves me and wants what's best for me."

"And if God's choice for you is a short, pudgy bald guy?"

Addy smiled at her. "Then I will think he's the hottest guy on the planet."

"Whatever." Kara laughed. "Maybe God's choice for Chad is a tall, spunky redhead."

Kara's phone rang, and she dug through her purse to find it. Her ring tone, the club version of a top-forties song, played at full volume. Kara apologized to the people in the terminal as she kept digging. When she finally found it, the call ended.

"Who was it?" Addy asked.

"I don't recognize the number." Kara looked at her screen. "It's New York, though, so it could be anybody. I'll just hit redial."

Kara waited as the phone made the connection. "Hello, this is Kara. Did you just call me? McKormick . . . Yes . . . Yes, I did." Kara stood and began walking up and down the hallway in front of the terminal. "I did? I am? . . . Next week? Of course . . . That's right . . . Yes, no problem. Bye!"

Kara screamed so loudly, everyone in the airport stopped to look at her. She stood on top of one of the chairs and announced, "I made it. I'm going to be on TV."

As Kara danced from chair to chair, the people around her began clapping.

"You were on *The Book of Love,* weren't you?" a man asked.

"I was." Kara jumped down. "But now I'm going to be auditioning for a new teen show. I'm going to Orlando."

Kara greeted people, shook hands, and signed autographs. In between, she'd run over to Addy, scream, and hug her.

Fifteen minutes later, the crowd dispersed and Kara sat beside Addy.

"Addy, I made it!" Kara gripped Addy's knee.

"I'm so happy for you." Addy beamed. "So, when do you get to come to Orlando?"

"Next week."

"That's not very long," Addy said.

"Are you kidding?" Kara stood and paced the aisle. "It's forever. One whole week of waiting and wondering. Oh, and writing."

"Writing?"

Kara sat. "Yes. The network is all about giving teens creative license, so all of us have to come with a monologue that we've written and memorized."

"Wow, that's a little scary."

"I know. It is." Kara sat still. "It really is. I've never written a monologue. I've performed them but never written one. What if I can't do it? Or what if it's so bad they send me home right when I get there?"

Addy placed her hand on Kara's arm. "Kara, calm down. You can do it."

"You really think so?"

"Definitely."

Kara hugged her friend. "Thanks, Addy. Okay. Deep,

cleansing breaths. I can write a monologue. I can write a monologue . . . How do I write a monologue?"

Kara stood again and Addy pulled her down. "I think that's a great start."

"What?"

"You should write a monologue about writing a monologue."

"That's not a bad idea." Kara stood again. "I could be a totally neurotic spaz. That would take real acting, of course."

"Of course." Addy laughed.

A voice over the loudspeaker announced, *"Flight 2352 to Islip, Long Island, now boarding."*

Kara grabbed her overnight bag and hugged Addy. "That's me. Thank you, Addy. For everything."

She returned the hug. "I'm so glad you came."

"See you in a week," Kara said with a squeal.

"I can't wait." Addy hugged Kara again.

Kara waited in line, showed the ticket agent her boarding pass, walked down the terminal onto the airplane, and finally found her seat. She buckled in and reached into her purse. No paper. A receipt and some gum wrappers, but no paper.

"Great." She sighed and picked up the in-flight magazine, hoping it had some blank pages inside.

"Excuse me." A huge man tried to squeeze past Kara to his seat. It was a no-go.

"I'll get up." Kara unbuckled as the man stepped aside so Kara could move into the aisle.

Great. Kara watched the man try to stuff himself into the window seat. *I get seated next to a sumo wrestler. Perfect.*

And I have no paper. Which doesn't matter since the ideas are all falling out of my head every minute I'm not writing. I'll be the only one at the audition with no monologue. The directors will send me home and pick some other girl who can actually write a monologue, and it'll be over before it even started.

Kara sat and tried to scribble some ideas on the back of her receipt from the airport lunch counter. But her pen refused to mark on the slick paper. It wouldn't even work when she laid it on the magazine. She was lifting the tray table with her left hand, her right elbow pinned to her side by Sumo Wrestler, when she saw white paper sticking out of the pouch.

Yes! The paper was halfway out when Kara realized it was actually the airline's barf bag. It was large and had plenty of room to write on. *But it's a barf bag. Can I write on this without thinking about what it's used for?* Kara turned it over, then looked inside just to make sure it hadn't been used. All clear.

Here goes nothing. At least I'll be able to say I have suffered for my art.

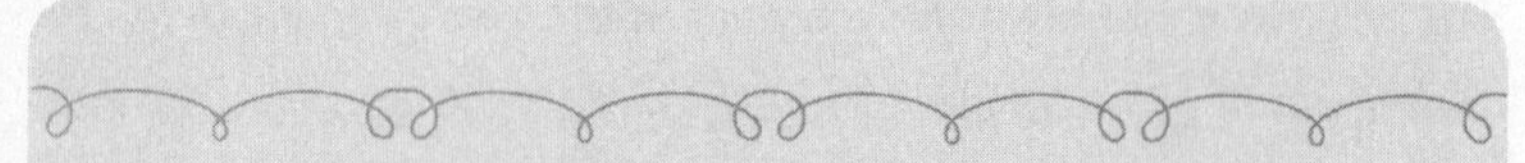

Kara's Monologue

(Kara looking at a sheet of paper) "Write a monologue." (She turns the paper over) That's it? "Write a monologue"? What kind of instructions are those? Am I supposed to write it like I'm me? Like I'm a little kid, a grown woman? An old lady?

Ooh, an old lady. That might be fun. I could be like, "Hey there, little missy. Have you seen my dentures? I'm going out to dinner with Gomer tonight. That's right. All the ladies want him, but he's mine. All mine. Only seventy-nine years old, with a head full of hair and only one hip replacement. He's taking me to the all-you-can-eat buffet at Bubba's Diner. They have the best cornbread. Mmmm-mmmm. I can't wait to sink my teeth into that. But first, I've gotta find my teeth. Where are they?"

I don't know. That may not be politically correct. Or what they're looking for. Maybe they want something more modern. Hip. Maybe I should be a gangster. I can get my swagger on, pull one pant leg up. "Yo, wassup. You know, I'm just here looking to get me another sick tat. I got a picture of my mom on this arm. A picture of my homey over here. Now it's time to get something written in some other language on my neck. Right here.

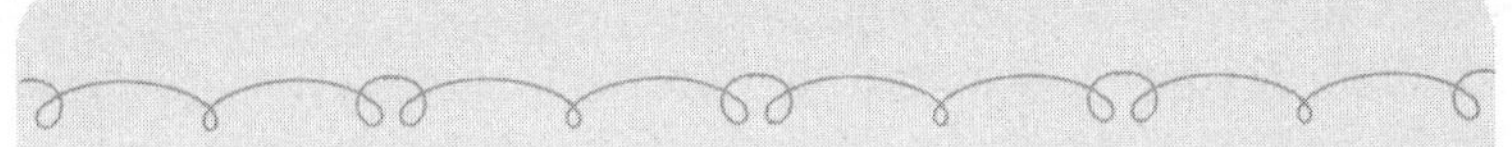

Something like, 'Don't you wish you could read what this says?' Or 'That's right, I got a tat on my neck so you know I'm scary.' Yeah. That would be wicked sick, yo."

That's not going to work. No one will buy me as a gangster. Not unless I am an Irish gangster. (Laughs) Right. So not modern. What else? Futuristic? It can be 2345. "The earth has been destroyed by mutant hedgehogs. That's right, hedgehogs. While everyone else was worried about nuclear war, alien invasions, and Texas-sized meteorites, a group of hedgehogs dug a home underneath a super-secret NASA testing facility. While the scientists were testing ways to grow plants on the moon, their chemicals leaked down through the dirt, into the hedgehogs' lair. The chemicals changed the hedgehogs' DNA, giving them superpowers. But they were evil, and they wanted to use their powers to rid the earth of all humans, making it a haven for mutant hedgehogs. But then, one day . . ."

Forget it. That's really dumb. Man, this is hard. If they just gave me something to work with. I can't come up with something out of thin air. "Write a monologue." Well, you know what? I can't. I'm sorry. I give up. (She throws the paper away and exits)

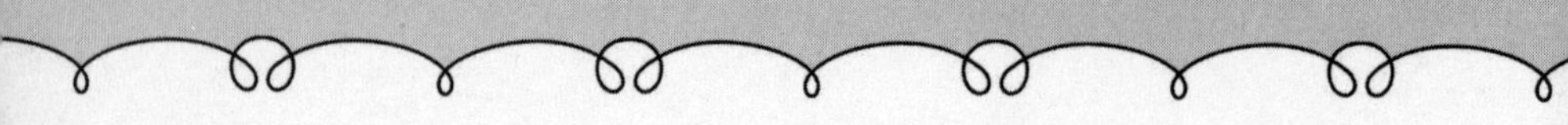

Chapter 11

"To Kara McKormick, next big star." Kara's brother Joey lifted his glass of sparkling grape juice into the air. Dozens of McKormicks joined him in the toast, all cheering and splashing juice around the dining room.

"Sit, everybody." Pop herded his large family into the living room. A blended family, Ma and Pop each had two children when they met and married almost thirty years before. Two more children followed. Kara was the youngest of the six and enjoyed that position in the family immensely. She loved that she had nieces and nephews just a few years younger than she, and she loved that when everyone was together, her house was so full it threatened to explode at the seams.

"Kara, are you nervous?" her sister Mary asked.

"A little, I guess." Kara reached for Mary's nine-month-old daughter, Ruth Ann. "But more excited than nervous."

"We'll sure miss you." Kara's brother Sam squeezed himself between Kara and Mary. Sam was twenty-seven—closest in age to Kara. "Who am I gonna tease now that you're gone? Little Ruthie Ann is too small. Right, little lady?" Sam pinched Ruth Ann's cheeks and the baby reached for her uncle with a smile. "She knows who loves her."

"Hey." Kara grabbed for her niece. "Always taking what's mine. Some things never change."

Ma walked to Kara. "You two fighting again?"

"He started it." Kara pointed to Sam.

Mary laughed. "We may have to send some siblings down every once in a while to check up on you."

"All right." Kara smiled. "But in birth order."

"So I'm last?" Sam bounced Ruth Ann on his knee. "Where's the love?"

"My little Kara." Pop nudged Sam over on the couch so he could sit next to her. "I'm going to miss you."

Ma pulled out a handkerchief and wiped her eyes. "We thought we'd have a few more years before you left the nest."

"You might," Kara said. "I haven't made it yet."

"But you will." Ma put her hands on her hips. "You're the most talented girl in the world."

"Too bad you're not the director." Kara laughed.

Her brother Patrick joined the family by the couch. "So, how are we going to keep you from getting a big head?"

"A big head?" Kara pushed her brother. "Me? How dare you. Hey, where's my bouncer? Get this guy outta here."

Patrick raised his hands in surrender and laughed. "That's my girl."

"So," Joey said, "a month of auditions, huh? What do you do for a month?"

Kara shrugged. "I'm not really sure. Different kinds of screen tests, I guess. Different types of sketches."

"So, no mud obstacle courses?" Joey referred to one of the competitions in *The Book of Love*.

"I doubt it." Kara pushed her other brother. "But if you recall, I did pretty well on that. Only missed one question, thank you very much."

"She's brilliant." Ma handed Kara a piece of chocolate from the crystal candy dish on the end table.

She refused the candy, and Patrick grabbed it from Ma's hand. "Watch it, Ma. You're making us think Kara here might be your favorite."

"All my children are perfect. Smart, beautiful, talented, every one of yous."

Kara turned to her mother. "Come on, Ma. We all know I'm your favorite. You don't have to pretend."

This statement caused a storm of good-natured protests from the other five siblings. Each child was sure he or she was the apple of their mother's eye.

Pop silenced them all with a clap. "All right, you hooligans. Your mother doesn't have any favorites. She loves you all the same. Now me, on the other hand . . ." Pop finished his sentence with a smirk and a shrug.

More shouting and laughing resulted, and Kara sat back and took it all in. *They are great. Loud and opinionated and awesome.*

The McKormick clan spent the day talking and laughing. Kara was sad to see the last of her siblings go.

I'm so used to seeing them all the time. I missed them like crazy while I was gone on The Book of Love, *and I knew that was just for a few weeks. If this works out, I'll live in Orlando for months at a time. Am I ready for that?*

Ma gathered up the plates and cups scattered throughout the living room. Kara helped, and the two walked to the kitchen in silence.

"It's going to be so quiet without you here." Ma teared up again.

"You guys could always move down with me." Kara looked at her mother. "Dad can retire from teaching, can't he?"

"Technically, he could. He's been at the same school since before we met."

"I know he doesn't enjoy it as much as he used to." Kara dried the dish her mother gave her and put it in the cabinet.

"That's true. The last few years have been tough."

"And with his cholesterol . . ." Kara put down the towel and sighed. "I worry about him."

"You and me both, honey." Ma scrubbed the plate harder than necessary.

"So if I make the show, be like every other New Yorker and retire to Florida. Pop can learn how to golf and you can join a book club."

"What about all the others? We can't leave your brothers and sisters."

"And the grandkids." Kara smiled.

"And the grandkids." Ma shook her finger as she spoke. "Patrick's in-laws, they moved down to Florida two years ago, remember? The grandkids barely know them. Last time they were up, little Ethan cried and cried, wouldn't even let Sally touch him."

"Ma." Kara placed another plate in the cabinet. "Sally and Dale barely saw Ethan and Emily when they lived here.

They were always traveling or out with their poker friends. You and Pop, you'll always make sure you have time with your grandkids. Plus, there's video chatting. You can call them every day if you want, even see them. They'll never forget who you are."

"This is home, Kara." Ma dried her hands and sat at the kitchen table. "Your pop and me have lived here in Smithtown our whole lives. We want you to follow your dreams. But we just can't go with you. Our roots are here."

"All right, Ma." Kara joined her mother at the table. "If I were Addy, I'd tell you I would pray that you changed your mind."

"I like that Addy." Ma smiled. "She'll be nearby to keep an eye on you."

"She will." Kara touched her mother's hand. "But I'll still miss you and Pop like crazy."

"And the others?" Ma dabbed her eyes with her handkerchief.

"Of course. I've got the best family on earth. I don't know what I'd do without you."

Pop walked in and joined Kara and Ma in the kitchen. "What's with the waterworks, ladies? This is a great day."

"I know." Ma motioned for him to sit at the table with them. "But she's our baby."

"Of course she is." Pop patted Kara's back. "That's not going to change."

"But she'll be so far away." Ma's tears flowed more freely. Kara felt her own tears spilling down her cheeks.

"Two hours in a plane." Pop hugged his wife. "That's nothing."

"I'll call every day, Ma," Kara promised. "And I'll show you how to use video chatting so I can show you around the house where I'll be staying."

Ma dried her eyes. "I'd like that."

"And we can come down," Pop said. "I've got another month and a half before school starts. Maybe we can take some of the grandkids and go to Disney for a couple days."

"That would be fun." Ma smiled. "Emily would love to see Mickey and Minnie."

"She sure would." Pop grabbed a cookie from the plate at the end of the table. "Can't you just see her little eyes light up?"

Ma laughed. "I sure can."

"So we're all good now?" Pop asked. "No more tears?"

"Not until I get on that plane," Kara said.

"The phone is lighting up." Ma picked up the receiver and dialed the number for voice mail. "With all the noise, I didn't even hear it ring."

"It's probably one of Kara's friends wishing her good luck." Pop gave Kara another hug.

Ma started pressing buttons on the phone.

"What is it, Ma?"

"I'm trying to get it on speaker." Ma handed the phone to Kara like it was a shard of glass. "You do it." Kara pressed the speaker button.

"So if you're interested, please give us a call back at this number."

"Who was it?" Kara pressed the Replay button.

"I don't know. It was for you. About the audition, I think."

"Here it goes." Kara kept the phone on speaker and they all listened in.

"Good evening. This call is for Kara McKormick." The man's voice was high and very proper. *"I am Jordan Sands, a Broadway producer and director. We are holding auditions for a new musical. I saw your work on* The Book of Love *and I'd like you to be part of these auditions. They will be televised live, just like* The Book of Love, *with the winner being chosen by audience vote. We have had great success with this model in England, and we believe this TV show and the musical will be huge successes here as well. Mary Kegel has agreed to be one of the guest judges, as well as Robert Van Zandt."*

Kara recognized the names—recent Tony Award winners and amazing actors. She and her friends had gone to see a musical that starred Mary Kegel the year before. Kara thought she was one of the most phenomenal actresses she had ever seen.

"We will hold the preliminary auditions on Monday, so if you're interested, please give us a call back at this number."

Kara saved the message and walked, in a daze, to the living room.

"What do I do?" She sat on the couch.

"This show would be on Broadway?" Pop sat next to Kara.

"Right here in New York." Kara stood and walked around the living room. "I wouldn't have to leave you guys."

"But what about the show in Orlando?" Ma stood in the doorway.

"That's incredible too." Kara swallowed hard. "This isn't fair. How do I choose? Why do they both have to be auditioning at the same time?"

"Could you fly back up Monday for these auditions?"

Pop looked at his watch. "It's just nine o'clock. Why don't you see if you can get ahold of this guy? Tell him your predicament."

"And ask him to hold those auditions for me? Right, Pop."

"You'll never know unless you call."

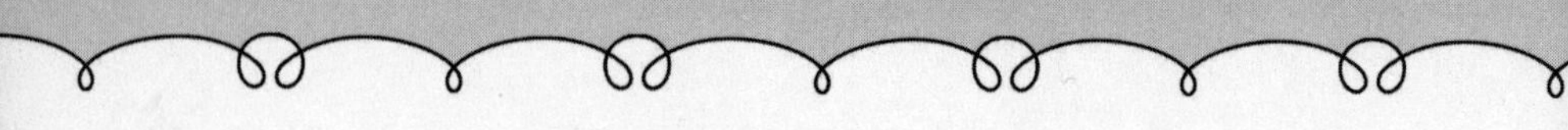

Chapter 12

"This water is freezing," Jonathon complained as he stepped into the raft.

Chad threw his friend an oar. "You really need to get out more."

Chad had convinced Jonathon to join him on a trip to North Carolina. His parents were no longer interested in white-water rafting, but that was an activity Chad loved. The president and First Lady agreed to let Jonathon come along for a few days, provided, of course, his Secret Service agents remained close by.

Bull, Jonathon's lead Secret Service agent, jumped in behind Jonathon, splashing the ice-cold river water all over Jonathon's back. "You're telling me. All this boy does is study and play baseball."

"And text his girlfriend." Chad nodded toward Jonathon's cell phone.

"She's not my girlfriend." Jonathon shut his phone and put it in a waterproof bag Chad had given him.

"Mmm-hmm." Bull clicked a life vest over his large chest. "Keep telling yourself that, boy. You forget I watched it all happen. There's no foolin' Bull."

Jonathon's face turned red. "Anyway, can you please tell me what I need to do to keep from drowning in the rapids?"

"Don't fall in." Chad laughed as he settled himself in the back of the four-passenger raft.

"Very funny." Jonathon looked at the churning water of the Nantahala River.

"Relax." Chad pushed them out into the current. "I've gone white-water rafting dozens of times. I'll steer. You boys just paddle when I say paddle. All right?"

Ten minutes later, the raft was stuck on a rock in the middle of the river.

Jonathon stared at Chad in disbelief. "Some expert you are."

"Don't worry. I got this. We'll be out of here in no time." Chad pushed against the rock with his oar. The raft didn't even budge.

An eight-person raft drifted past them. A six-year-old inside waved and laughed at the three large men.

"Very nice," Bull said. "We just got passed up by a kindergartner."

"We'll just have to get out and push it off. No big deal."

Jonathon stuck his hand in the water. "No way am I getting in there, man. You got us stuck. You get us unstuck."

Chad struck his oar in the water, sending an icy spray of water raining down on Jonathon. "You big wimp."

"I'm not a wimp." Jonathon smirked. "I just don't want to die of hypothermia in June."

"You won't die of hypothermia." Chad laughed. "We just need to give the raft one big push. Then we can jump back in and keep going. We haven't even hit the big rapids yet."

"Seems to me like all we've hit is this rock," Bull said.

"Come on, get out and help me push." Chad jumped into the water.

Bull crossed his arms. "I'm with my buddy here. You push us out."

"You guys together weigh over three hundred pounds." Chad crossed his arms over his chest. "I know I'm strong. Real strong"—he flexed his muscles to prove his point—"but that's too much weight, even for me."

"Boy, you sure talk a lot of smack." Bull jumped into the water, towering over Chad.

Chad slapped Bull on the back. "I know, man. But when you're built like me, you can."

Bull came up behind Chad, lifted him up, and threw him several feet away. Chad came up spitting out water.

"That's right." Bull laughed. "Who's the man?"

Chad coughed, then ran for Bull. Bull jumped to the side, causing Chad to run right into the raft. Jonathon fell backward as the raft slid off the rock and began speeding down the river.

"Hey, wait!" Chad swam after the raft. Bull joined him.

"How do I stop this thing?" Jonathon held an oar in the air. The raft drifted underneath a tree, pushing the oar into the water. Jonathon reached for a second oar, but it slipped out of his hands. Chad and Bull stopped swimming to laugh at their friend as the "kindergarten raft" pulled up beside Jonathon.

"Need a hand, mister?" the little boy asked as his father held an oar out to Jonathon.

While the two rafts floated to a calmer portion of the river, Chad and Bull swam up to meet Jonathon.

"One, two, three." Chad and Bull grabbed the side of their raft and flipped it over, causing Jonathon to tumble out.

"Hey." Jonathon scrambled to right the raft. "What was that for? Chad's the one who started this."

Chad laughed. "I know. But you looked way too dry sitting up there. Now we all match."

"You boys all right?" the father from the next raft called out.

Bull pulled himself into the raft. "Yes, sir. I've just got to keep an eye on these little ones. You know how it is."

The man nodded. Chad and Jonathon looked at each other and tried to flip Bull out of the raft. The larger man, however, anticipated their move and pushed each of them underwater.

"I am a trained agent, boys." Bull flexed his very large muscles. "Youth and energy are no match for these brains and brawn."

"Okay." Jonathon panted. "Truce. White flag. Uncle. Whatever you want to hear. Just get me back on dry land."

Bull laughed, helping the boys back into the raft and pulling the raft toward the lost oars.

After two more hours and three more trips into the river, Bull, Chad, and Jonathon pulled up to shore. Soaking wet, they wrapped up in towels and begged their driver to stop off at the nearest coffee shop for the largest, hottest drinks they could buy.

"That was fun," Chad said, hands wrapped around his coffee cup.

"It was." Jonathon nodded. "Even if you two did try to drown me."

Chad looked out the coffee shop window, the Nantahala rushing beside them, green trees leaning over the churning water. "You know, if show business doesn't work out for me, I could live here. Be a guide. That would be awesome."

"Sure." Jonathon laughed. "You'd be in high demand too. Not everybody can guide a raft onto a huge rock."

"Hey." Chad set down his coffee. "That current is strong."

"Yeah, well. I still think you better stick to your day job."

"Here's hoping I can." Chad lifted his cup in a mock toast.

"So, what's next?"

"I'm going to try something new," Chad said. "Acting."

"Really?"

Chad shrugged. "I love being onstage. And not just singing, but connecting with the audience and telling a story. It's like nothing else."

"Better than white-water rafting?" Jonathon smiled.

"Definitely."

"Don't you have to record more songs?"

"Yep." Chad watched out the window as a kayaker made his way down the river, gliding between larger rafts and rocks. "But I'm not bound by a contract anymore. So I'm free to do what I want."

"And you want to act?"

"Not just act." Chad took another sip of his coffee, finally warming up. "I'd like a chance to do it all. Act, sing, even write."

"I thought you already wrote your music."

"I do." Chad leaned back in his chair. "I mean, write the stuff I'll be performing. Be a part of the whole artistic experience."

Jonathon shook his head. "Artistic experience?"

"Don't laugh, dude."

"Sorry." Jonathon cleared his throat.

"You like editing, right?"

Jonathon nodded.

"That's artistic."

"I don't know about that," Jonathon said. "It takes a lot of work. But I don't know if it's art."

"Sure it is. You decide what clips to show and which to throw away. You pick music to play underneath. I've seen some of your stuff, remember? You're good."

Jonathon sighed. "Thanks, man, but it doesn't matter. It's just a hobby. I'm destined for politics."

"Says who?"

Jonathon lowered his voice, looking back at Bull, who was sitting at the table behind them, reading the paper. "My dad. I'm expected to study law, practice for a few years, then run for some kind of office. Just like he did."

"But is that what God wants you to do?"

"Doesn't God want me to obey my parents?" Jonathon asked.

Chad nodded. "But God's will trumps your parents'."

"I don't know . . . I don't want to disappoint them."

"Have you ever really talked to them about it?" Chad knew Jonathon's parents loved their son deeply, and he doubted they really wanted him to pursue a career he didn't want to pursue.

"No," Jonathon answered quickly. "I don't need to. It's just a given."

"Maybe they think it's what you want to do."

"What?"

Chad leaned forward. "My parents own an orange grove. Quite a successful grove, one that's been in the family for three generations."

"I know." Jonathon's face was blank. "I've been there, remember?"

"I'm their only child. For three generations, the fathers have passed the grove down to their sons."

"You were supposed to run your family's business." Understanding dawned on Jonathon's face.

"Right. But from the time I was ten or eleven, I knew that wasn't for me. I loved growing up there, don't get me wrong. And there's nothing in the world I love more than the smell of orange blossoms. It's in my blood. But having that be my life . . . that's just not in me."

"But if you don't take over, what will happen?" Jonathon asked.

"I worried about that for years. I felt like I had to take it over. So I wrote songs and sang and hoped that doing that in my bedroom for the rest of my life would be enough."

"So how'd you end up on *America's Next Star*?"

Chad gazed back out at the water. "I didn't even know about the show."

"Right." Jonathon smiled. "No TV."

"But when I was fifteen, I felt like God was telling me I needed to talk with my parents about how I felt. So I did."

Jonathon leaned in, his elbows on the table. "Were they mad?"

"They were more upset that I had waited so long to tell them than that I felt the way I did."

"Really?"

"Yeah." Chad looked at his friend. "They said God would take care of the groves, and that if he had something else for me, then I should go for it. They were the ones who found out about the auditions in the first place."

"Wow."

"You should talk to your parents," Chad concluded.

"But what if they don't respond well?"

"Do you believe God wants you to be a politician?" Chad asked.

"No," Jonathon said, exhaling.

"Then trust God to help your parents see that too. Give them a chance."

"That's not going to be easy."

"Neither was white-water rafting." Chad motioned to the window. "But you survived that."

"Barely." Jonathon laughed. His phone chimed, and he pulled it from his back pocket.

"Addy?" Chad smiled.

"Yes." Jonathon's face turned red.

"Tell her I said hi." Chad sipped his coffee.

Bull, who had just come to stand beside their table, said, "Me too."

"Yeah, yeah." Jonathon continued texting.

"How's Kara?" Chad asked.

"That was smooth, boy." Bull grinned and pulled a chair to the head of the table.

"What?" Chad asked.

"Aw, come on now. I saw you looking at that girl last week. Sitting next to her, asking about her family, holding the door open. Don't try to act all shy now. We all know you're not shy."

"I just asked how she's doing. That's all."

"You forget I live with Jonathon." Bull laughed. "I've heard all that before."

"But she lives in New York. I live in Florida. The fact that we met was just a coincidence."

"Do we believe in coincidences, Mr. Jackson?"

"No, sir." Jonathon smiled and laid his phone on the table. "We do not."

"I didn't think so."

Chad shook his head. "She may be the prettiest girl I've ever seen. Ever. With perfect hair and the creamiest skin on the planet. With a great sense of humor. And almost as tall as me in heels . . ."

"But?" Jonathon looked at his friend.

"She's not a Christian, so I've got to stop thinking about her."

"Uh-huh." Bull snorted. "Good luck with that."

"No kidding." Chad sighed.

"What is it you've been telling me, Chad? God has a plan for everything, right?"

"Yeah," Chad said. "And for everyone."

"So we'll keep praying for Kara, that she sees God's plan for her."

"Thanks, man."

"And I'll pray for you too." Jonathon smiled at Chad. "I think you need it."

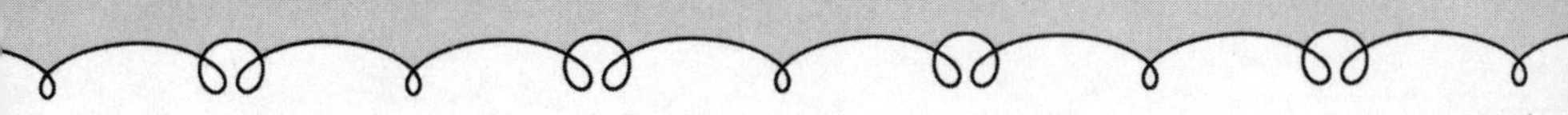

Chapter 13

"Emergency McKormick family meeting now in session," Joey announced in true lawyer fashion. His love for the profession had begun when he initiated McKormick family meetings over two decades before. Trials were held over who ate the last Popsicle in the freezer, who forgot to flush, and who was spying out the window when the girls were getting good-night kisses on the porch. The tradition had waned in the last few years, but Kara's dilemma brought all her siblings over and Joey's gavel back on the table.

"Kara, please rise." Joey motioned in a mock judge-like manner.

"Joey, this is serious."

"This is the most serious McKormick case to date." Joey's hands emphasized his words. "New York or Orlando. Broadway or TV. Ladies and gentlemen of the jury, the fate of a teenage girl is in your hands."

"Enough, Judge Joseph." Kara grabbed one of her mother's

sandwiches and stuffed it in his mouth. "All right, here's the deal. You all know I'm in the top ten to audition for a show in Orlando."

"That's right, sweetie." Ma handed Joey a napkin.

"And I'm supposed to get on a plane for Orlando this afternoon."

"Yes, so let's move this along." Sam looked at his watch. "All in favor of Kara staying in New York, raise your hand."

"Sam." Kara shoved her brother's hand down. "You need to know all the facts."

"Go ahead." Sam folded his arms and sat on the couch. "But I already know I'd rather have you fifty miles away than a thousand miles away."

"Sammy, this isn't about what you want." Mary looked at Kara and smiled. "This is a big deal. Come on, Kara. Give us the details on each of the opportunities."

"Mr. Sands is a Broadway producer, and he is casting a new musical that will star a teenage girl."

"The magnificent Kara McKormick." Sam clapped.

She glared at him until he stopped applauding. "Anyway, he's having auditions for this part on TV, with people voting each week for their favorite. At the end of six weeks, America will choose the star of the show, kind of like on *The Book of Love*."

"And when do those auditions start?" Mary asked.

"They start Monday with twenty girls," Kara said. "There are two weeks of rehearsals, and then the show starts."

"The show starts in two weeks, and they're just calling you now?" ever-practical Patrick asked.

"No, a girl got hurt and dropped out, and they called me because I'm already here in New York."

"Hey, that's what happened with the guy on the dancing show," Mary said. "And he ended up winning. Remember?"

"That's true. I forgot about him."

"Which will be you." Sam winked at Kara. Kara was not amused.

Mary leaned forward. "But the Orlando auditions are for a TV show, and the winner will be chosen by . . . ?"

"I don't know, exactly." Kara shrugged. "One of the directors, I guess."

"But not us?"

"No, those auditions won't air until right before the show premieres in October. The star will already be chosen."

Joey tossed his gavel from one hand to another. "So, why have these auditions in July if the show doesn't start until October?"

Sam rolled his eyes at his brother. "Because, genius, they prerecord those shows."

"How did I know they weren't live? She did say it was like a teen version of *Saturday Night Live*. Emphasis on the *live*."

"Yous both need to be quiet." Pop waved the boys back down to their seats. "The point is both of these are great opportunities for Kara, but they are at the exact same time and neither will let her do both. It's gotta be one or the other."

Patrick, an accountant, held up a hand. "You got twenty girls competing for one spot here in New York, and only ten in Orlando. Your odds are better in Orlando."

"But the New York auditions are won or lost by viewers,

and Kara already has fans," Mary said. "She made it to the top three in *The Book of Love*. All the folks who voted for that will be voting for this one too."

"All of them?" Patrick asked.

"You know what I'm saying."

"I know, but it's still twice as many competitors."

"Stop!" Ma rarely raised her voice, but when she did, her kids got quiet and listened. "This isn't about the odds. Kara can win this one or that one, doesn't matter about numbers or fans. Kara, you gotta choose the one you want."

"Ma's right," Joey said. "When you were describing the two shows, your eyes lit up when you talked about Orlando."

"They did," Mary agreed.

"But what if I'd have a better chance at winning the show here?"

"Which would you regret more?" Sam held Kara's hand.

"I'd regret not going for the show in Orlando."

"Then there's your answer."

"But—"

"No 'buts,'" Ma said. "We had enough of those. The Buts and the Ands, remember me telling you about that?"

The siblings all smiled.

"You wanna be on TV, then you should try to be on TV." Pop stood behind the couch and rubbed Kara's shoulders. "Go for it."

Kara looked around the room. "You sure?"

"Of course not." Patrick laughed. "But you have to take risks every once in a while."

"So the jury is unanimous with its verdict?" Joey asked.

Her brothers and sisters each picked up a pillow and threw it at his face.

"Well then," Joey mumbled under the pile of pillows, "court is adjourned."

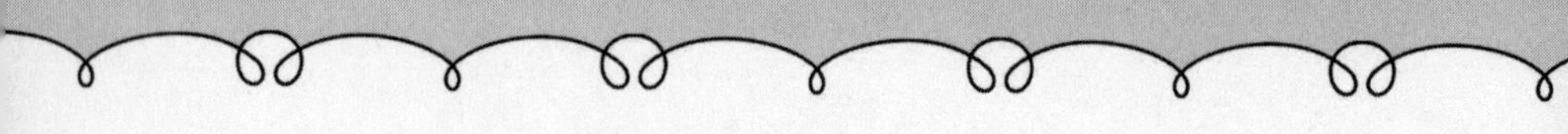

Chapter 14

"So the house is super boring." Kara eased herself into the seat at the deep end of the pool. The hot July sun was only bearable while immersed in water. "But this pool totally makes up for it."

Kara had called Addy as soon as she arrived in Orlando. The few girls who had gotten there before her were out on a shopping spree, according to the note left on the refrigerator. The rest, Kara supposed, were still flying in.

"So it's not The Mansion, huh?" Addy's voice sounded strange when on speakerphone.

"The outside is yellow stucco. One story. I was really hoping for one of those big old Florida homes with the wraparound porches and the shutters and all that. This one is big, but there's nothing special. No history."

"No trailers?" Addy laughed. When the two roomed together on *The Book of Love*, they lived in trailers because The Mansion in central Tennessee, where the show was filmed, was too old to allow for thirty girls to pad around in its two-hundred-year-old halls.

"No, we'll be living here."

"All ten of you?"

"And the housemother," Kara said.

"It must be big."

"Six bedrooms, each with its own bath." Kara floated backward and began treading water.

"Wow."

"Yeah, but every bedroom looks the same. All browns and creams. This place has no personality. I hope it's not an omen. Maybe I made the wrong choice? I should have gone for the Broadway show."

"Are you seriously second-guessing yourself based on interior design?" Addy asked.

Kara swam back to the pool seat and sighed. "Stupid, right? I just can't stop thinking about it. If I lose this, I'm always going to wonder if I could have won that one."

"But if you went there and lost it, you would have wondered about this show, right?"

"Exactly."

"So you'll just have to win this one so you won't have any regrets."

"Of course." Kara got out of the pool and dried herself with a large cream towel. "Easy as pie."

Kara heard the front door open. "Some of the girls are here. I'd better go."

"I'm praying for you," Addy said.

"You know what?" Kara wrapped the towel around her lean body. "I'll take it."

"Wow, is this all they can afford?" an annoyingly familiar voice drawled from the living room. "When I was on *The Book of Love*, we lived in a mansion."

"It must have been great to live there," another girl answered.

"Sure was," the first girl said. "Too bad I didn't make it all the way."

"I heard Jonathon didn't even like the girl who won."

"Lila? No. He took her to prom, but that was it. I heard he didn't even kiss her good night."

"Wow, all that and not even a kiss. I guess you're glad you didn't win that date."

"Sure am."

"And now he's dating that girl Addy?"

"That's what I hear, but I don't know why."

Kara turned the corner into the living room. "Well, if it isn't Anna Grace."

Looking like a teen Reese Witherspoon with her tiny frame and blond bob, Anna Grace Austen appeared sweet and innocent. But Kara knew better.

"Kara McKormick," said a Hispanic girl with long, shiny black curls and curves Kim Kardashian would envy. "What, is this a *Book of Love* reunion?"

"Well, I guess so, Miss Haley. But where's little Addy?" Anna Grace drawled. "You girls go everywhere together, don't you, Kara?"

"Actually, I just got off the phone with her."

"She's not auditioning?"

"Addy?" Kara laughed. "Do you not know her at all?"

"No, I don't," Anna Grace said. "She was too good for the likes of us, remember?"

"She didn't want to gossip with you, you mean."

"Girls," a third girl, with dark brown hair pulled into a long ponytail, interrupted. "New day, new show. I'm Ava, by the way."

"Kara." Holding her hand out to Ava, Kara smiled at the petite brunette.

"Don't get sucked in by her," Anna Grace said. "That girl just attaches herself to whoever she thinks is going to win."

"I am friends with people who are genuine." Kara walked up to Anna Grace.

"Well then, you can just genuinely get out of my way because this show can only have one star, and that's me."

This is stupid. I'm not going to get into it with her. It's not worth it. This is exactly what Ma doesn't *want me to be.*

Kara turned to walk away.

"That's right," Anna Grace said, walking behind her. "Just go back to your room, tail between your legs. Loser."

Kara kept walking. *It's not worth it. It's not worth it. It's not worth it.*

A hand on Kara's shoulder stopped her.

"I don't want to get into an argument with you, okay?" Kara turned around to see a tiny woman staring up at her. Her hair was purple and spiked, her shirt was neon green with paint splatters, and her stirrup pants were purple with polka dots.

"I'm not one of them," the woman said. "I am Flora, the housemother. I wanted to see if you needed any help."

"I'm so sorry," Kara said. "I didn't mean to be rude. I was just—"

Flora put a hand up. "I know. I heard. Think of me as

Miss Temple in *Jane Eyre*. I'm on your side, and I'm not going to believe the horrible things people say about you. Unless you prove them right, of course."

"I saw that movie in class last year." Kara nodded. "It was good."

"The book is even better." Flora smiled, revealing a gap between her front teeth.

Kara glanced down at the suitcases in Flora's hands. "Hey, can I help you? Those look heavy."

Kara grabbed the suitcase on the right. She could barely lift it. "What's in here? Rocks?"

"Books." Flora hefted her remaining suitcase and the two walked down the hall to Flora's room. "But I'm supposed to be helping you."

"Oh, there will be plenty of time for that, I'm sure."

"Well, thank you . . . ?"

"Oh, sorry. My name's Kara. Kara McKormick."

"Very nice to meet you, Kara. Irish?"

"How'd you guess?" Kara laughed.

"Typically, last names that begin with *Mc* denote an Irish etymology. Not to mention that redheads are often associated with Ireland. Wait, you were being sarcastic, weren't you?"

Kara smiled and laid Flora's suitcase on the floor in her room, situated at the end of the hallway. A queen-sized bed was in the center, but other than that, the room looked just like Kara's. "Do you need anything else? I'm all unpacked, so I've got time."

"That's very nice. I need to determine what we're going to eat for dinner tonight. I haven't had a chance to go shopping yet, so we'll have to send out for something. I was thinking pizza, though that's not very healthy."

"Some pizza places sell salads too."

"I would love a big Caesar salad." Flora opened her suitcase of books and placed them on the nightstand.

"That sounds good to me," Kara said. "How about if I look up some places nearby that sell pizza and salads and see if we can get some delivered out here?"

"Stupendous suggestion, my dear."

Kara returned to her room and pulled out her phone, scrolling through local listings to find just the right spot. She walked out into the living room to ask the girls what kind of pizza they'd like.

"Sucking up to the housemother, Kara?" Anna Grace laughed. "The lawn guy's out front. Maybe you should cozy up to him too."

"Did you see what she was wearing?" Haley laughed. "Where did they dig her up? The Woodstock Museum?"

The other girls laughed. Kara folded her arms. "Two cheese, a pepperoni, Caesar and house salads. Right?"

"That's right," Anna Grace said. "Go back and tell Miss Matched our order."

"Her name's Flora." Kara glared.

"I don't care," Anna Grace said.

"What is your problem?" Kara came to stand next to Anna Grace.

"My problem is that I don't want to lose another competition."

"And acting like a jerk will win this for you?"

"It worked for Lila."

"That's a great role model." Kara rolled her eyes. "Lila was awful the whole time we were on *The Book of Love*."

"But she knew to stay away from you and Addy." Anna Grace put her hands on her tiny hips. "Now she's got her own show. No competing for one role. My agent said if I want that, I *should* make her my role model. That's how you get ahead in this business."

The other girls in the living room listened to Anna Grace and nodded.

"My agent said the same thing." Haley shrugged. "If we get too close, we might not do our best in the auditions."

"Boy, this is going to be a great month." Kara shook her head.

The pizza deliveryman came forty-five minutes later. The girls were hungry and cranky, pouncing on Flora as soon as she paid the bill.

"The house salad is mine," Anna Grace called out.

"No, I ordered a house salad," Ava yelled.

Flora, balancing three pizzas and two salads in her thin arms, tripped over a rug and fell, food flying everywhere.

"Great." Anna Grace stepped back. "What a klutz. Now we'll have to wait another forty-five minutes for more food."

Haley, Anna Grace, and Ava left Flora on the floor, surrounded by lettuce and upended boxes.

"I'm sorry, Flora." Kara helped her up, then bent down to pick up the pizza and salad scattered throughout the entryway.

"You don't need to do that." Flora joined Kara on the ground, scooping handfuls of lettuce into the plastic containers. "I am a bit uncoordinated."

"We should have helped." Kara walked to the kitchen. "I'm sorry the girls were so rude."

"I appreciate your help, Kara." Flora smiled up at the younger woman. "More than you know."

"Do you want me to call in another order?"

"Would you?" Flora asked. "That would be wonderful. I have to make a quick phone call."

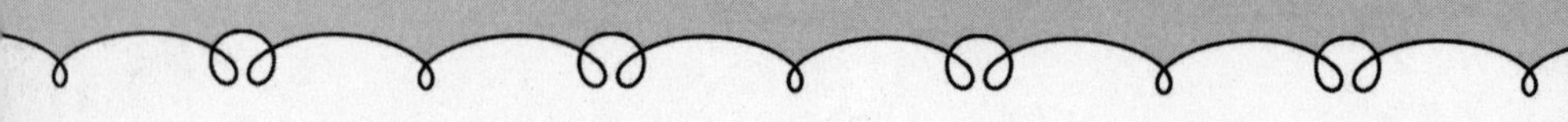

Chapter 15

"Call off the auditions." Flora's face filled the computer screen in the Beacons' living room. "I have found the girl."

Chad squeezed in beside his mother, trying to hear Flora over the loud clanking of the metal bracelets on her arm.

"It's the first day," Mom said. "You can't know already."

"All the girls aren't even there yet, are they?" Dad asked.

"No, but that doesn't matter." Flora's purple head bounced back and forth. "I've found her."

Chad leaned in front of his mother so Flora could see him. "What does she look like?"

"No, no." Flora waved her hand. "I don't want you to know anything about her. Not until you meet her."

"Aw, come on, Flora." Chad smiled. "Just a hint. Give me her name at least."

"Absolutely not." Flora's thin eyebrows rose. "I know how the Internet works. You'd type in her name and see her, and then you'd know all about her before you meet. No way. This has to be a surprise."

"Why?" Chad asked.

Flora cocked her head to the side. "St. Augustine once wrote, 'Patience is the companion of wisdom.' I want you to be wise."

"Mom, Dad." Chad looked to his parents. "A little help, please?"

Mom smiled. "I'm not opposed to making you wait until the decision has been made about the girl. But, Flora, I do want you to wait the full month before making that choice."

"I agree," Dad said. "This is a big decision. We've all put a lot of prayer into it. We want to make the right choice."

"But I don't need a month to make the choice," Flora insisted. "I know she is the one. Remember I told you I prayed that God would show me clearly the first day who that girl is? He answered that prayer."

"Is she a Christian?" Dad asked.

"I don't know yet."

"Flora." Dad rubbed his temples. "The whole reason we're doing this is so we can find a Christian to work with Chad."

"But, Mr. Beacon, I know—"

"Flora." Dad's voice was firm. "How many girls are at the house?"

"Four."

"Four?" Mom said. "Not even half."

"I'm telling you, it doesn't matter."

"It does to us, Flora," Mom said. "Get to know all of them, all right? Give them a chance."

"Oh, ye of little faith." Flora shook her purple head.

"Flora, we trust you," Mom said. "You know that. We just want to be sure."

"Not to mention the executives have a whole month of auditions planned plus a television special they're putting together." Dad leaned back in his chair.

"I suppose they wouldn't look kindly upon me calling the venture to an abrupt halt." Flora gave a half smile.

"No, they wouldn't," Mom said. "We'll check in with you in a few more days."

The Beacons clicked End on their computer and leaned back on the couch. Chad looked at the painting above their mantel, a portrait of their family completed when he was twelve.

"Did we make a mistake sending Flora?"

"No." Dad wrapped an arm around Mom. "I trust her. She's unique, but she knows the mind of God. You know how much prayer she's put into this job."

"And research." Chad laughed. "She's taking the role of housemother very seriously."

"And she loves Chad almost as much as we do," Mom said. "I just don't like that she's made such a hasty choice. Good decisions are rarely made quickly."

"That's why we're making her wait out the full month," Dad said. "She doesn't have a problem admitting that she's wrong."

"When she *is* wrong." Chad looked at his father. "Which isn't often."

"True." Dad yawned. "I've gotta get to bed. I have a meeting tomorrow with a potential client. See you two in the morning."

Dad said good night, leaving Chad and his mother alone on the couch.

"So, what kind of girl are you hoping will be chosen?"

"A girl who's just like you, Mom." Chad grinned.

She reached over to rumple his hair. "Very good answer, my dear. But really, what are you hoping for?"

Chad closed his eyes. "Tall, with auburn hair and green eyes, outgoing and funny."

"That's quite specific." Mom turned to look at him.

"I met this girl named Kara at Jonathon's a couple weeks ago. She was amazing. We spent the day together."

"The day your father and I went out to Hagerstown?"

"Yeah."

"Why didn't you tell us about her then?"

"We were so busy with history," Chad said.

"You like her?"

"I don't really know her." Chad shrugged.

"But you're still thinking about her."

"I am."

"What about her attracted you?"

"She was just really fun," Chad said. "She didn't flirt with me like other girls do. She treated me like a normal guy. I like that. She was at the White House with her friend Addy."

"The one Jonathon likes?"

Chad nodded. "He's crazy about her. But I really admire what they're doing. Getting to know each other and praying about how God wants them to proceed."

"That is admirable. So this Kara is a Christian, then?"

"No." He sighed. "But we're all praying for her. Me, Jonathon, and Addy."

"Then I'll be praying for her too."

"Thanks, Mom." Chad stood. "I better get to bed too. Calculus tomorrow, right?"

"That's right."

He groaned.

"Chad." Mom stood and looked up at him. "Be careful with your heart."

"I'm fine. I only spent one day with the girl. I probably won't even see her again."

"But you're thinking about her." She patted Chad's arm. "Guard your heart, son."

"I know, Mom. I will."

Chad walked up the stairs, his mind wandering back to Kara McKormick.

God, help me guard my heart. I know it's silly, but I feel like I'm losing it to a girl I barely know. If we have a future, work it out. And if we don't, help me to stop thinking about her so much. Actually, God, either way, help me to stop thinking about her so much. I don't have room in my brain for Kara and *calculus.*

Chapter 16

"I thought we should have a little get-to-know-you time since we'll all be together for the next four weeks." Flora gazed at each of the girls. She had made them all sit in a circle in the living room.

"Look, this isn't necessary," Anna Grace said. "We all know why we're here. We don't need to be friends. We just need to be well rested and well fed and have our laundry done."

"Anna Grace, right?" Flora asked, her hair a muted shade of burgundy today.

"Yes," Anna Grace hissed.

"I do believe it's necessary. I want us to be peeps."

The girls laughed. Anna Grace rolled her eyes at the housemother.

"It's like in *The Lord of the Rings*; we are the fellowship of the rings, guardians of a sacred trust. And we must all work together to accomplish our goal."

"My preciouuuus." Kara mocked Gollum's voice.

"What?" Flora asked.

"You know, Gollum, the little bald guy in the movie?"

"There's a movie?"

Most of the girls looked at Flora like she was crazy.

Kara touched Flora's arm. "I'm guessing there's also a book?"

"Of course, J. R. R. Tolkien. He and C. S. Lewis and Dorothy Sayers and several others were part of a group called the Inklings. They would meet to discuss their writing and their thoughts, and—"

Anna Grace yawned dramatically. "Please, Miss Flora. We are still on summer vacation. Spare us the history lesson."

"Actually, it would be classified more as a literature lesson than a history lesson." Flora looked around the room. "But I understand your point. We should move on. So here's my suggestion. Let's go around the circle and everyone give me your name, where you're from, and your favorite book."

"Favorite book?" Haley was brushing her thick black hair. She barely even looked at Flora.

"Yes." Flora clapped once. "I'll start so you all have time to think. My name is Flora. I was born in Paris."

"Wow, really?" Kara asked.

Flora laughed, a high-pitched giggle that caused the other girls to wince. "Paris, Tennessee. I always get people with that. But I've lived just south of here for the last twenty years."

"And your favorite book?" Kara noted most of the other girls were either texting or having their own conversations.

"Oh dear." Flora paused. "I don't think I can choose just one."

"You're the one who came up with these questions," Sophie said, looking up from her phone.

"That I did." Flora nodded. "I offer my sincerest apologies. How about if I tell you my favorite literary genre? That's a bit easier. I love Regency romance. Jane Austen, in particular."

Most of the girls weren't listening. Kara tried to revive the group by going next. Anna Grace, however, had already informed the others that Kara was a "brownnose," so they barely acknowledged what she said. As the group got louder, all involved in their own conversations, Flora put two fingers in her mouth and let out an earsplitting whistle.

"Girls, I would prefer not to resort to such base vociferations. However, I expect you to behave with decorum."

"What did you just say?" Anna Grace peered at Flora.

"She said shut up or she'll let out another whistle," Sophie interpreted.

"Not exactly," Flora said. "But I do want you to remain silent when others are talking."

"Look, lady." Anna Grace stood. "You are the housemother. To me, that's just a slight step up from house help. You're not telling me what to do or how to act or making me sit in a circle and talk about myself. I'm out of here, y'all."

Flora stood with her. "I didn't want to have to resort to this, but I will call your mother if I have to."

Anna Grace walked away, her cell phone raised in the air. "Go ahead. She's the one who told me I don't have to listen to you."

Flora sat down. Most of the other girls followed Anna Grace's lead and walked out of the room. Only Haley, Jillian, and Kara stayed behind.

"I'm sorry, Flora," Kara said.

"I appreciate you three staying," Flora said with a sad smile. "Why don't you tell me about yourselves?"

Jillian leaned forward. "I'm Jillian Lane and I'm from San Diego. My favorite book is *The Lion, the Witch and the Wardrobe*."

"A C. S. Lewis fan." Flora clapped. "Even though I do prefer nineteenth-century British literature to the more modern writers, Lewis is one of my favorites. Have you read his Space Trilogy?"

"No, ma'am, I haven't," Jillian said.

"Oh, you should. They are just wonderful. A man named Ransom is sent to another planet to . . . well, I don't want to give it away. I think I have it with me if you'd like to borrow it."

"Thank you, Flora, but I have summer reading for school to finish."

"All right, then." Flora sighed. "And you? Haley, right?"

"Haley Maxwell." She was French-braiding her long hair. "I'm from Chicago. I don't really like reading. No offense."

"I appreciate your honesty. What do you like to do?"

"I like to act." Haley looked at Flora as if that were the dumbest question ever. "I've been doing commercials since I was two. Last year I played a lead role in a big professional theater downtown."

Jillian leaned forward. "I've been in small roles on some television shows."

Kara felt her stomach drop. *All I've done is school plays and community theater. How can I compete with these girls?*

"That's wonderful," Flora said. "But you really should

read. It will help broaden your horizons. As actresses, you have to portray many emotions and many characters. Reading helps you get inside people's minds and live experiences you might not have on your own."

"That's a great point, Flora," Jillian said. "If I finish my summer reading, do you think I could maybe borrow one of those C. S. Lewis books?"

"I would love that." Flora smiled.

"It's late." Haley stood, finally finished with her hair. "Tomorrow we have our first cold reading. Well, the first for *this* show. I'd better get some sleep."

"Splendid idea." Flora stood and straightened her floor-length, quilted skirt.

Kara sat in the living room as the others filed out. *Do I really have a shot at this show? It's not just agents these girls all have. It's experience. I am way out of my league. Is it too late to ask to be on the show in New York?*

"Kara, are you all right?" Flora poked her head around the living room wall.

Kara stood. "Yes, I'm just a little nervous about tomorrow."

"Do you know what I do when I'm nervous?"

"Meditate?"

"Close." Flora looked up at Kara. "I pray."

"You sound like my friend Addy. She prays about everything."

"She's a wise young woman." Flora walked to the lamp on the end table to turn it off. "Martin Luther once said, 'Pray, and let God worry.'"

Kara closed the venetian blinds. "I don't really believe in God."

"That's all right." Flora smiled, walking out.

"It's nice to hear someone say that."

Flora turned to her. "God believes in you."

Unsure how to respond to that, Kara watched Flora walk to her room at the end of the hallway.

God believes in me? Kara spent the rest of the night trying to get that thought out of her mind.

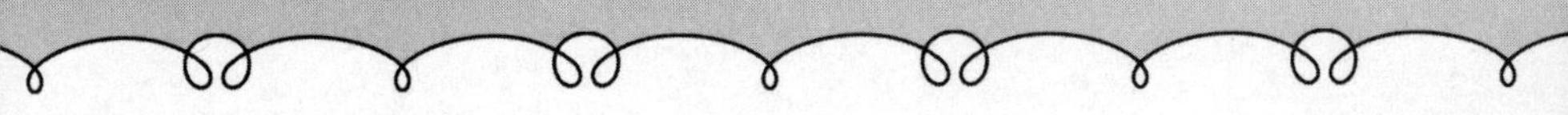

Chapter 17

I'm on an actual set. A real, live set with lights and cameras and props and people everywhere. Kara tried her best not to scream. She didn't want to appear unprofessional. Not when the other girls walked on the set for their first screen test like they had been to a million of these before.

"When I was in an episode of *Dark Forces* last year"—Haley referred to a popular crime drama on network television—"we were shooting in the tiniest space you've ever seen. But when I watched the show back, it looked huge. It's amazing what camera angles can do, you know?"

When you were on Dark Forces, Kara thought, trying not to make a sour face. *Yes, well, when I starred in my high school's production of* Our Town *. . . no, not so much. How about when I played Tiger Lily in the community theater's* Peter Pan? *No. All right. Just keep your mouth shut, Kara, and maybe they'll think you know what they're talking about.*

Anna Grace walked up to the couch on the set and lay down. "This is all mine, ladies. I am going to *own* this audition."

"Don't get too comfortable." Ava pushed Anna Grace's legs off the couch and sat down. "I think I see my name right here."

"All right, girls." Ashley Win entered through the fake front door on the set and motioned for them to have a seat. "In the chairs back there. No sitting on the actual set until the auditions begin."

The girls did as they were told and Ashley pulled up a director's chair and sat, her small legs not even reaching the footrest. Her formidable demeanor, however, prevented the girls from any sort of laughter at Ashley's expense.

"You'll be given scripts and numbers," Ashley said. "The scripts are all the same, the numbers are different. You may not switch your numbers, you may not complain about your numbers, and you may not have your agents call me with their complaints about your numbers. Got it?"

The girls nodded and Ashley went on. "You must have your script completely memorized when you perform. You should make sure you also note the blocking in the script. If the script says to stand by a chair for a line, you stand by that chair."

Anna Grace raised her hand. "But what if that doesn't feel right?"

"Then go home and do school plays where you can 'feel' your blocking." Ashley glared at Anna Grace. "Here we have cameras set up. Those cameramen have the same script you do. So if you're supposed to stand by a chair and deliver your line, then that's what you do."

"I-I'm sorry, Miss Win," Anna Grace stammered. "I wasn't trying to argue."

"Moving on." Ashley waved her hand. "You will be joined in this scene by Devlin Tyne."

The girls all began talking at once. Ashley folded her arms and stared at them until they were silent. "Do not think of him as a teen star. He is another actor playing a role."

Kara looked at the other girls. They were squirming with excitement. She thought back to her time with Chad Beacon. She had already spent a day with a celebrity. *I was tongue-tied at first, but then I saw he was just a regular guy. Well, as regular as a Greek god on earth can be. Devlin Tyne is cute, but he looks like a skinny little kid next to Chad. Come to think of it, no guy looks good next to Chad Beacon. That boy has seriously ruined me for all other guys.*

"Anna Grace," Ashley called out. "You're first."

"Me?" Anna Grace pouted. "That's not fair."

"Are you complaining about your number?"

"No, ma'am."

"Good." Ashley handed her the script. "You have thirty minutes."

"Ava, you're next." Ashley handed the script to Ava. "We are going in alphabetical order. Gina, Haley, and Jennifer, you're numbers three, four, and five."

As those girls walked up to receive their scripts, Ashley kept talking. "You will all perform before lunch."

Yes. I've got at least four hours to work on this. Thank you, God. Or Universe. Or luck. Whatever. Just thank you!

"Jillian, Kara, Kylie, Sophie, and Zoey." Ashley waved them forward. "You've got more time, so I'll expect better work."

"Of course," Jillian said. "Thank you, Miss Win."

Kara ran outside but found that the Florida humidity

was not her friend. And unlike Haley, her hair was not naturally perfect. Walking back into the building, she overheard Jillian on the phone.

"Yes, I'm working on the lines . . . I know it is . . . Not yet, but I will . . . Okay, bye."

"Hi, Jillian." Kara smiled. "We really lucked out, huh? Getting to go after lunch?"

"I don't believe in luck." Jillian returned her smile. "I believe in God."

"Wow, you too, huh?"

"You don't?"

"Not really." Kara shrugged. "But I'm open to spirituality."

"Good for you." Jillian opened her script.

"Really?"

"Sure." Jillian's eyes stayed on her script. "We should all be free to believe whatever we want, right?"

"Right. I guess."

Jillian glanced up at Kara. "Christianity works for me, but maybe it won't work for you."

"My friend Addy doesn't think that."

"Some Christians are very narrow-minded." Jillian rolled her eyes. "They mean well, but they just don't get it. God loves everybody, right? No matter what."

"Addy isn't narrow-minded." Kara was upset that her friend was being painted negatively by this girl who claimed to share Addy's faith. "She's very sincere. She says that God just gives one way, and his love is what allows us to choose that one way."

"I wouldn't buy into that if I were you." Jillian turned to walk away. "You need to be true to yourself. Don't forget that."

Kara didn't have time to dwell on the thought too much. She wanted to memorize the script and find a way to add her own personal spin on the character. *I need to be memorable. I need to say the right lines and move to the right spots, but be me*. Exhilarated at the prospect, Kara found a quiet spot in the corner of the building and skimmed the sketch.

All right. Kara began to pace. *Airheaded girl. Everybody is going to play her like a dumb blonde. I need to bring something different. Something that will make my audition stand out. But what? An accent?*

Kara read through the script again, trying first a southern, then a British, and finally a surfer girl accent. *No*. She rolled up the script and tapped it with her hand. *Too cheesy for this one. I don't want to go over the top. The other girls will be doing that. This would be funnier if the character was more believable. But she's totally out of it. How do I make her out of it without acting like a complete ditz?*

Kara's phone vibrated, and she pulled it from her back pocket. A text from her brother.

"That's it!" The concrete walls made Kara's exclamation echo in the large soundstage.

"Shhh," Kylie hissed. Kylie was a consummate actress, and she hated being interrupted when she was preparing for a role.

"Sorry." Kara put her hands up in surrender. *Sorry I just came up with a great idea*. Kara unrolled her script and read through it again, her characterization coming to life as she read. *I can be texting through the whole skit. That's why I don't really pay attention to Devlin's character. I'll look up just enough to catch the gist of what he's saying. I'm not an airhead; I'm just shallow. Yes. It's perfect! Now to memorize.*

Kara rehearsed her lines and her blocking, adding in her phone as a prop. In the middle of her seventh run-through, she heard Ashley calling the girls to lunch. Kara followed them to a small cafeteria on the other side of the soundstage. Devlin Tyne had already gone through the buffet. Kara, too nervous to eat much, just grabbed a salad and made her way to the long table in the center of the room.

"You can sit by me." Devlin motioned Kara toward his end of the table. His little arms reminded Kara of sticks that fell off the oak tree in her backyard.

"I'm fine over here."

"Don't be shy now." Devlin flashed what Kara was sure he thought was a million-dollar smile. "I won't bite. I save that for the scene."

Kara couldn't join him in laughing at his lame joke, but she did reluctantly scoot her plate a few chairs closer.

"Hoping for your fifteen minutes of fame, huh?" Devlin winked at her. "I started so young, I never really had to compete for roles. They just came to me. Is it hard?"

"Actually, the auditions are fun." Kara stabbed her lettuce with gusto. "You're really missing out. I feel bad for you, not getting to experience the thrill of not knowing. It must be so boring."

Kara was satisfied she had wiped the smug grin off Devlin's face. The other girls came through the line and surrounded the young star, treating him like he was royalty. Kara's mind drifted back to the audition piece.

Oh yes. Ignoring him won't be hard at all.

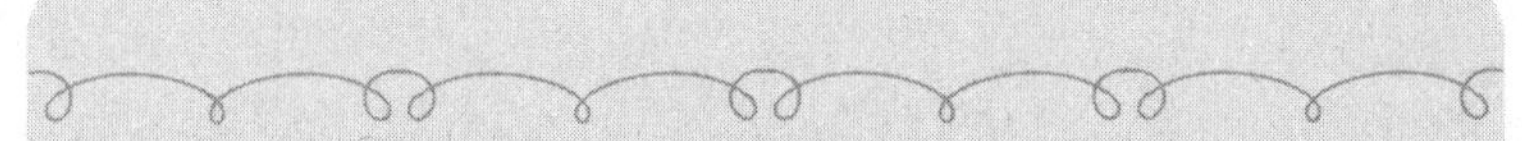

"You Suck"

HOPE: (Standing by a tree) I hate this new city. It's nothing like home. I wish I'd never moved here.

VAN: (Suddenly appearing from behind the tree) I am glad you are here.

HOPE: Who are you?

VAN: (Standing beside Hope) My name is Van.

HOPE: Why are you so pale?

VAN: I am from the north.

HOPE: Why are your eyes red?

VAN: Genetics.

HOPE: Why are your teeth so . . . pointy?

VAN: Okay, okay, so I am a vampire. You got me. (He walks to the park bench)

HOPE: (Walks in front of him) Really? Cool. I'm on the swim team.

VAN: What?

HOPE: You're a vampire, like in baseball, right? Well, I'm on the swim team. At my old school, I was the record holder for the five hundred meter.

VAN: (Stands and walks to Hope) No, I'm not an umpire. I'm—

HOPE: (Crosses to the tree) I know what you're thinking. The record holder for the whole school? But I am.

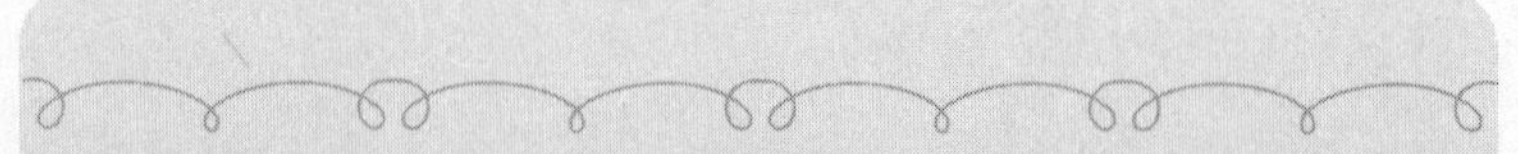

VAN: That's impressive.

HOPE: I know, right? But no one here seems to care.

VAN: (Standing close to her) I care. I have been watching you for a while. And I think I—

HOPE: I mean, I can swim circles around these other girls. And does anyone care? No. It's like they're ignoring me.

VAN: (Touches Hope's neck) I'm not ignoring you. Since the first day I saw you—

HOPE: (Walks away) Well, that's nice and all, but I don't want to get on the baseball team. I want to swim.

VAN: Forget swimming. I can take you far away. We can fall in love and get married and have babies that crawl out of your belly and have weird names and—

HOPE: Whoa, dude. I don't really go for ballplayers, okay?

VAN: I'm not a baseball player.

HOPE: So you lied to me?

VAN: No. What?

HOPE: You come over and tell me you play baseball and get me to talk to you and then you tell me you don't play baseball?

VAN: (Yelling) Vampire. I am a vampire.

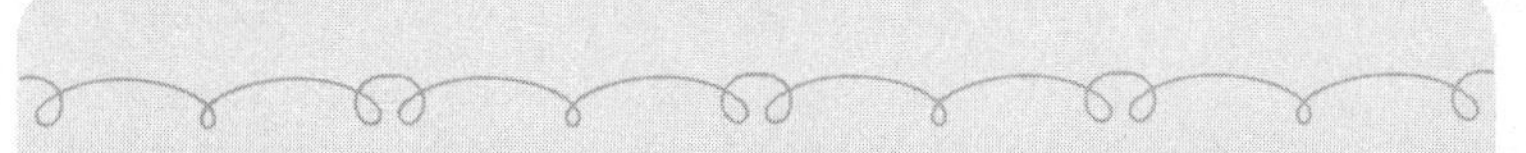

HOPE: Make up your mind. Do you play baseball or don't you?

VAN: Pale skin, red eyes, pointy teeth . . . vampire.

HOPE: (Walks past Van) Oh, I get it.

VAN: Thank you.

HOPE: You have issues because you're ugly, so you pretend to play baseball.

VAN: (Walking away) Forget it.

HOPE: (Calling after him) You could try spray tan. Colored contacts.

(Van exits.)

HOPE: Oh well. Some guys are just losers.

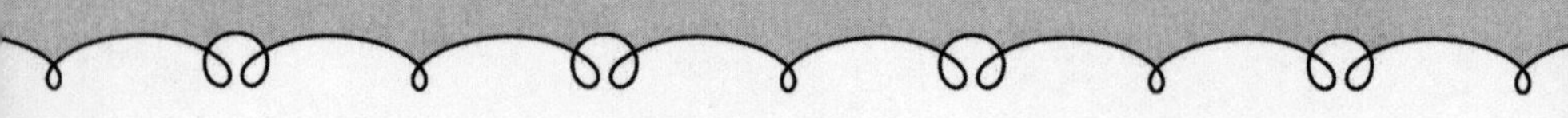

Chapter 18

"That was so fun." Kara turned to Haley on the ride home.

"I don't know about fun," Haley said. "I hated feeling so bound to their lines and their blocking. I agree with Anna Grace. I wish we had a little more freedom."

"Isn't this network supposed to be all about teens bringing our ideas to the show?" Anna Grace said. "I mean, they have us write and perform our own monologues to get on this, then they put us in this tiny box once we get here."

"Forget today." Zoey leaned up from the backseat of the van. "Tonight we get to have dinner with Devlin Tyne."

"I can't believe he's coming to our house." Sophie grinned.

"That is one hot boy," Anna Grace said. "I bet he's the star."

"But he's on *Boys Underground*." Sophie twisted in her seat to face Anna Grace.

"He's one of five on that show," Anna Grace said. "Why wouldn't he want to be on his own show?"

"Good point," Zoey said. "I sure wouldn't mind looking at him every day."

"Too bad, then," Anna Grace said. "Because this show is all mine. I killed it in the auditions today. Sparks were flying between Devlin and me like you wouldn't believe."

"That's because *he's* a good actor," Ava said, a hard edge to her voice.

"Just watch tonight." Anna Grace crossed her arms. "You'll see. He won't be able to keep his eyes off me."

The girls in the van grew silent. Kara closed her eyes. *And the game has begun.*

She looked back and noticed that neither Jillian nor Kylie was involved in the conversation. Jillian watched the other girls. Kylie was engrossed in a book. Kara knew that girl was very serious about her art. She was always reading a book about acting or the biography of a famous actress. Kara had tried to talk to her, but Kylie wasn't interested in doing anything but reading about acting or actually performing.

So maybe Jillian and I can be friends, Kara hoped. Jillian was Miss America pretty, with blond-on-blond highlights, perfect hair all the time, huge blue eyes, and teeth that Kara was sure had been covered in braces and whitening trays. *No one's teeth can be that perfect.* But she seemed pretty nice. That was certainly a rarity around here.

Two hours later, Devlin Tyne entered the girls' house. Kara found her impressions of the teen star were exactly right.

Those girls were swarming to Devlin like ants to a lollipop. If she learned nothing else from Addy, it's that going crazy for a boy did not endear a girl to him. Kara looked at Devlin once more, his thin frame enhanced by skinny jeans and a tight-fitting shirt.

Plus, that boy is a stick. I want a man with some muscles. Now, if Chad Beacon were coming over for dinner, I might be in trouble. But of course, he's not. He's a singer, not an actor. He's probably out in California somewhere, recording his next album.

"Ladies, ladies," Devlin said, parting the girls like Moses parting the Red Sea. "Thank you for the enthusiastic greeting. But I can't talk to you all at once. Why don't we just go in order, like we did at the auditions today?"

Anna Grace thought the idea was "stupendous" and suggested they go out to the pool for their talk.

"Did you bring your suit?" Anna Grace asked Devlin as she sashayed past the others.

"No, I'm afraid I didn't."

"Well, would you mind terribly if I got into mine? It's been such a long day, and I've been just dying to soak in the hot tub."

Devlin thought that was a great idea, and Anna Grace changed into her suit, a bikini that left little to the imagination, in world-record time.

Wow. Kara watched Anna Grace lower herself ever-so-slowly into the hot tub. *And the auditions continue.*

"I don't approve of bikinis." Flora joined Kara at the refrigerator where Kara was getting a bottle of water.

"I don't approve of throwing yourself at a boy to get his attention." Kara laughed.

"Good for you, Kara." Flora patted her on the back. "You just keep being yourself."

"Myself is not making too many friends here."

"That's all right." Flora sat at the kitchen table. "I'm not too popular either."

Kara looked out the window. Ava, who had also changed into her bathing suit, motioned for Anna Grace to go back inside. A slight argument ensued, but Anna Grace eventually submitted.

"Do you think Devlin is the star of this show?" Kara asked.

"What do you think?"

"It doesn't really matter, I guess. It's just acting."

"But . . . ?" Flora smiled at Kara.

"I don't know." Kara looked at Devlin, allowing Ava to take off his shoes so he could put his feet in the hot tub. "He just seems kind of fake. If I was going to be working with someone every day, I'd want it to be with a friend."

"You sound like Elizabeth Bennett in *Pride and Prejudice*. Except she was talking about marriage, not a TV show. But the same principle applies to both situations. Elizabeth was beautiful and smart and caring, and she didn't want to be with someone who didn't share those qualities."

"You really do love books, don't you?" Kara smiled at Flora. Today she was wearing a beret over her burgundy hair. Her dress was a wraparound Hawaiian print dress, held on her shoulder by a huge daisy pin.

"I do." Flora nodded.

"And you're a Christian?"

"I am."

"One of my best friends is a Christian."

"What is she like?"

"She's one of the best people I know."

Flora nodded.

"But a girl I knew at school said she was a Christian, and she is one of the worst people I know," Kara said. "All I was to her was a project. When she finally realized I wasn't going to believe what she believed, she was done with me."

"I have known people like that too."

"How can people who believe the same thing behave so differently?"

"That's a good question." Flora took an orange from the fruit bowl and began peeling it.

"Are you going to answer it?"

Flora kept peeling. "No. I think our questions are best answered by God. You should ask him."

"Ask God?"

"Yes." Flora peeled a section of the orange and ate it. "If you really want to know him, he'll answer you."

"But what if I don't?"

"Then you wouldn't be asking these questions." Flora handed a slice to Kara.

"You're not really a housemother, are you?"

"I am for the next month." Flora stood to throw her orange peel away. "I need to get dinner together. You go have your talk with Devlin."

Kara watched Flora open the stove and check on a casserole inside. *Ask God, huh? Maybe I should. Just to see. Not that I think he'll answer. But if he doesn't—when he doesn't—at least I can go back to Flora and tell her she's mistaken.*

"You don't want to swim?" Devlin asked Kara when she walked out the sliding glass door in her shorts and T-shirt.

"Not right now." Kara sat in a lounge chair. "I just want to rest."

"I guess it is tiring," Devlin said. "I've been doing this for so long, it's just second nature. I did my first commercial when I was six months old."

"Really?" *He doesn't even remember having this conversation with me at lunch.*

"Yes." Devlin sat next to Kara. "From there, I was on TV shows, a few movies, some music videos. I did anything and everything. I was even in a band for a little while."

"Really? Do you know Chad Beacon?"

"Sure I do," Devlin said. "We go way back. We used to go to acting school together."

Kara sat up. "Chad's homeschooled."

"Yes, but this was outside of school."

"Really?"

"Oh yes," he said. "My parents and his are good friends. His little sister and mine really hit it off. They have play dates all the time."

"Are we talking about the same guy?" Kara looked at Devlin. "Chad is an only child."

"What, are you some stalker of his or something?" Devlin's eyes hardened.

"No, I was just confused."

"I'm just trying to make small talk, all right?"

"Sure. Fine." Kara forced herself to smile. "So tell me a little about yourself."

Devlin's face brightened. He launched into a Devlin Tyne autobiography, and Kara sat back, pretending to be interested in his accomplishments, his fans, his future plans.

". . . And this fall, I start shooting my first film." Devlin smiled. "It's going to be a trilogy. I'm the star."

"That's wonderful," Kara said, meaning it. "Really, really wonderful."

Especially since that means you can't possibly be the star of this *show.*

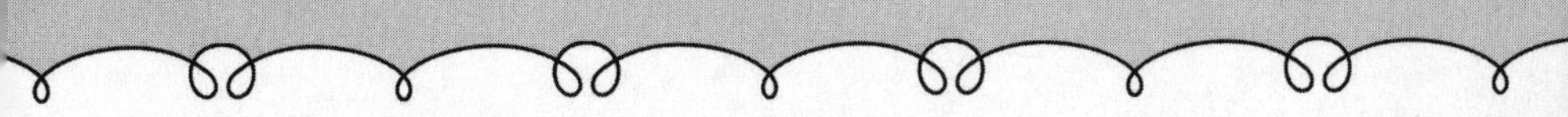

Chapter 19

"Oh, Addy." Kara hugged her friend as soon as she stepped out of her car. "I'm so glad you came."

Addy returned the hug. "Of course I came. I can't wait to explore Orlando with you."

"Let me just tell Flora I'm going." Kara walked into the house and called for Flora. That woman, sporting pink hair and a full-length purple plaid shirtdress, came out of her room. "My friend Addy is here. She's going to take me out for the day."

"Kara speaks very highly of you." Flora shook Addy's hand. "Very nice to meet you, my dear. Enjoy your day off."

"Do you want me to pick anything up for you?" Kara asked Flora.

"No, thank you."

"Are you sure you want to stay here all by yourself?"

"Oh, Kara." Flora patted her arm. "I love solitude. I have my books and my organic green tea with pomegranate. And silence. I couldn't ask for anything better."

"What are you reading now?"

"C. S. Lewis's *Till We Have Faces.*" Flora's face brightened. "It's based on the myth of Cupid and Psyche, written by Psyche's sister, Orual. Orual hates the gods for all the horrible things she believes they have done. But at the end, she finally recognizes they are real and powerful and she submits to their authority."

"Interesting," Kara said.

"It's a parallel, written about Lewis's own conversion from atheism to Christianity."

"Well, enjoy then." Kara waved good-bye to Flora and walked out to Addy's car.

Kara heard the front door open and shut behind her. Turning around, she saw Anna Grace walking toward them.

"Tweedledee and Tweedledum." The blonde shook her short hair and laughed. "I guess you don't need to go to Disney, do you? You have your own little freak show all the time."

"You seriously came all the way out here to say that?" Kara turned around and started walking back to the car.

"No, I was checking to see if our ride was here." Anna Grace huffed. "But seeing you two, I just couldn't help myself."

"Ah, self-control," Kara said. "Another defect to add to the list." She slammed the car door before Anna Grace could retort.

"Is that what they're like all the time?" Addy asked as she pulled out of the driveway.

"Anna Grace is definitely the worst. Some of the other girls have moments when they're nice. But then they remember this is a competition, and they get all nasty again."

Addy laughed. "No kindred spirits?"

"Not really." Kara looked out the window as Addy merged onto I-4. "This girl Jillian is all right. I don't think we'll be best buds or anything, but she doesn't call me names or lock me out of my bathroom."

"Your roommate?"

"Haley." Kara sighed. "I swear, that girl spends so long in the shower she should have shriveled up like a prune. I wish she would."

"I'm sorry."

"Thanks." Kara pointed to the Mickey Mouse–shaped electric poles that lined the interstate. "I love this city."

"It is fun. And I have all day to show you around."

The girls spent the morning wandering around Downtown Disney, a tourist trap that housed dozens of shops. Kara loved seeing the larger-than-life characters inside and outside the stores. She was especially excited to see Cinderella walking around. Kara posed next to the princess, immediately making that her Facebook timeline picture.

The pair looked at prints of Disney cartoons, listened to music, even rode in a simulated roller coaster. For lunch, they ate at Planet Hollywood.

"Someday my red-carpet gown will be hanging here." Kara pointed to a glass case housing a decades-old gown belonging to Marilyn Monroe.

Addy took Kara to Old Town next. Designed to resemble Main Street USA circa 1950, Old Town had a Ferris wheel, a merry-go-round, and an Old General Store. Kara loved seeing the *I Love Lucy* memorabilia and bought a huge poster of her favorite actress to go on the wall in her room.

"I've got to liven that place up a little." Kara picked up an *I Love Lucy* pillow as well.

"You'll have to show me your room when we get back."

"It's not too exciting." Kara walked past a life-size poster of Elvis. "But I've added some McKormick touches."

"Such as?"

"A Hollywood Star with my name on it—Sam made that for me. Painted gold and everything." Kara picked up a snow globe with the Three Stooges inside. "Of course, the other girls love to make fun of it."

"Really?"

"You have no idea, Addy. People in your world are so nice."

"What did they say?"

"Trash talk." Kara walked out of the store into the warm Florida evening. "Telling me that's the only star I'll ever get, making fun of it because it's homemade—Anna Grace supposedly has one made out of real gold."

"Right."

"She says all kinds of stuff." Kara held her stomach. "Being a tourist really works up an appetite. Ready to grab some dinner?"

"You really need to warn me when you change subjects." Addy laughed.

"It was a natural progression." Kara wrapped her arm through Addy's. "Hollywood Stars made me think of Anna Grace who makes me sick to my stomach. My stomach needs to be filled with food, therefore—dinnertime."

"Of course." Addy walked with Kara to the parking lot. "Makes perfect sense."

Addy knew a Bahamian restaurant just miles from Old Town.

"Island food?" Kara licked her lips. "Sounds great. Lead on, mon."

Because it was a weeknight, the wait was short, and the girls were sitting down to eat in half an hour. Kara enjoyed her mahimahi and steamed vegetables. Addy, not a fan of seafood, ate chicken with fries.

"You really need to branch out more." Kara looked at Addy's plate. "You can get that at McDonald's."

"Hey, I don't make fun of your fish." Addy popped a fry in her mouth. "Don't mock my meals."

"You sound like Pop. I can't make him eat healthy for anything."

"How are your parents doing?"

Kara shrugged. "As well as can be expected, considering the light of their lives is a thousand miles away."

"But the grandkids are there." Addy winked.

"They're cute." Kara smirked. "But the house just isn't the same without me."

Kara's phone rang. She picked it up to see Flora's name on her screen. Kara answered. "Time to go home already? . . . But I'm having so much fun, Mom."

"Actually, this is Flora. But it is time to return. You have a busy day tomorrow, and I want you to be well rested."

"All right. We're just finishing up dinner." Kara took a sip of her water. "You sure I can't bring you anything?"

"No, dear. But I do appreciate you asking. And I appreciate you not complaining about the curfew."

Kara thought of the other girls. "Have you gotten a lot of complaints?"

"Not all the girls are as respectful as you are."

"I'm sorry."

"No, no," Flora said. "Such is the nature of teenage girls today. I've read all about it. Although I must admit, viewing the reality is much more disturbing than reading about the proclivity."

"Thanks for calling, Flora." Kara smiled, not really sure what Flora had just said. "I'll be home soon."

Kara ended the call. "Sorry, fairy godmother, but my carriage is about to turn into a pumpkin."

"Oh yes." Addy laughed as she finished off her chicken. "You have definitely had too much Orlando today."

"Is it possible to have too much Orlando?"

"You really like it here."

"You have no idea." Kara waved the waitress over and the girls put their money in the black folder she provided. "Everything about this is so fun. The auditions, the cameras, memorizing lines. I love it."

"You weren't even this excited about Tennessee." Addy walked with Kara out to her car.

"That was a dating show. It was exciting to be on TV. But the best part, for me, was the first week when we got to perform on that stage."

"I hated that week." Addy groaned.

"Not me." Kara climbed into the passenger seat of Addy's small car. "The end of *The Book of Love* was just a date. The end of this is a real show. I want to do this forever, Addy."

"I hate having cameras all around. It makes me so nervous."

"When I'm really into a scene, I forget they're even there."

"That's a gift, Kara." Addy turned onto the interstate. "I could never get used to that."

Kara looked at her phone. "We're not too far away, are we? I don't want to come in past curfew. Flora has enough problems. I don't want to be one of them."

"Just a couple more minutes. Flora seems very nice."

Kara smiled. "I love that lady. She knows who she is and doesn't care what anyone says about her."

"Sounds like somebody else I know."

"Except she's a Christian."

"I thought so." Addy turned off on the exit back to Kara's neighborhood. "Especially when she got so excited about that C. S. Lewis book she was reading."

"You know what she told me when I asked her about God?"

"What?"

"She told me if I wanted to know something about him, I should ask him."

Addy looked at Kara. "And what did you say?"

"Nothing. But when I got back to my room, I tried to pray."

Addy turned in her seat. "You prayed?"

"Don't get all excited." Kara unbuckled. "Nothing happened."

"But you tried."

"You and Flora are making me think." Kara shrugged.

Addy reached into her backseat and pulled out a leather-bound book. Her Bible. "Take this."

Kara pushed it back. "No way. You read this all the time. I'm not that serious."

"I have others," Addy said. "Besides, if you want to know more about what we believe, you need to read it. Start with John."

"John?"

Addy opened the Bible and laid a black ribbon between the thin pages. "Right there. Jonathon read that and he loved it."

"Jonathon could read the back of a cereal box and love it if it came from you." Kara laughed.

"Very funny." Addy pointed to the dashboard clock. "You better go, Cinderella."

Kara got out, leaving her sparkly flip-flop in the car.

"Kara," Addy yelled out of the window. "Get your shoe."

"Hang on to it," Kara shouted back. "I'm going to need you to bring it the next time you save me from the ugly stepsisters!"

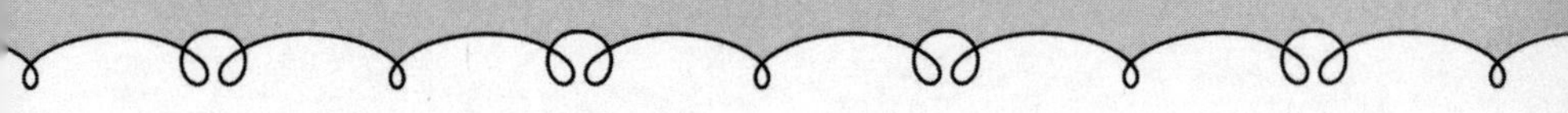

Chapter 20

"I think we got it that time, Chad." The producer's voice blared through the speakers in the recording studio. Chad turned down the volume and spoke into the microphone.

"Great." Chad peeled the headphones off and hung them on the rack to his left.

The door opened and Jim walked in, then pulled a stool up beside Chad. "I want to talk to you."

"Okay."

"We've been working together awhile, right?" Jim asked.

"Since I won *America's Next Star*. Hard to believe it's been two years."

"Two great years." Jim nodded. "And you're just getting started. Each album gets better and better. This one is amazing. Your fans are going to go crazy. I've got some ideas for the tour I want to run past you."

"I'm not touring with this one, Jim." Chad sighed. They

had already had this conversation. "I'm taking a break from music for a while."

"You're still planning that TV show?"

"Yes." Chad looked at Jim. His thinning hair was plastered to his head, caked with sweat. Chad loved making music, but he didn't love touring or having girls scream his name and cry when he came near.

"Look." Jim rubbed his hands together. "I wasn't going to say anything because I hoped this was just a phase. But, dude, going from pop star to hosting a TV show is a huge jump down. People will talk. This could kill your career. I mean, all of it—music, acting, you name it. You could be a laughingstock in the business, end up flipping burgers for the rest of your life."

"I appreciate your concern. But I can't live my life worrying about what people are going to think. If they laugh me out of the business, then so be it. I'll run my family's orange grove and take my guitar out to the streets on the weekends."

"Sure, make jokes." Jim stood. "But I'm telling you this for your own good. Drop this show."

Chad didn't like Jim's tone. And he really didn't like the fact that the man made sense. This thought was not a new one. He had considered it before. No pop star had ever done what he was considering. *What if this is career suicide?*

Jim slammed the door as he walked out. Chad looked past him to see his parents come into the small office. They were in their work clothes.

I know what that means.

"SOSYDGABH Day, son." Mom handed Chad a canvas bag with jeans, a T-shirt, and some old sneakers.

SOSYDGABH was an acronym for "Serve Others So You Don't Get A Big Head." A tradition Chad's parents started right after he had won the music competition, these days were filled with helping people in need. The Beacons had served meals at homeless kitchens, cleaned out flooded houses, and cleared out gutters. They never let the press know what they were doing, wanting to serve others in secret.

"Today we're helping a family from church," Dad explained.

"The Millers' house burned down last week." Mom frowned. "Get changed now. We have a busy day ahead of us."

Chad changed from his button-down shirt and khaki pants into his work clothes, wondering what project they would be doing for the Millers.

"The Millers are staying at a seedy little hotel in a bad part of town," Mom said once the family was in their SUV. "Pastor Greg told us they didn't have insurance, so they have literally lost everything."

"That's terrible," Chad said. "Do they have kids?"

"Three little guys." Dad shook his head. "They don't need to spend another day in that awful place. We put a call in to Janet, and she said the apartment complex she manages has a three-bedroom that's available."

"Now, this stays between us, all right?" Mom said.

"Of course." Chad nodded.

"We've paid for their first year's rent, and we've furnished the apartment. But we're not telling the Millers that. We don't want them to feel obliged to us. Pastor Greg is calling them right now to tell them an anonymous giver has done that and that our family is coming to help them move in."

"Here's where you come in." Mom smiled at Chad. "Once we get the Millers to their apartment, we want to take Mrs. Miller shopping for some household items."

"I'm babysitting the boys," Chad concluded.

"That's right."

"You always said you wanted a brother." Dad smiled.

"All right," Chad said. "I can handle that. I think."

"Little boys have lots of energy," Mom said. "But the complex has a pool and a playground, so you'll have plenty to keep them busy."

Mom wasn't exaggerating about the hotel, Chad thought as they walked to the Millers' door. Paint fell in sheets off the antiquated walls, and the metal door looked like it had been on the losing end of a schoolyard fight. After one knock, Mrs. Miller opened the door. Peering under the chain, she smiled as she saw Chad's family. After quickly shutting the door to remove the lock, she opened the door wide.

"Thank you so much." A baby on one hip and two other boys attached to her legs, Mrs. Miller looked like she would topple over at any moment.

"When Pastor Greg called and said someone had paid for an apartment"—Mrs. Miller began to cry—"I was just about at the end of my rope. I was praying this morning for some help. I didn't think I could go on."

"One thing we know is that God answers prayer." Dad held his arms out to the baby. "We are glad to be used by him to help you."

"We haven't been formally introduced." With the baby safe in Dad's arms, Mrs. Miller was able to take Mom's outstretched hand. "I'm Maria Beacon, and this is my husband, Bill, and my son, Chad."

"Of course. I know who you are." Mrs. Miller smiled and invited the family into the tiny room. Two double beds crowded the space. A chair was butted against the window and one small suitcase lay on the dresser. "I'm Karen Miller. My husband, Allan, is at work right now. But this is Allan Jr. We call him A.J."

The five-year-old stood next to his mother, his big brown eyes staring up at Chad.

"How are you, buddy?" Chad knelt so he could be at eye level with the boy. "My name is Chad. My parents are going to let me have a playdate with you today. What do you think about that?"

A.J. looked at his mother. When she smiled, A.J. nodded. "Can Robby come too?"

Chad looked at the three-year-old, who was flashing a wide grin at Chad. "I wike bafeball."

"I like baseball too, Robby." Chad laughed. "Maybe we can pick up a ball on our way out."

Dad tickled the baby. "And who is this little guy?"

Robby pulled on Dad's shirt. "That's my brover."

"Is he your brother?" Dad looked down at Robby. "Are you sure? I thought this was your dad."

"No." Robby giggled.

"Your uncle?"

"No."

"Your pet turtle?"

A.J. stepped out from beside his mother. "He's our little brother, mister."

"Well, if you both say he's your brother"—Dad looked at the baby again—"then I guess he must be."

Chad looked at the boys. "You'll have to excuse my dad, kids. He's old. Sometimes he gets confused."

The adults shared a laugh while A.J. and Robby looked at Dad with suspicion.

"All right now," Mom said. "We have a busy day. You boys ready to see your new place?"

"Yeah," Robby and A.J. yelled. The baby joined in with a squeal.

Karen Miller was able to gather all her belongings in just five minutes. Chad watched as she placed everything she owned into the one suitcase in the room. The apartment complex was south of Orlando. Janet White was a longtime friend of the Beacons. They had been part of the same small-group Bible study for years, and Janet's husband, Dan, ran a marketing firm that his parents used to advertise their oranges.

"We're going to wiv *dere*?" Robby pressed his face against the SUV's window.

Mrs. Miller patted her son's head. "Not in all of that. Just a part."

The apartment community had a gate at the entrance. Once they passed that, the boys saw the huge pool and play area.

"I wanna go there," A.J. said quietly.

"I was hoping you'd say that." Chad smiled. "Me too."

"Chad will watch the boys while we go shopping and get you settled," Mom said to Karen.

"Oh, are you sure?"

"Of course," Dad said. "Chad is great with kids."

"But he's a big star."

"Today he's just a young man wanting to help," Mom said.

"Really." Chad pinched baby Trevor's cheeks. "I love kids. It's my pleasure to get to spend a day with these guys."

Karen Miller wiped her eyes. "Thank you. Are you sure you can handle all three?"

"Yes, ma'am," Chad said. "Don't worry. I won't take my eyes off them."

The afternoon went by faster than Chad had expected. He and the boys went to the pool, to the playground, and back to the pool. The older boys loved having Chad throw them into the deep end. The baby sat in a float and laughed as his brothers begged to "go higher." Chad enjoyed watching their faces light up. But keeping three young boys entertained was exhausting. He was relieved to see his parents wave him over to the apartment at five o'clock.

"The Millers have invited us to dinner." Dad opened the door for Chad and the boys.

"Wow." Robby looked into the apartment, his eyes wide. "This is awesome."

"I want to see your room." Chad turned to A.J.

"Where is my room, Mama?" A.J. asked.

"I think you should try to find it yourself," Karen said with a smile.

A.J. darted through the living room and down the hall. He peered in the first room. "Hey, those beds are too little for me."

"You're right." Chad stood behind the little boy and looked at the room. A crib was on one wall, a toddler bed on the other.

"Thomas the Tank Engine." Robby ran past Chad and A.J. to the toddler bed. "Dat's my favowite!"

His wall was filled with prints of Thomas and Friends. His comforter matched the prints, and a table with Thomas trains and tracks sat below the window. Robby sat by the table and began playing.

"I think Robby found his room." Chad gazed down at A.J. "But where's yours, buddy?"

A.J. looked at the room across the hall from his brothers'. "That's not mine."

The master bedroom was spacious. A queen-sized bed filled the center of the room, with a dresser and chest of drawers against the walls.

"Maybe you'll have to sleep outside in the pool," Chad said.

A.J. looked at Chad and frowned.

"Oh, wait," Chad said. "I see one more room down there."

A.J. ran to look in the last bedroom. "This is mine! And it's got baseball stuff everywhere."

Chad walked in and saw a twin bed topped with a baseball quilt, pictures of baseball players on the walls, and a shelf with baseball caps above the dresser.

"I even have my own bat and glove." A.J. pointed to the spot beside the door where the equipment hung.

"Awesome," Chad said. "Maybe we can go throw the baseball a little before dinner."

"I think that's a great idea," Mom said.

Chad and A.J. stayed outside until their mothers called them in. The dinner, spaghetti with garlic bread and a Caesar salad, was delicious, and the little boys were asleep before the Millers could serve the chocolate cake Karen had made for dessert.

"We can't thank you enough," Allan Miller said after tucking A.J. into his new bed for the night. "This is so generous."

"We just helped get you in and get you set up," Mom said. "And it was a joy to be able to do that. You have a beautiful family."

Karen Miller wiped her eyes. "Thank you. And thank you, Chad. My boys had such a great day. You have no idea how difficult the last week has been for all of us. This is the first time I've really seen them happy since the fire."

"I should thank you." Chad smiled. "And if it's all right, I'll come back again. Maybe you guys can go out one night and I'll watch the boys."

"I'd love that." Allan winked at his wife. "Wouldn't you, dear?"

"Chad Beacon, babysitting our sons?" Karen laughed. "That is something."

The families said good-bye, and a fatigued Beacon threesome got back in their car to drive home.

"That was great," Chad said. "Thanks."

"Better than the recording session?"

"So much better." Chad laughed.

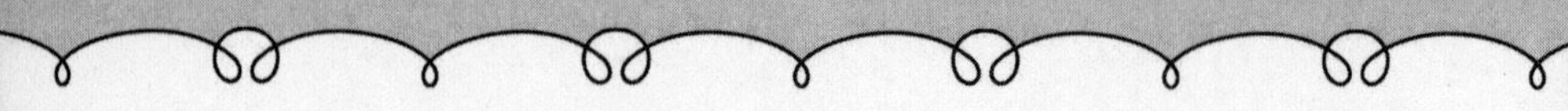

Chapter 21

"Today I'm taking you to the set of *Morgan's Road*," Ashley Win informed the girls the next morning. She had arrived at the house at eight o'clock. Most of the girls weren't even awake. Kara, an early bird, had been up, had her morning jog and shower, and was just sitting down to breakfast.

"*Morgan's Road*?" Sophie asked. "I love that show. Will we get to meet the cast?"

The other girls all talked at once about the teen show, a soap opera–type drama on a popular teen network.

"I've seen every episode."

"Will we be on it?"

"I want to do a scene with Zach."

"No way, he's mine."

"Not with that big old pimple on your face. He'll take one look and go running."

"Girls." Ashley silenced the girls with a wave of her hand. "You are auditioning to star in a show that will be just as, if not more, popular than *Morgan's Road*. Don't get starstruck. You'll be performing a scene with the actors from that show, just as if you were starring with them. It will be taped. Just like your scene with Devlin, this will be shown on television too."

"When?" Anna Grace asked. "When I did *The Book of Love*, our episodes were shown that same week."

"This is not a reality TV show." Ashley folded her arms. "This is a television show that will, hopefully, be on for years. Your auditions will be aired the month leading up to the show's premiere. The premiere is scheduled for the first week of October."

"She's already told us that." Haley looked at the petite blonde. "Pay attention once in a while."

"Enough." Ashley tapped the screen on her phone. "We begin at ten o'clock. The van will be pulling out of the driveway at nine thirty."

"That's not enough time to get ready." Zoey ran her fingers through her curly brown hair.

"That's all the time you get," Ashley said.

"It'll be fine." Jillian smiled at the girls. "We can do this."

Flora, sitting in the back of the room, stood. "We have six bathrooms. Let's make a sign-up sheet for each one, and that will allow each girl to have thirty minutes in a bathroom. That will be . . ."

The girls, ignoring Flora, ran for their rooms. Doors slammed. Ashley walked out, leaving Jillian and Kara standing with Flora.

"I thought it was a good idea, Flora," Jillian said.

"These girls don't listen." Flora shook her head.

"Don't worry about them." Kara hugged the smaller woman. "You're the best housemother I've ever had."

"Have you had other housemothers, Kara?" Flora asked.

"No, I was being silly." Kara laughed. "But even if I'd had others, you'd still be the best."

"I'm not sure how you could come to that conclusion, based on such hypothetical assumptions."

Jillian grabbed Flora's hand. "Don't mind Kara. We all think you're great. The other girls are just focused on getting this part. Too focused on that, if you ask me. I think there are more important things in life than that."

"Do you, Jillian?" Flora smiled. Kara walked out slowly, listening to the conversation. "Like what?"

"Like God."

"Are you a believer?"

"Yes, ma'am. I sure am."

"Well, isn't that wonderful." Flora patted Jillian's hand. "I'd love to hear your testimony."

"Of course," Jillian said, her voice sounding strained. "But right now, I really should get ready."

"Oh yes. You do that. Have a good time now."

The girls barely made the nine thirty deadline. By the time Kara got to her room, Haley was in the bathroom. *Of course.* Once again, Kara was forced to put her makeup on in her bedroom, opening the blinds to let in more light and holding her compact out at arm's length to check her hair. Haley waltzed out of their bathroom at 9:25, freshly showered, her hair and makeup perfect.

"You could have let me in the bathroom to fix my hair." Kara threw her compact in her purse.

Haley looked at Kara. "I could have."

"I knocked a dozen times."

"I know."

"Well?"

"What are you upset about? You look fine." Haley put her makeup bag in the dresser drawer.

That was the closest her roommate had come to a compliment, so Kara chose to smile and say thanks.

The ride to the studio was silent. The girls were either texting or listening to their iPods. Kara glanced over at Ava's cell phone. "Agent Kelly" was advising her to befriend the stars on *Morgan's Road*.

"Stop looking at my phone." Ava covered the screen with her hand.

Kara sighed.

Sitting next to her, Kylie had her eyes closed. Kara knew from their oh-so-brief conversations that the girl was mentally preparing for the audition.

Kara decided she'd close her eyes too. No one in the van needed to know it was out of sheer boredom.

As soon as the vans pulled up, the girls scrambled over each other to get out and greet the waiting stars. The five teen celebrities hugged each girl as she introduced herself. Kara waited at the end of the line. She noticed Flora pulled into a parking space at the corner of the lot.

"You're Kara McKormick," Paige Hanson, Morgan of *Morgan's Road*, said when Kara reached her.

"I am." Kara extended her hand.

"I loved you on *The Book of Love*," she said.

"Wow, thanks." Kara smiled. "I'm excited to be here."

"Come on in," Paige said. "I'll show you around."

The other girls, most of them vying for the attention of Zach Stone, the show's handsome costar, were ahead of Kara and Paige.

"You'll love it here," Paige said. "And you'll be great. You were a natural in *The Book of Love*."

Paige showed Kara the dressing rooms and the set. She introduced her to their director and stage manager.

Wow, a down-to-earth star. What a nice change.

"And there's Ashley Win." Paige pointed to the small woman walking into the building.

"Oh yes." Kara winced. "I know her."

"She talks tough, but she's really a sweetheart once you get to know her. She just has to be like that for auditions. Once you're in, though, she's great."

"Let's hope I get to see that side of her." Kara looked across the room as several of the other girls roared in laughter at something Zach said.

Paige looked at Kara and must have guessed what was going on in her mind. "Everything is better once the auditions are over. Trust me. When you're in a show together, the cast really does become like a little family."

Paige's assurance gave Kara hope.

Ashley gathered the girls in the green room as the show's stars went into their dressing rooms to prepare for their day's work.

"All right," Ashley said. "This is a little different from your last audition because you'll be working with two actors, not just one. We want to see how you interact with the other actors. And *Morgan's Road* is a drama, so we'll be looking at how you can perform in that arena."

"But isn't our show going to be a comedy-sketch show?" Haley tossed her perfect curls behind her shoulder.

"*You* don't have a show." Ashley walked over to Haley, her stiletto heels clicking with each step. "If you ever hope to have one, you better show that you can perform in any venue, any style, under any circumstances."

The door opened, and the man Kara recognized as the stage manager brought in a handful of scripts.

"Thanks, Randy." Ashley smiled and took the scripts from him. "We don't have as much time as we did with Devlin. The *Morgan's Road* actors have graciously agreed to give us their morning. I purposefully didn't give you the scripts until now because I want to see how you do with just a few minutes to memorize your lines."

The girls gasped.

"There will be monitors on the sides of the stage with your lines on them," Ashley said. "But you can't be attached to those. It will be obvious."

"This isn't fair," Gina said. "You're just rewarding those who can memorize quickly."

Ashley looked down at Gina. "This is fair, my dear. And this is show business. If it's too tough, then go home. I can guarantee you there are plenty of other girls who won't complain."

Gina opened her mouth to say something, but nothing came out.

"All right, then," Ashley said. "I will give you your script ten minutes before your audition. You must stay in here and wait for your turn so no one sees the scenes and comes in with an advantage."

Flora entered with a tray full of fruits, vegetables, and cheese. "I've got snacks so you won't go hungry."

"Thank you, Flora," Ashley said. "We'll go in reverse alphabetical order today. So, Zoey, you're up."

Kara ran through the list of girls in her head. *Zoey, Sophie, Kylie, me. Fourth. Not bad. Enough time to mentally prepare, not so much time that I go crazy. I can handle that.*

Ashley left the room with Zoey and the girls began to gripe.

"This is ridiculous," Gina said. "None of the *Morgan's Road* cast is given a script a few minutes before performance."

"How do you know?" Kara asked. "Maybe they are."

"That's not how it works."

Anna Grace walked up to Gina. "And you're an expert?"

"This isn't my first audition." Gina pursed her lips.

"Well, it may be your last," Anna Grace said, "if you keep mouthing off to Ashley like that. Actually, never mind that. Keep it up. You're digging your own grave. One less competitor for me to have to beat out."

"This is about our acting abilities." Gina took a step closer to Anna Grace.

"Strike two."

Jillian stepped between Gina and Anna Grace, her eyes on Flora. "All right, girls. No need to get upset. We're all tense. This is nerve wracking. But getting angry at each other won't make us audition any better."

Anna Grace walked away. "Whatever. You're not worth it. None of you are."

The room grew silent and remained so as the minutes ticked on. Sophie was called out twenty minutes later, then Kylie. The girls didn't return once they performed. *They could, though.* Kara looked around the room. *If Ashley is worried that they might tell us what the scene is like, she's crazy. They'd be more likely to make up some stuff just to throw the rest of us off.*

Kara was called next. She read through the script quickly. *This is definitely dramatic. Melodramatic, if you ask me. But I just have to prove I can do it.*

Kara spent the next few minutes trying to understand her character and find some qualities in her that could bring her to life on-screen.

Her mind went blank. Normally, a million ideas were zinging through all at the same time. This time, nothing.

Come on, Kara. Think.

She looked at her phone; two of her ten minutes had passed and she had no plan. Her stomach began to turn, and she worried that she'd spend another two minutes losing what she had eaten for breakfast.

Trying to ignore her churning stomach, Kara began to work on memorizing her lines. When the director called her in, Kara was only partially sure of her lines and not at all sure of her character.

I'm going to blow it right here. I should have stayed in New York, tried out for the Broadway show. I bet they don't make their actors perform with only ten minutes of prep.

Paige welcomed her warmly, as did Zach.

"All right, Kara." The director looked at her. "You'll be Morgan's classmate Brittany. I'm sure you've guessed from the scene that you aren't a very nice girl. You're trying to steal Jake away from her. We want to see nasty from you, all right?"

Oh, I think I have lots of experience watching "nasty." Kara thought of her housemates. *Now if I can just not think about throwing up for the five minutes it'll take to play this part.*

"And . . . action."

Morgan's Road Screen Test

BRITTANY: (Walking toward Morgan) Oh, look, if it isn't Morgan.

MORGAN: Hi, guys! I'm all ready to get started decorating. This year's prom is going to be great, isn't it, Jake?

BRITTANY: I was just telling Jake the same thing.

JAKE: Brittany has some ideas.

MORGAN: Do you? That's great. I'm always up for some help.

BRITTANY: I'm sure you are. But, actually, I need Jake to help me. There are some columns in the basement that would be perfect.

JAKE: Sure.

MORGAN: I was just in the basement, Brittany. There aren't any columns there.

BRITTANY: You must have missed them.

MORGAN: Where did you see them?

BRITTANY: In the back, behind some pieces of wood. You have to really look.

JAKE: Why don't we all go together?

BRITTANY: No. I don't want to keep Morgan from her work. All those balloons won't blow themselves up. You and I can take care of the columns.

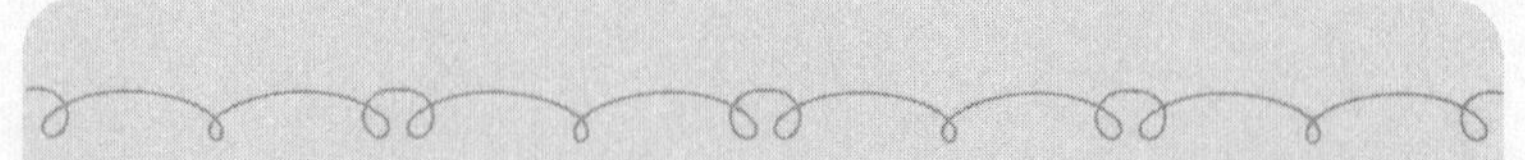

JAKE: That makes sense. (Turns to Morgan) We'll be right back.

MORGAN: All right. I guess.

(Cameras switch to the basement set. Brittany and Jake enter from the left. Brittany shuts the door.)

JAKE: Be careful with that door. It only locks from the outside.

BRITTANY: I know.

JAKE: What?

BRITTANY: (Standing close to Jake) You and I both know Morgan isn't for you.

JAKE: What are you talking about? Where are the columns?

BRITTANY: Jake, you knew I wasn't asking you down here to look for columns.

JAKE: No, I didn't. Brittany, I don't know what you're trying to do.

BRITTANY: (Pushes Jake onto a chair) I'm trying to get you to see what a waste of time Morgan is. You don't want to take her to prom.

JAKE: (Standing) Yes, I do. We've been through so much. The tornado, her parents' accident, the fire.

BRITTANY: I understand your wanting to help a

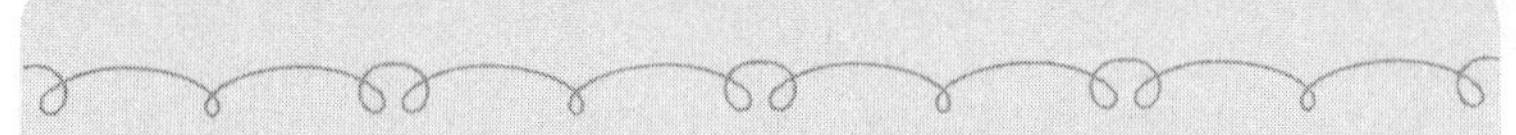

damsel in distress, Jake. But why don't you let someone take care of *you* for a change?

(Brittany leans forward to kiss Jake right as Morgan bursts through the door.)

MORGAN: (Running in) Jake? How could you?

JAKE: (Pushes Brittany away) No, Morgan, you don't understand.

BRITTANY: No, *you* don't understand, Morgan. And that's why Jake needs me.

MORGAN: (Crying) Fine, then. I hope you're happy together.

(Morgan runs out and Jake follows. Brittany sits.)

BRITTANY: Oh, we will be, Morgan. We will be.

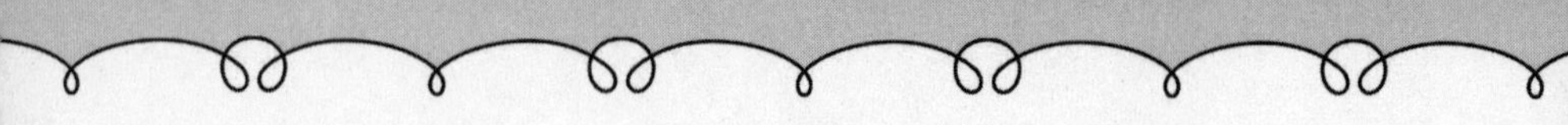

Chapter 22

"That was great, Kara," Paige said after the director yelled "cut."

Along the way, Kara's nausea had disappeared. But she knew this was far from her best performance. Paige was just very kind. "Thanks."

"Okay, Kara." Ashley walked onto the set. "We have a room set up for you right through there. You get to meet some of the other *Morgan's Road* stars and relax until all the girls are finished."

Kara replayed the scene in her head as she walked down the hallway. *I looked at the monitor too much. It's going to look like I was just reading the lines. That was such an amateur audition.*

"Excuse me," one of the show's other stars yelled at a caterer. "I specifically requested *diet* raspberry tea. Is this diet raspberry tea? I don't think so." She threw the bottle down on the table and walked away. The caterer was forced to rush after the rolling bottle, catching it before it fell on the floor and shattered.

Kara turned to see Sophie poking her head through the door to the girls' waiting room.

"Did you see that?" Kara said as she walked through the door.

"I sure did." Sophie's eyes sparkled. "I can't wait until I have that kind of power."

"She's terrible. That poor guy brings food and drinks right on the set and all she can do is yell at him because he didn't bring the exact right drink? There were dozens of others."

"These people work for *her*," Sophie said. "She has every right to expect them to bring her what she needs. She's a celebrity, after all."

Kara looked around the room. It was a large rectangular game room, with couches, recliners, a pool table, an air hockey table, and video-game consoles throughout.

Zoey was playing pool with one of the show's stars. Kylie, of course, was reading a book on the craft of acting. Sophie went back to the door to spy on the "celebrities."

Pool looks fun. I haven't played that in a while. That boy with Zoey looks like he's fifteen. Oh, Chad Beacon, yet another young man you've ruined me for. I'm beginning to think meeting him was a curse. No boy on earth can compare to him. That blond hair. The muscles. Hazel eyes. The muscles. Tall. The muscles . . . Kara sighed.

"Can I join you?" Kara asked Zoey.

"Only two pool sticks." Zoey shot Kara a mock "Oh, I'm so sorry" look and resumed her conversation.

Kara stood at the pool table for a few minutes, hoping

the actor would at least offer her a turn. But, no, he was enjoying having Zoey throw herself at him too much. Both people ignored Kara until she decided to leave and go sit by herself on another of the room's couches. Sophie entered the room with the now-happy actress drinking her diet raspberry tea. The pair took the seats across from Kara.

"That's how you get things done," the actress told Sophie. She looked at Kara. "My name's Lacy."

"Kara." Smiling at Lacy, Kara held out her hand.

"Sorry, I don't touch people." Lacy held her palms up to Kara. "Germs, you know. I can't afford to get sick. Not in this business. They could write me off if I missed a day. Nope, I stay healthy and take the spots of the people who do get sick."

"Wow," Kara said.

Lacy leaned in. "It's just a matter of time before I get Paige Hanson's spot. She's constantly shaking hands and hugging people. She goes to the malls and lets everybody breathe on her and share their pens and their paper for autographs. Just wait. She'll come down with some awful disease, and I'll be waiting."

"I never thought of that before." Sophie looked down at her hands, her eyebrows wrinkled.

"Most people don't." Lacy sipped her tea. "Everybody says stars just disappear because they lose their popularity or get involved in bad stuff. I say it's all germs. The healthy ones are the wealthy ones."

"You've put a lot of thought into that, haven't you?" Kara tried not to laugh out loud at Lacy's insane logic.

"Of course." Lacy set down her drink and tightened the

top. "There's more to this business than just being a good actress. That's what I was just telling Sarah."

"Sophie."

"Right." Lacy tossed her short strawberry-blond hair. "Be healthy, know who you are and what you want. And don't let anybody change you."

"My agent says the same thing," Sophie said.

"Who's your agent?" Lacy asked.

"The Jefferson Group out of Atlanta."

"Never heard of them." Lacy picked a speck of lint off her designer jeans. "Who do they represent?"

"They have hundreds of clients," Sophie said. "The walls of their offices are filled with pictures."

"But who do they represent? Who that is famous?"

"I don't know." Sophie's face fell.

"Then dump them." Lacy crossed her legs. "If you want to make it, you have to have good representation. You want to impress people. Take me, for instance. I'm represented by Jermaine Lockhart. Do you know who he is?"

"No." Sophie leaned in.

"He's the agent for Devlin Tyne and Felipe Barbot, and, of course, me."

"Really? We just met Devlin Tyne a few days ago. He's wonderful."

Get me out of here, Kara thought, making her way back to the pool table. *I cannot handle hearing one self-absorbed actor talking about another self-absorbed actor. I'd rather be ignored by Zoey and Twig Boy.*

"And I said, excuse me? I asked for a red Marsha Lane dress. You gave me a maroon Marian Long," Zoey said.

Twig Boy nodded his agreement as he lined up his pool cue for a shot. "It's good that you know what you want."

Zoey waited until the young man looked up from the table. "Oh, I do."

I am going to vomit all over the pool table. Kara walked away.

The door opened and Jillian entered. Kara walked over to greet her. "How'd it go?"

"All right, I guess," Jillian said. "A little more drama than I like."

"I know, right?" Kara laughed. "'No, *you* don't understand, Morgan. And that's why Jake needs me.'"

"Have you seen Flora?" Jillian asked, not even laughing at Kara's melodramatic interpretation.

"No, why?"

"I just wanted to talk to her."

"Is everything all right?"

"Of course," Jillian said.

"I think Flora is in the first green room with the other girls. We've got plenty of snacks here, though."

"I'm not hungry." Jillian walked to a recliner and sat down.

"Want to play a video game?"

"No."

"Want to talk? Tell me your most embarrassing moment ever." Kara sat opposite Jillian and smiled.

"Actually, I'm tired," Jillian said, closing her eyes. "I think I'm just going to rest for a while."

"Okay, sure."

Bored, Kara pulled out her phone. "Great, no bars. What am I going to do?" She spotted a bookcase in the corner and walked over. "All right, Flora, you'd be proud. I'm looking at books. I'm looking at books and talking to myself. But no one cares because they're all wrapped up in their own little worlds."

Kara bent down and scanned the titles. *Northanger Abbey* caught her eye. "Flora loves Jane Austen. I guess I could try her out."

Lost in Regency England, Kara barely noticed as the rest of the girls came in over the course of the next hour and a half.

"The best was saved for last," Anna Grace announced as she walked into the game room. "Y'all can all go on home now."

Flora came in behind Anna Grace. "The young woman is correct. Your auditions have concluded. Our van is waiting in the parking lot. Miss Win has requested we keep our voices down as we exit so we do not disturb the performers."

"We won't get to spend more time with the *Morgan's Road* cast?" Sophie complained.

"No, dear, I'm afraid not." Flora ushered the girls outside. "They have work to do."

"All this for a five-minute audition?" Haley said. "I don't think Ashley Win even knows what she's doing. This is ridiculous. Why not just spend five intense days auditioning us? She can get the same amount of taping done, the same scenes, and then we're done."

"Good point, Haley," Zoey said, her hands on her hips. "Who wants to tell that to Ashley?"

The girls were silent.

"Why don't we all call our agents and have them call her?" Gina suggested. "That way none of us gets in trouble."

"I don't think that's a good idea," Jillian said. "We're here for a month for a reason. We should just enjoy it and be grateful. Not look for ways out."

Flora patted Jillian's back. "Thank you for that word of wisdom, Miss Jillian. Excellent point."

The girls didn't hear Flora. Most were digging through their purses, reaching for their phones. By the time they were in the van, most of the girls were talking at once, begging their agents to end this month-long audition. Kara rolled her eyes, wishing she had taken the book with her.

Anything is better than listening to this.

"Hey, Flora." Kara leaned forward. "I started reading a Jane Austen book in there."

Flora turned to Kara. "Oh, that's wonderful. Which one?"

"*Northanger Abbey.*"

"Magnificent." Flora clapped. "Austen makes quite a caustic commentary on those who read gothic romances in that, don't you think?"

"I don't know." She hoped that by the end of her time in Orlando, she would be able to interpret Flora-ese. "But does Catherine end up with John or Henry? That's what I want to know."

"Oh, my dear." Flora's eyes widened. "I couldn't rob you of the pleasure of your first read-through of an Austen novel. To not know which. How delightful. You must finish it. I'm sure I brought my copy with me. I'll give it to you as soon as we return. John or Henry. It's quite a dilemma for our dear Catherine, isn't it?"

Kara laughed. "All right, Flora. I'll find out for myself. It better be good, though."

"Of course it is. It's Jane Austen," Flora said, her hands extended. "And how did you enjoy today?"

"It was wonderful." Kara beamed.

Jillian perked up. "Oh yes. I had a great time too."

"Tell me about it." Flora looked at the girls.

Kara was surprised to hear Jillian jump in and begin talking.

". . . but I didn't care for how some of the actors behaved," Jillian said.

"No kidding." Kara leaned in. "I saw a girl throw a bottle of tea down on a table because it wasn't what she wanted."

"Even worse." Jillian lowered her voice. "I heard some of the girls here saying how they can't wait to be like that."

Flora sighed. "Pride comes before a fall, you know. Those girls might be permitted to behave like that now. But it won't last forever. Then they will live with deep regret."

"I agree," Jillian said.

"You girls behaved yourselves very well, though." Flora smiled at Kara and Jillian. "I am quite proud of you both."

"Thank you." Jillian beamed now. "You don't know how glad I am to hear you say that."

Kara made it home in time to watch *Broadway Bound*, the show she gave up to be in Orlando. The girls auditioning were amazing. Kara wasn't sure if she could have looked that graceful, dancing all over the stage while belting out a show tune. *But I couldn't be any worse at that than I was at today's audition.*

Kara listened to the directors talk about the musical the girls were auditioning for. A modern take on Shakespeare's *A Midsummer Night's Dream*. "Did he just say two teenage leads?" Kara asked the other girls watching the show.

"Helena and Hermia." Zoey leaned back. "Haven't you ever read the play?"

Two leads? They said it was just one. That makes it the same odds as this show. But it's a vote-in, so my chances might have been better. Kara rubbed her temples, fighting off the beginnings of an "Oh great, I just made a huge mistake" headache. *I knew I should have stayed in New York. I'm such an idiot.*

Kara couldn't stand to watch any more of the auditions, auditions she should have been on. She crawled into bed, but it was several hours before she finally drifted off to sleep.

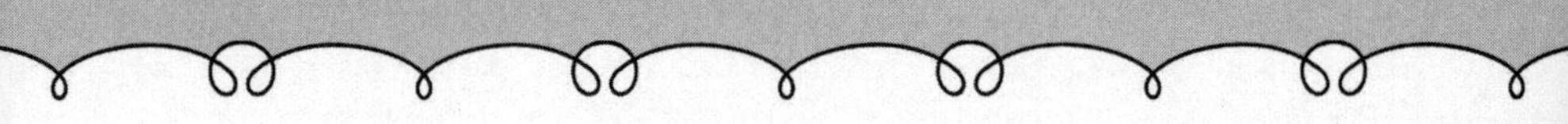

Chapter 23

"And let's give a big round of applause to today's special guest judge: Mr. Chad Beacon!" Jack Patrick, host of *America's Next Star,* motioned for Chad to come onto the huge stage in an arena in downtown Orlando.

Chad had been invited to sit in on the first-round auditions. Standing next to the longtime judges, Chad waved at the crowd. Thousands of people clapped and cheered, hoping today would be the day that their lives changed, that they were discovered. Thousands of people hoping to be the next Chad Beacon.

Little do they know that Chad Beacon doesn't even want to be Chad Beacon.

Looking up into the crowd, Chad recalled Jim's words from the recording studio. What was he thinking giving this up? Would people think he was throwing away the opportunity he was given when he won *America's Next Star*? Would they be angry at him?

"All right, let's head out," Derek Falcon, dubbed "the

angry judge," said as he walked off the stage. Chad and fellow judge Tina Kincaid walked behind.

"We love you, Chad!" a group of teen girls called out in unison. Chad turned to wave at them.

"Never gets old, does it, Chad?" Tina smiled.

Chad wanted to scream that not only did it get old, but it got lonely. Instead, he just looked at Tina and smiled back.

"You get enough breakfast, Chad?" Derek opened the door to the limo that would take the threesome to the hotel where the auditions were being held. The angry persona, Chad had learned, was just for television. Derek was actually a very nice man.

"I did, thanks."

"Good. Looking forward to being behind the table this time?"

"I guess." Chad leaned back in the plush leather seat. "I don't feel very qualified to be a judge, though. I've only been doing this a couple years."

"Don't worry," Tina said. "You let us be the bad guys. Your fans are just excited to see you. The producers will put together a package that talks about where you came from, how you won, what you've been up to, all that. This will air in January, so they'll promote your new album too. It'll be out about then, right?"

"Right."

Derek took a sip from his stainless-steel water bottle. "So we'll be airing just in time to promote the tour. That'll work out great for you. Have they talked to you about singing on one of the episodes?"

"No, not yet." For once, Chad was relieved that he

couldn't talk about the upcoming television show. If Derek and Tina knew, they might spend the whole day trying to talk him out of it. Even if they didn't, their presence alone made him feel guilty.

Two hours later, Chad was exhausted. "How do you do this all day? I'm ready for a nap."

"No one believes us when we tell them how tough it is." Derek took another sip of water. "And we've only just gotten started."

Chad stood and stretched while he and Derek waited for Tina to return from the restroom.

"Chad Beacon!" A very large African American girl ran into the room, security guards right behind her. "I'm here, Chad. I'm coming, baby. Hold on."

Chad didn't have time to react before the girl leaped over the table and landed on top of him. He fell backward with the girl crushing his chest.

God, please do not let this be the way I go out. Unable to breathe, unable to remove the girl, Chad knew he was seconds away from losing consciousness.

The security guards grabbed the girl from behind, but she resisted, and Chad felt an explosion in his side.

"Please . . . get . . . off," he squeaked, the girl's braided hair slapping his face as she fought the guards.

"Oh, baby, I'm sorry." Chad's captor lifted herself off his chest, bringing her face within inches of his. Chad got a sudden whiff of what he was sure were her armpits and decided that passing out definitely would have been better.

"I love you, Chad. I've loved you from the first time I saw you."

Backup had been called in, with two more guards assisting in lifting the girl from the floor. She fought hard, falling back down on Chad's chest. "No, I need a minute. We belong together. You and me, sugar. Ebony and Ivory." Her voice stank even worse than her armpits, and tears stung his eyes.

"I know, baby, I know." The girl wiped Chad's eyes with her thumb. "I knew you'd love me. I felt it." She put her palm to his chest. "In here."

Finally, the guards, with the help of the crew and Derek, pulled the girl off Chad.

"Live together in perfect harmony . . . ," the girl sang as she was escorted out, tears rolling down her face. "They can't keep us apart forever, Chad. I'll be back. We belong together. Ebony and Ivory . . ."

~

"A cracked rib?" Chad looked at the medic and groaned. "Are you serious?"

"Sorry, man." Several ambulances had been posted by the arena in case of emergency. Chad never thought he would be the emergency, though.

"You need an X-ray to confirm. And an MRI. I heard you hit your head pretty hard going down."

"No, I'm fine." Chad tried to sit up but was stopped by a searing pain in his side.

"That was about 350 pounds of fan you had on you, bud," one of the cameramen said, trying not to laugh.

"Please tell me you did not get that on tape."

"Are you kidding?" Derek put an arm around Chad and helped him stand. "That's going to make a great promo."

Chad groaned.

"But you do need to get checked out. We'll just have to judge the rest of the day without you. If you're better, you can come out tomorrow."

Any doubts Chad had about getting out of the music business were gone. *Let the fans get mad at me*. He winced with every breath. *Fame is definitely not worth this much pain.*

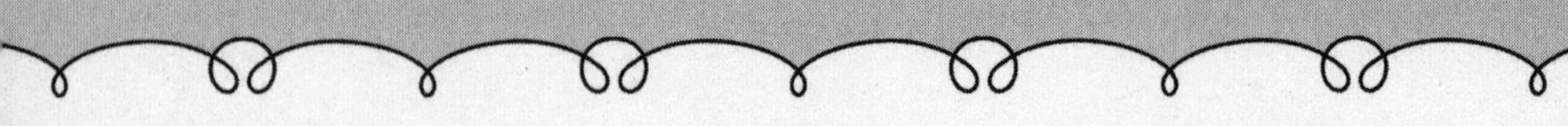

Chapter 24

"Ma." Kara looked at her mother's face filling her computer screen and groaned. "We have to sing."

"You're a beautiful singer." Ma shifted, revealing only the lower half of her face.

"Ma, move the camera up. I can't see your eyes."

She adjusted the camera, revealing the white ceiling of her kitchen.

"Ma." Kara laughed. "Can't you see that little screen at the bottom?"

"What?" She leaned forward, giving Kara a close-up view of the top of her mother's head. "All I see is gray."

"That's your hair, Ma. Sit back."

"Oh, oh." She looked down and smiled. "There I am. How's that?"

"Better." Kara leaned back. "But I'm nervous about singing."

"Oh, honey. You've sung lotsa times at the theater here."

"I know, but the girls here have more experience. They're going to be so much better than me." *Not to mention my last audition was a huge failure. I can't afford another one.*

"That doesn't sound like my girl." Ma frowned. "You worked hard to get there. You can do it."

"Thanks, Ma. I miss you."

"We miss you too, Kara. The house is so quiet without you."

She laughed. "I'm sure. How's Pop?"

"He's a little under the weather," Ma said. "I think it's just a cold."

"Oh no," Kara said.

"Don't worry." Ma looked at the bottom of the screen and fixed her hair. "He's resting, and I'm making him drink plenty of liquids. He'll be fine."

"All right." Kara sighed. "Are you guys still going to bring the kids down to Disney? There're only a couple weeks left."

"We want to. We just gotta wait until your pop is better. As soon as he's up to it, we'll pack the car and come down. Little Ethan asks about you every day."

"I miss them." Kara thought of her four-year-old nephew. "Give them all big hugs and kisses from Aunt Kara."

"Of course I will."

Kara hung up and popped her earphones back in, listening to her song again. The girls had been walking around the house singing all day. Haley, of course, locked herself in the bathroom, leaving Kara with their bedroom to rehearse in. The other girls came in and out of their rooms. Anna

Grace had made her rounds, reminding everyone she had "seven years of vocal training by one of the premiere vocal coaches in the United States." Having heard her sing in *The Book of Love,* Kara knew the petite southerner had the pipes to back up her big mouth.

Well, I've had two years in concert choir with Mr. Jones. So there.

Kara sang her song several times, trying not to strain her voice. Later that afternoon, all the girls were taken over to a recording studio downtown.

"That's Chad Beacon." Zoey pointed to a picture on the studio's wall.

"Yes." Jim, the manager, straightened the photograph. "He was just in here last week, as a matter of fact."

"Will he be in today?" Anna Grace stepped forward.

"I'm afraid not." Jim led the girls to the green room. "I heard he got hurt. Broke a rib or something."

"What?" Kara's voice was louder than she intended.

"Calm down, Kara." Anna Grace flipped her short hair. "Good grief."

"He was a guest judge for *America's Next Star* auditions and a fan attacked him."

Kara wondered where Chad was, if he was all right. She pulled out her phone and texted Addy to see if she knew anything. The girls all looked up as the door to the studio opened and Ashley Win walked in.

"Sit." Ashley pointed to the couches. "We need to talk before we begin recording."

The girls obeyed and Jim left the room. The tiny woman looked at each of the girls before continuing. "Don't worry. This won't take long."

Kara heard the clock ticking as Ashley pulled her phone out of her purse.

"Over the last few days, I've heard from several of your agents and parents. Calls, texts, e-mails, all telling me how to run this audition." She narrowed her eyes. "All suspiciously similar."

The girls looked at each other. No one spoke.

"I am the casting director." Ashley pointed her phone at the row of girls. "You are not. I'm not out to win a popularity contest. I'm here to do my job. I make the rules; you don't. If you don't like them, go home. That'll make my decision that much easier."

Kara glanced around. Only she, Kylie, and Jillian were actually looking at Ashley. All the rest of the girls' heads were down, examining the carpet.

"Am I clear?" Ashley asked.

The girls mumbled, "Yes."

"Very good," she said. "This better not happen again."

Anna Grace raised her hand. "Ashley, I hate to be a tattle, but this was really Haley's idea."

Haley stood. "Excuse me?"

"Come on, girls." Anna Grace's southern drawl became even more pronounced. "I know we all want to protect our friend, but we have to tell the truth."

"If you want some truth"—Haley's voice was shrill—"how about we tell Ashley how you've been acting around the house, telling everybody you have this audition in the bag and we should pack up and go home?"

Several of the other girls piped up, complaining about each other, agreeing with Haley about Anna Grace.

"Enough!" Ashley waved a hand in the air. "You two have just earned the first spots in today's recording session. Let's go."

"But I'm not warmed up," Anna Grace whined.

Ashley ignored her and walked to the door. Anna Grace and Haley followed.

As soon as the door shut, the girls all began talking at once.

"Well, I think this is all good," Sophie said, shaking her short black hair. "Two girls down. No way Ashley casts them."

"What about the rest of us?" Zoey said. "She knows we had our agents call her."

"She can't take all of us out," Gina said. "Then she'd have to start over."

"This is about talent, girls." Ava sat on the tan couch and crossed her legs. "Ashley is looking for a star, not a Goody Two-shoes."

The door opened and Ashley walked in again. "We need some quiet in here, please. Take out your cell phones or your iPods or read a magazine." She pointed to a rack on the wall. "But no talking. Got it?"

"Thank you." Kylie sighed as the door shut behind Ashley. She pulled out a book on the art of comedy and opened it to the middle.

Kara took Kylie's cue and pulled *Northanger Abbey* out of her purse. Flora had been helping her understand the novel, and to Kara's surprise, she was actually beginning to like it.

Her cell phone chimed and she picked it up. Addy had

finally texted back: CHAD'S RIB IS CRACKED, BUT HE'S OKAY. AT A HOSPITAL IN ORL. J WANTS ME TO GO SEE HIM. WILL U COME WITH?

Did Addy really have to ask? RU KIDDING? YES!!

TOMO MORNING?

Kara couldn't wait. YES, YES, YES!

PICK U UP AT 9.

Kara was so excited about getting to see Chad, she completely forgot to be nervous about singing. Until Ashley called her name, that is.

Jim walked with Kara and Ashley down the hallway to a small room divided by a sheet of Plexiglas. A microphone with a circular shield was on one side of the room, the sound equipment on the other. Glancing down the hallway, Kara saw Flora sitting on a chair watching a TV set up in the corner.

"Put those headphones on," Jim instructed. "A thumbs-up means 'turn the music up,' thumbs-down means 'turn the music down,' and an okay sign means it's perfect."

"I think I can remember that." Kara smiled and put on the headphones. The manager walked into the other half of the room and sat behind the desk, turning dozens of tiny knobs and pressing buttons.

Okay, feeling a little nervous. Kara tried to will away the knots forming in her stomach. Her throat suddenly felt coated with peanut butter. She was sure when she opened her mouth to sing, nothing would come out.

I can't have another bad audition. Kara thought back to the *Morgan's Road* fiasco. *I've got to do my best. Come on, Kara. You can do it.*

The music blasted through the earphones, and Kara gave the thumbs-down sign with one hand while yanking the headphones off with the other.

"Sorry about that," Jim said. Kara replaced the headphones. "Let's try that again."

Kara's music came through at a more reasonable volume. *I can't believe I'm going to record a song.* Kara took a deep breath. *I can do this. I can do this.* Just as she opened her mouth to sing the first note, Jim stopped her CD.

"All right," he said. "We've got the music levels where they need to be. Now for you. Count to ten right into the mic."

Kara did as instructed. Jim turned a few more knobs and put his hand up for Kara to stop.

"Very good. We're on a schedule now, so you'll get one rehearsal and one recording. Got it?"

Kara's heart hammered in her chest. *One rehearsal? What if I mess up? What if my voice cracks during the recording? What if I forget my words?*

"You stand right there," Jim said. "We'll adjust the balance between your voice and the music. You don't need to move."

"No problem." Kara laughed.

"All set?"

All right, God. I know I don't talk to you much. Or ever. I don't even know if you're real. But if you can help me get through this without messing up, maybe we can spend some more time together.

Kara remembered one of Addy's comments. *"God isn't your personal genie. He's the creator of the universe."*

All right. Just help me. If you're there. I'd really appreciate it.

Kara listened to her voice coming through the headphones. *Wow, is that me? They really can do wonders in that little box. No peanut butter voice. No shaking. Awesome.*

At the end of the rehearsal, Kara felt ready to record.

"What are you doing in there?" Kara asked.

Jim furrowed his brow. "What?"

"I sound so much better in here than I do in real life." Kara pointed to her headphones.

Jim pointed to the soundboard. "This baby is a miracle worker."

"Now I know why singers sometimes sound so much different live than they do on their CDs."

Jim needed a minute to get everything set for the recording, so Kara took that time to stretch and breathe. *One shot. You can do this. I think.*

With a point toward Kara, the manager started the music. She had chosen Carrie Underwood's "Before He Cheats." She loved the song, and she loved that it told a story. In her rehearsals back at the house, Kara had come up with a whole background story to go along with the song: young girl right out of high school has been dating this boy since her sophomore year. They were going to get married as soon as they graduated college. They'd work a few years, then settle down and have kids and their lives would be perfect. On their three-year anniversary, they go out to a fancy restaurant and have a beautiful, romantic, candlelit dinner. Then as they walk out of the parking lot, the boy asks to run back in for a minute. Scared to be waiting outside by herself, the girl walks in to see him talking to their waitress. The waitress hands him her number with a wink and he walks out. The girl says nothing, and he drives her home. Getting into her car, she follows him to his favorite hangout, a greasy diner. He's there. And a few minutes later, so is the waitress. And the song begins . . .

Kara imagined herself as the jilted woman. Forgetting she was singing in a studio, Kara closed her eyes and tried to "be" this girl, her song telling the story. She could see the truck, feel the baseball bat in her hand.

The song ended and Kara opened her eyes, exhilarated.

"Excellent," Jim said. "Great choice."

"Thank you!" Kara said, her heart racing.

"It's interesting. Your tone and volume are almost an exact match to one of the singers we work with."

"Really? Who?"

"Chad Beacon," he replied. "You've heard of him, right?"

"Yes. I've heard of him." *And I'll be seeing him tomorrow.*

"You guys would sound really good together."

"Okay." Kara smiled. "If this show doesn't work out, maybe you could hook us up."

Kara thought she saw a scowl pass over Jim's features. "I'd like nothing better, sweetheart."

Ashley walked back in, escorting Jillian. "This is Jillian, Jim."

Jim looked up quickly, his eyes brightening. "Jillian, yes. I think we have a mutual friend."

Kara didn't hear any more of the conversation because she was being escorted back to the waiting room. And because she was thinking of Chad.

"You guys would sound really good together." So maybe she

didn't need to do this show. Maybe she could come back and they could record CDs and tour together. *Kara and Chad. Okay, maybe Chad and Kara. Oh yes, we could definitely make beautiful music together.*

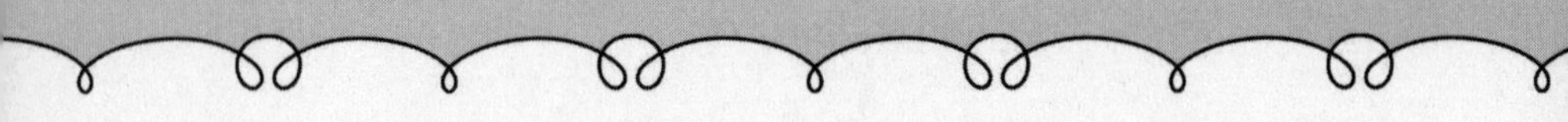

Chapter 25

"Kara." Chad sat up in the hospital bed and winced. "And Addy. You guys shouldn't have come."

"We didn't want to." Kara smiled. "But Jonathon forced Addy, who forced me."

Chad laughed. "Ouch."

"You okay?"

"Just a cracked rib. And a bruised ego."

"I understand that." Kara knew Addy was referring to her stint in the hospital after being bitten on the rear by a brown recluse spider.

"But what are you doing here in Orlando?" Chad looked at Kara.

She had already decided she didn't want to tell Chad about the show. If she told him and she didn't make it, she'd be humiliated.

"I'm just hanging out with Addy." *Not a lie. Just not the whole truth.*

"I wish I'd known," Chad said. "I would have invited you over."

"It's not too late for that." Kara grinned.

"Actually"—Chad took an unsteady breath—"I've got a thing in Phoenix at the end of the week."

"A thing?"

"Yeah, a thing." Chad smiled.

Perfection. "Can you sing with a cracked rib?"

"Are you kidding? No way." Chad held his side. "But I'm not singing for this event. I'm visiting a little boy who has leukemia. We're just hanging out for the day. But I can't postpone it. This little boy has been waiting for a while. And he isn't doing well."

Kara pictured one of her little nephews being in that position. A thought she did not want to dwell on. "So I've read what the blogs are saying. But what actually happened?"

Chad closed his eyes. "What are the blogs saying?"

Kara held up one finger. "You and Derek got into a fistfight." Kara held up a second finger. "You got angry at a guy for singing one of your songs so you got into a fistfight with him."

"Do they all end with me getting in a fistfight?" Chad interrupted Kara as she lifted a third finger.

"Not all." Kara walked to the foot of the bed. *He even looks good with bruises.* "One blogger said you faked it because you're trying to promote your new album."

"Which isn't out until January."

Kara held up her hands. "Hey, you asked."

"Forget I asked."

"So, what really happened?"

"I got pounced on by a huge fan."

"I did hear that story." Kara walked closer. Only Chad Beacon could look hot in a hospital gown. "Does that happen often?"

"Girls breaking my rib? No, that was a first."

"Crazy girls trying to get to you?"

Chad closed his eyes. "Sometimes."

Kara looked at Addy. "Look at him, trying to be modest."

Addy touched Chad's arm. "The reason we're here is because Jonathon sent us to check up on you. I have orders to report back."

"Orders, huh?" Chad pushed the button on the bed so he could sit up. "Tell him I won't recover until he has that talk with his dad."

"What talk with his dad?"

"The talk about not going into politics."

"Oh, that talk." Addy raised her eyebrows.

"I don't know why he's so scared."

Kara read the cards on the flowers by the window. "His dad is president of the United States. I'd be scared too."

"But he doesn't want to be president," Chad said.

"Easy for you to say." Kara walked back to the bed. "You're living your dream."

Chad's smile melted away. "You're right."

"That wasn't a criticism." Kara looked into Chad's hazel eyes. She hated the thought that she may have hurt his feelings.

"I know." Chad's gaze seemed to go straight through her. Kara couldn't look away.

Chad cleared his throat. "I thought of you last night. I was watching TV."

He thought of me. Last night.

"There's this show on called *Broadway Bound*. Have you heard of it?"

The show I should have chosen? The one I might have actually had a chance to win? "Yeah, I think I've seen an episode or two." *Or every one, sometimes twice. But whatever.*

"You seem very dramatic." Chad smiled. "I bet you could do something like that."

Addy looked at Kara over the hospital bed. "She definitely could."

Kara shot a warning glance at Addy. "I don't know."

"But you like performing?"

Just dig that knife in a little deeper, Chad.

Addy glared at Kara again, a "Why don't you just tell him?" look on her face.

"Doc says you are free to go. Your brain is going to be all right," a gray-haired nurse announced in a loud voice, pushing her tray past Addy and, thankfully, putting an end to the conversation.

"Good to know," Chad said.

"You never know about falls. Concussions don't always show up right away. That's why we needed to keep you overnight for observation."

"You sure he should go already?" Kara eyed Chad. "I heard lunch was mashed potatoes and lime Jell-O. Don't want to miss that."

"All right, girls," the nurse said. "I've got to do some looking. You better get out so this young man doesn't lose his dignity."

"Right." Chad glanced down at his hospital gown. "I'd hate to lose my dignity."

The girls said their good-byes. Kara hoped to get some more time with Chad. *At least give him a chance to ask for my number*, she thought. But the nurse made it clear it was time for the visitors to leave.

Buckling up in Addy's car, Kara sighed. "You're welcome, by the way."

"Really?" Addy pulled out of the parking lot.

"Not just any friend would come out to a hospital to see a hurt friend. But I'm just great that way."

"Yes, I know it was difficult for you."

Kara closed her eyes and thought of Chad. She could still feel his skin on hers when she patted his hand good-bye. "You have no idea."

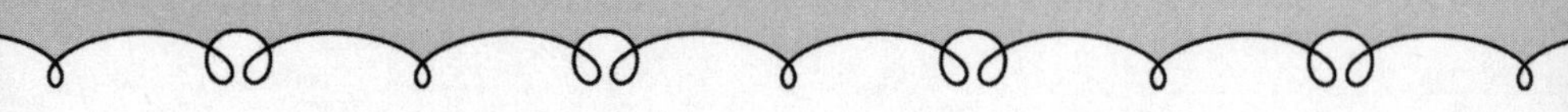

Chapter 26

"Welcome back, Kara," Flora greeted from the kitchen. Today she was wearing a vintage floral 1960s maxidress. "Did you have a good morning?"

"Very good." The girls were given a free day, but Addy had to get back to Tampa to help a friend. So Kara decided she'd spend some time in the pool. Daydreaming about Chad Beacon.

Flora took a chicken from the refrigerator and laid it in the sink. "Now for the pot." Flora turned faster than her dress did, and when she took a step, her leg twisted and she came crashing down on the tile floor.

"Oh no." Kara knelt beside the housemother. "Are you okay? You fell hard."

Flora tried to push herself onto her knees. Her dress turned into a burrito and Flora fell on her back. "It was just a minor accident. And you know what Aristotle says about accidents: 'The ideal man bears the accidents of life with dignity and grace, making the best of circumstances.'"

Kara pushed Flora's dress up and looked at her leg. Her ankle was already starting to swell. "This is not time for your authors, Flora. We need to get that ankle taken care of."

"No, no. Aristotle was a philosopher."

"Really?" Kara walked to the freezer for ice.

"Oh yes. You should have studied him by now. What is education coming to?"

"Flora, the 'really' was as in, 'Really? You're going to discuss philosophers while your ankle swells up?'" Kara wrapped the ice in a towel and laid it on Flora's foot. "We need to get this leg propped up. Keep the ice on it. I'll get a chair ready for you to sit in."

"No, I'll be fine. Go ahead out to the pool."

Kara looked down at her bathing suit. "I'm not going to the pool when you're hurt. Now give me your hands, but don't put any weight on your foot. Ready?"

Kara steadied herself and helped the small woman stand and hop over to the waiting chair. Kara placed Flora's injured ankle on the seat across from her and positioned the ice back on Flora's foot.

"All right. Now stay there. I'm going to call my mom."

"Why would you call your mother?" Flora asked. "I just slipped. No problem."

"My mom's a nurse. And your ankle looks bad. It may be broken." Kara ran back to her room, threw a shirt and shorts on, then walked back to Flora, dialing her mother's number as she walked.

Her ma, a registered nurse working at a hospital for more than thirty years, was immediately in medical mode.

"Yes, Ma, I have it elevated and iced." Kara cradled the phone between her jaw and shoulder. "Hang on."

Kara knelt by Flora's leg. "I'm going to have to poke around a little." Pushing the speaker button on her phone, Kara handed it to Flora. "Okay, Ma. I'm here. It's purple."

"Where?" Ma asked.

"Right by the ankle bone."

Ma's voice crackled over the cell phone. "All right. It could be a break or just a sprain. Touch around the ankle, Kara. Gently."

Kara barely touched Flora's skin when the older woman sucked in a deep breath.

"I'm sorry." Kara pulled her hand back.

"No, no." Sweat was beginning to bead up on Flora's forehead. "I'm sorry."

"That was very painful?" Ma asked.

"Yes, I'm afraid so," Flora said. "But it isn't Kara's fault. I'm afraid I just don't do well with pain."

"Oh, honey, none of us likes pain," Ma said. "You just relax. Tenderness and bruising, huh? How about swelling? Kara, compare Flora's injured ankle with the other one."

Kara moved around the chair to look at Flora's left foot. "Oh wow. That right ankle is a whole lot bigger than her left."

"Can you be more specific?"

"She's a little lady, Ma. Not much body fat. Her ankle bone on the left foot really sticks out. Like a mountain. The ankle bone on the right looks more like a little hill."

"That's not good," Ma said. "She definitely needs to get checked out. You got someone there who can take you to the doctor?"

"We have a driver," Kara said. "But I don't know how to reach him. Flora?"

"No." Flora straightened herself in the chair. "I'll be fine. I don't need to go to the doctor."

"Yes, you do," Ma and Kara said in unison.

"The sooner you get this taken care of, the sooner you'll be up and around," Kara said.

"All right." Flora sighed. "The driver's name is Harold, and his number is on the pad of paper in the drawer next to the silverware."

Kara called Harold, hanging up right as Sophie came in the kitchen.

"What happened to you?" Sophie barely glanced at Flora before opening the refrigerator.

"She's hurt." Kara folded her arms, watching with disgust as Sophie opened the fruit and vegetable drawers in her search for the perfect snack.

With a bright red apple in her hand, Sophie walked out. "Hope you feel better."

Kara looked around. A couple more girls were by the pool. *There's a sliding glass door right there. Why aren't they helping? And the girls in the living room are just watching a movie. I know they can hear us. I can't believe this.*

"I'm sorry, Flora."

Jillian walked in as Kara replaced Flora's ice.

"Oh no." Jillian stopped. "What happened?"

"Nothing, nothing," Flora said, her head down.

"She hurt her ankle," Kara said. "I called Harold, the driver. He's on his way."

Jillian knelt to look at Flora's ankle. "That looks terrible, Flora. Have you taken anything? I have some ibuprofen in my room."

"Normally, I try to avoid medication," Flora said. "But I might make an exception. Just for today."

Harold rang the doorbell just a few minutes later.

"Jillian, can you help me get Flora to the van?"

"Of course. I'm coming with you. She takes such good care of us. I wouldn't leave her when she is in need."

"All right, then," Kara said. "Let's get you out to the van, Flora. Don't put pressure on that ankle, okay?"

The girls helped Flora into the van, and Jillian buckled the small woman's seat belt.

"I can do that," she said.

"I know." Jillian smiled. "But I don't want you to have to strain yourself."

"I hate to be such a bother." Flora looked at her ankle, propped between the two front seats on a cooler.

"You're not a bother." Jillian put her hand on Flora's arm. "I'm going to be praying that you get better soon."

"That's the best medicine you could give me." Flora settled in as the van took off. "We have a few minutes. Why don't you tell me about how you came to know Jesus, Jillian?"

"What?" Jillian looked at Flora.

"You told me you are a believer. I've been looking forward to hearing your testimony."

"Oh, my testimony." Jillian relaxed. "Yes. I'd love to

share that with you. I was raised in church. Both my parents are very good people. They taught me to obey the Bible."

"Wonderful," Flora said. "What church do you attend?"

"W-well, it's in San Diego," Jillian stammered. "I'm sure you've never heard of it."

"You'd be surprised. I have traveled quite a bit. San Diego is one of my favorite cities."

"Oh, well, it's a small church. Um, Central Christian."

"You're right," Flora said. "Never heard of it. But I'll look it up next time I'm there."

"Flora." Kara leaned toward the older woman. "What did you do before you were our housemother?"

"This is Jillian's time to talk." Flora patted Kara's knee. "We can talk about me later."

"I was wondering the same thing." Jillian spoke quickly. "We know you traveled. And you know so much about books. What else?"

"One more question for you, Jillian, then we can talk about me. All right?"

Jillian gave a slow nod.

"Tell me something wonderful Jesus has done for you."

Jillian's face turned white. "Something wonderful?"

"Yes." Flora smiled. "There are so many things, I know. But tell me just one. I love hearing how he is working in the lives of other believers."

Jillian looked up. "Jesus, um, he got me an audition on this show. Out of the thousands of girls who tried out, he helped me to get chosen."

"And why do you think he allowed that?"

"I don't know." Jillian shrugged. "Because he knows how much I want this, I guess."

"All good and perfect gifts come from above." Flora nodded, her smile not quite reaching her eyes. "That is true."

"Okay, ladies." Harold leaned back. "We're here. Are you okay on your own? Some of the girls want me to take them to the outlet stores this afternoon. You can just call me when the little lady is all patched up."

"Sure, Harold," Jillian said.

The emergency room smelled like sweat and Pine-Sol, and Kara put a hand to her nose to keep from gagging. Her other arm supported Flora. Jillian was on the other side of the injured woman, and the pair managed to get Flora into a brown plastic chair, with another chair set in front of her for her leg.

"Wait there," Kara said. "I'll get you signed in. Do you have your insurance card?"

"Yes, let me just find it." Flora tried to bend down and reach for her purse, but the pain on her face reflected how difficult that was.

"I'll get it." Jillian lifted the large woven purse into Flora's lap.

Kara walked to the front desk and wrote Flora's name on the sign-in sheet, handing over Flora's insurance card and ID. *I can't believe I'm at the hospital for the second time in two hours. Too bad Chad has already checked out. I sure wouldn't mind popping in to see him again.*

"So, about how long will the wait be?" Kara asked when the receptionist finished making copies.

"Half an hour or so."

Kara walked back to Jillian and Flora."The receptionist said half an hour. In ER time, that means about two hours."

"You seem quite at home here." Flora took the insurance card from Kara's hand.

"Oh yes," Kara said. "Emergency rooms were my second home growing up. I've broken two bones, had stitches three times, and I've had two concussions."

Jillian looked at her. "Daredevil?"

"That and just dumb." Kara laughed. "When I was seven, I was totally into Tarzan, so I decided I'd make myself some vines like he had. I got rope and tied it to a tree in my backyard."

"Oh dear," Flora said, her eyes wide.

"Yeah, the rope was about eighty years old. I found it way in the back of the storage shed. I got a ladder and tied it to the tallest limb I could find, then I climbed up on the roof of my tree house."

"Was that the concussion or broken bone?" Jillian leaned in.

"Actually, it was all three—broken leg, eleven stitches in the back of my head, and a concussion."

"How terrifying for your poor mother."

"She says she used her nursing skills on me more than she did with all the other kids combined."

"That sounds very much like a boy I know," Flora said.

"Really?" Kara asked. "Who?"

"A friend." Flora cocked her head to the side. "He grew up on a—well, a farm of sorts. His parents would go looking for him, and he'd be out climbing trees or swimming across lakes. He only had a couple trips to the ER, but that was just from luck, not because he was careful."

"Sounds like we would get along well." Kara laughed.

"Oh, I daresay you would get along splendidly."

"All right." Kara scooted her chair closer to Flora. "We've got time, and you have no excuses. Tell us who you really are."

"I am Flora Lopez." She sat up straight.

"And what did you do before you came here?"

"I work as an assistant to a business owner."

"What kind of business?" Kara probed.

Flora shook her finger. "The kind that prefers to stay anonymous."

"The mob?" Kara jumped up.

"No, no."

"CIA?"

"You have a very active imagination, Kara." Flora shook her head and motioned for Kara to sit back down. "Just a business."

"But you said you've traveled all over," Jillian said.

"I have." Flora smiled. "I am a single woman, and I use my extra money and vacation time to see the world."

"That sounds fun."

"It is quite enjoyable." Flora nodded.

"Flora Lopez," a nurse called from the door.

Jillian and Kara helped Flora to an examining room. A few minutes later, the doctor pulled the curtain and stopped short. "Flora. Nice to see you again."

"Again?" Kara looked from the doctor to Flora.

"We're old friends."

"You've been here before?"

"Plenty of times," the doctor said. "In fact, Ch—"

Flora waved her hands to stop the doctor. "No, no. Um, girls, I do believe I am fine where I am. Would you mind going back to the waiting room while Dr. Smith completes his examination?"

Kara noted the blush on Flora's cheek and winked at Jillian. "Sure, Flora. No problem."

The doctor shut the curtain and Kara stood still, trying to listen to their conversation.

"Kara," Jillian whispered. "Don't eavesdrop. That's rude."

"It isn't eavesdropping," Kara whispered back. "It's spying."

A nurse stopped to look at the girls and they made their way quickly back to the waiting room.

"Don't you want to know the story behind those two?" Kara asked when the two were seated in the smelly waiting room once again.

"Only if Flora wants to tell us."

"But she doesn't," Kara said. "Which makes me even more curious."

"I'm sure it's nothing." Jillian picked up a magazine from the table beside her.

"Then why send us out?"

"Maybe she had to come in here before for something embarrassing, and she doesn't want us to know about it?"

"Or"—Kara pushed Jillian's magazine down—"Dr. Smith and Flora had a romance long ago. He left to pursue his dreams of practicing medicine among the sick and dying in Africa and she stayed here, working like a slave for the

Mafia. He tried to get her to come along, but she refused. She couldn't or the people she worked for would kill him. She loved him too much for that, so she sacrificed her happiness for his life. That's why she's never married. She's never gotten over her first love."

"You really have an active imagination, you know that?" Jillian opened the magazine to an article about Chad Beacon.

"I saw him this morning. Right here." Kara pointed to the picture. "He got pounced on by a fan, and I came to check on him."

"Right." Jillian looked at the magazine cover. "Was Prince William there too?"

"I'm being serious," Kara said, but Jillian kept reading, obviously not interested in conversing with her.

Kara pulled her book from her purse. *Jane believes me, don't you, Jane?* She returned to the world of *Northanger Abbey.*

Kara looked up half an hour later to see Flora hobble out on crutches, Dr. Smith behind her.

"You girls need to make sure she stays off that foot for a while, all right?" the doctor told Jillian and Kara.

"Yes, sir." Kara smiled. "But that won't be easy."

"Just because you have crutches," Dr. Smith said, "doesn't mean you should be on them all the time. A couple hours a day, at most."

"But that's impossible," Flora said. "I have far too much work to do."

"I'm sorry," said the doctor. "But if you want that ankle to heal, you've got to rest."

"Don't worry," Kara said. "We'll make sure she stays off it. Right, Jillian?"

"Of course."

"And don't worry." Dr. Smith put a hand on Flora's shoulder. "You-know-who is just fine."

"Thank you." Flora sighed. "I'm glad you were here to take care of him."

Kara looked over at Jillian. She raised her eyebrows toward Flora. Jillian rolled her eyes, but Kara knew there was more to Flora's story than she was telling. And she was determined to find out what that woman was hiding.

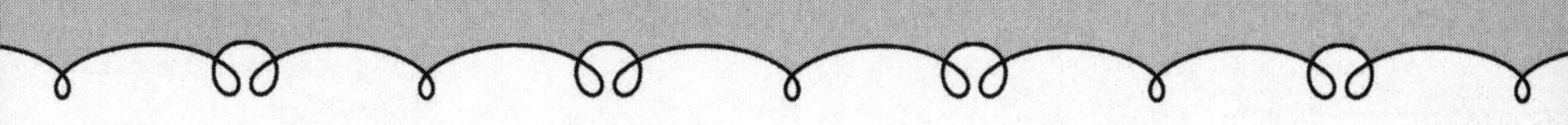

Chapter 27

Kara walked into the kitchen to find Jillian preparing a salad while Flora sat at the table.

". . . I guess I like the story of Noah because it shows that God's promises are true." Jillian slid sliced carrots into the large wooden salad bowl.

"Very true, my dear." Flora noticed Kara and smiled. "What about you, Kara? Do you have a favorite Bible story?"

"Not really." Kara shrugged, reaching into the refrigerator. "I've never really read much of the Bible."

"But it is God's Word."

Kara rinsed a carton of cherry tomatoes. "There are so many different religions out there. How can you be sure yours is right? That your God is *the* God?"

"The Bible says if anyone lacks wisdom, he should ask for it," Flora said. "If you want to know what is true, ask God to show it to you."

"And if he doesn't?"

"Four thousand years of biblical history have stood

firm, proving that he does answer those who diligently seek him."

Jillian leaned forward. "She's right, Kara."

Kara laughed. "It's like a conspiracy. First Addy, then Flora, now you. I'm being surrounded by Christians."

"Perhaps this is God's way of showing you he exists."

"Maybe." Kara thought about the chapters she had read in the book of John the night before. She didn't have an overwhelming sense that God existed from those few pages. But it *was* interesting.

Anna Grace walked into the kitchen. "Where is lunch? You said it would be ready by noon. We have to be at the studio by two o'clock for our dress rehearsal."

"And good afternoon to you." Kara glared at the young woman. "Sure, we'd love some help."

Anna Grace pointed to Flora. "That's the help. But she just 'happens' to be injured. Must be nice, getting paid to sit around and let other people do your work for you."

"You need to stop." Kara walked over to the angry Alabaman. "You'll get your lunch, and you'll get to the studio. You can either go back to the pool and wait, or you can come in here and help us."

"Like I'd lift a finger for you losers." Anna Grace walked around the kitchen, bumping into Flora's foot on her way out.

Kara started to walk after her.

"Kara." Flora's determined tone stopped Kara in her tracks. "'Do not associate with one easily angered.'"

"What?"

"It's from the book of Proverbs," Flora said.

"Then you two are the only people I should associate with," Kara said.

"Some girls are just so self-absorbed," Jillian said. "Anyway, I love cooking. And hanging out with you, Flora."

"Thank you, dear." Flora smiled. "Let's get that fish cooked, and then I think lunch will be ready."

After all the girls had eaten, Flora excused herself to take a nap. Jillian put the last of the dishes in the sink and turned to Kara. "So you really like Flora, huh?"

"Sure." Kara sprayed the counter with cleaner and wiped it. "Don't you?"

"Of course. She's great."

"I know. You guys have a lot in common."

"We do?"

"You know, you're both Christians."

Jillian blinked. "Right. Yes, we do share our faith. I think I'm the only one here who is a Christian, don't you?"

Kara thought. "I guess you're right."

Jillian relaxed into a chair.

"Is that hard for you?" Kara sat next to her.

"What?"

"Being the only Christian."

"Oh no," Jillian said. "Not at all. I kind of like it."

"Really?"

Jillian looked at her phone. "We're leaving in just a few minutes. I better fix my hair."

"Right. Me too."

Thirty minutes later, Kara stood looking at an actual set built just for the girls. One side looked like a typical suburban living room. The other was decorated like a retro loft. Both were three-sided, with cameras and lights all around.

"While you were working with the help"—Anna Grace walked past Kara and whispered—"I was studying my lines. I guess we both spent our afternoons preparing for our futures."

Ashley walked into the room before Kara could respond. "All right, girls. Time to start. As you know, you're all doing the same scene. Five in one, five in the other. The first group to go is Jennifer, Gina, Haley, Zoey, and Kylie."

Haley raised her hand. "But I went first last time."

The other girls began complaining as well. Ashley held up a tiny hand to silence them. "First group, you're wasting time. You get an hour to rehearse and then thirty minutes to tape."

"Miss Win." Anna Grace's accent was even more pronounced than usual. "I just want to say thank you for this opportunity, and—"

Another wave of the hand. "The rest of you will be in the green room. Let's go."

Ashley's high-heeled shoes clicked loudly on the cement floor. The girls in group two followed her through the set to the lounge on the other side of the building. Ashley held the door open and the girls filed in.

Anna Grace stopped beside Ashley. "As I was saying, I'm just so grateful—"

Ashley looked down the hallway to make sure all the girls were in, shut the door in Anna Grace's face, and clicked her way back to the set.

Anna Grace looked around, her jaw firm. She sat next

to Kara and said, "Listen, you better give me something to work with today."

"What?"

"Everybody knows you're the weak link in this group." Anna Grace lowered her voice. "No agent, hardly any experience. It's obvious you don't know what you're doing. I didn't mind when we were on different teams. But if you're going to work with me, you need to step up your game."

Anna Grace was trying to make her nervous. *And she knows exactly what to say to do it.* Refusing to let that girl win, Kara stood and walked to another chair.

"Are you going to answer me?"

Kara looked up, refusing to let Anna Grace intimidate her. "No. You've got me so nervous, I don't even know if I can remember my lines. I may just fall apart and start crying in the middle. Ruin the whole scene. Destroy your chances of winning."

"You think you're so funny." Anna Grace's face turned red. "Whatever. Just don't blow this."

Kara closed her eyes and drew in several deep breaths. She had read a little of Addy's Bible the night before. John was basically stories of Jesus. She wasn't sure what to think of it yet, but she did know that when she was reading, she felt calmer. *I could use a little of that calm right now.* She opened her script.

Reviewing her lines, Kara thought about her character and got excited about performing, in spite of Anna Grace's efforts to unnerve her.

Girl 2. I need to give her a real name. Something cool. Ooh,

I can make her a Native American. She will be Girl Who Wins Contest and Becomes Super Famous. Or Mary.

She isn't the funniest one in the skit. Ava gets that one. But I need to show I can support her, that I'm not trying to get all the attention. Anna Grace always tried to go over the top. Girl 4 was not the crazy one, so she might just blow it for herself if she tries to overdo it. *A girl can dream, right?*

"All right, girls." Ashley opened the door to the green room almost an hour later. "Places."

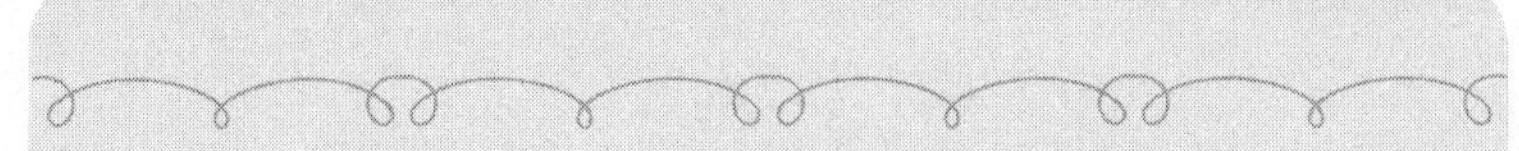

Radioactive Monkey Brains

Scene 1

(Five girls are in their living room. Girl 1 is staring at the phone.)

GIRL 1: Ring.

GIRL 2: You know it can't hear you, right?

GIRL 3: I don't know. Once, I told the radio to play my favorite song, and it totally did.

GIRL 4: What if they don't call?

GIRL 5: They said they'd call either way.

GIRL 1: Ring.

GIRL 2: Seriously, stop staring at the phone. It's not listening.

GIRL 3: It might be.

GIRL 4: It's a phone.

GIRL 3: Or maybe it's not. I saw a movie once where aliens invaded people's electronics. That's how they got to know the earthlings before they ate them and took over the world.

GIRL 5: The phone is not an alien.

GIRL 1: Ring. *Ring.*

GIRL 2: I want this so much.

GIRL 3: We all do. But it's not up to us anymore.

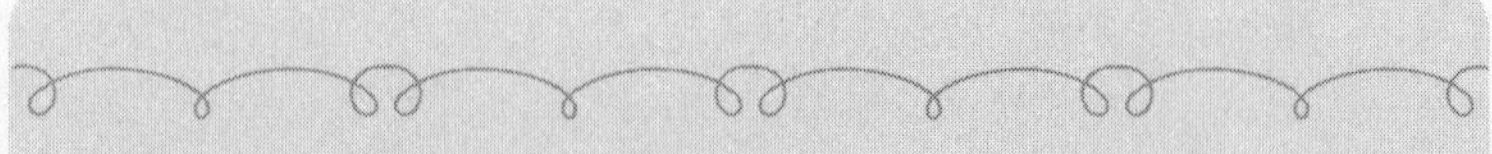

GIRL 4: We left it all out on that stage. You know we did.

GIRL 5: But there was some fierce competition.

GIRL 2: Those girls from Detroit were amazing.

GIRL 1: *Ring!*

GIRL 3: One time, I saw a show about competitive yodeling. It was intense.

GIRL 4: Competitive yodeling?

GIRL 3: It's totally legit. I swear.

GIRL 5: If this thing doesn't work out, maybe we should look into it.

GIRL 1: Just ring, stupid phone. Ring.

GIRL 2: You're saying more words. Good.

GIRL 3: When I was in sixth grade, my teacher taught us the longest word in the English language. It's . . .

(The phone rings. The girls freeze.)

GIRL 1: It's—it's ringing.

GIRL 2: I know.

(The phone rings again.)

GIRL 4: It might be them.

GIRL 5: This is it.

(The phone rings again.)

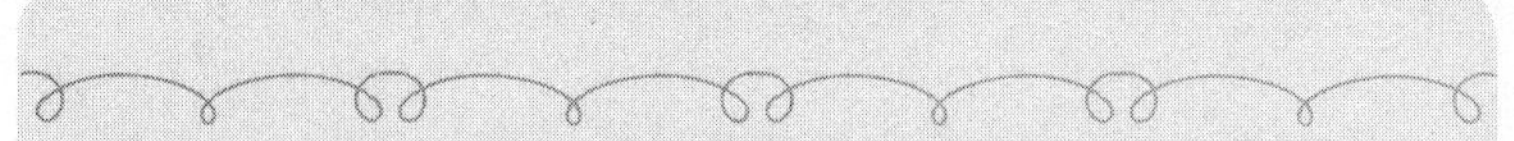

GIRL 3: One time, I got this phone call that was super important, but right when I was about to hear the big news, my battery died.

(The phone rings again. Girls 1, 2, 4, and 5 lunge for the phone at the same time. It falls on the ground. They follow. Girl 1 presses the Speaker button.)

GIRL 1: (Out of breath) Hello?

MAN ON PHONE: Hi, this is Rex Fanner, from the Unlimited Music Company.

ALL 5 GIRLS: Yes?

REX: Am I speaking to the band Radioactive Monkey Brains?

GIRL 3: Yes, we came up with the name one day when we were bored in science, so we started surfing videos and saw this one about a zoo in Japan . . . (Girl 2 clamps a hand over Girl 3's mouth)

GIRL 2: Sorry. Yes, we're Radioactive Monkey Brains.

REX: I was at your concert last night.

ALL 5 GIRLS: Yes?

REX: And I think you're terrific. I want to sign you on with our company.

(The girls scream.)

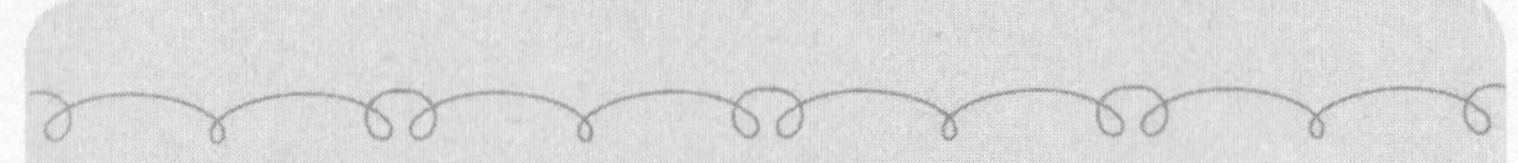

REX: How soon can you come out to Los Angeles?

Scene 2

(The girls walk into their apartment in LA.)

GIRL 1: Wow.

GIRL 2: This is unbelievable. Look at this place.

GIRL 3: When I was three, I had a clock just like that cat clock. I used to sit and watch its tail go back and forth until I fell asleep.

GIRL 4: (Pushing Girl 3 toward the clock) Then, please, look at this. Look at it a lot.

GIRL 5: (Sitting on the couch) Our very own loft apartment.

GIRL 1: (Pointing to a picture on the far wall) Look! Our poster. It's us, guys.

GIRL 2: The Radioactive Monkey Brains are taking over LA, baby.

GIRL 3: I saw this movie once where mutant anteaters tried to eat the Hollywood sign. But their mouths were too small. All they could eat were the *L*s.

GIRL 4: I can't believe this is happening. We're making our own CD. We have a poster.

GIRL 5: And a concert.

GIRL 1: What?

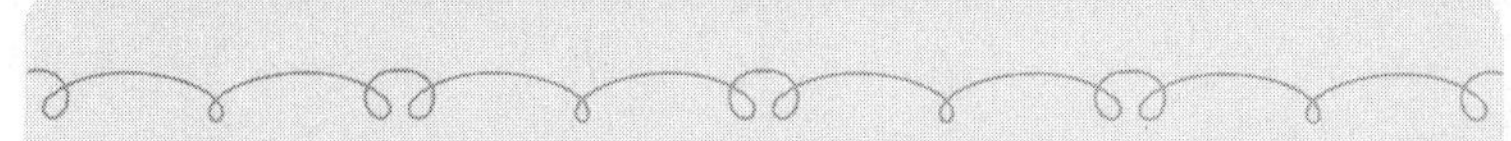

GIRL 5: Yep. Rex just told me. We're singing downtown tonight.

(All the girls scream.)

GIRL 2: That is awesome.

(Someone rings the doorbell.)

GIRL 3: Coming.

(She tries to open the door, but it won't budge.)

GIRL 3: This . . . won't . . . open.

GIRL 4: (Pushing Girl 3 aside) Let me try. You're right.

GIRL 5: You guys must not be turning the lock the right way.

GIRL 1: What lock?

GIRL 5: What do you mean what lock?

GIRL 2: There's no lock. Not anywhere. It's just a big slab of metal.

GIRL 4: We're trapped.

GIRL 3: Once, my mom and I got trapped in a roller coaster for, like, thirty minutes. We couldn't get out of our seats.

GIRL 4: Be quiet. This is serious.

GIRL 3: But . . .

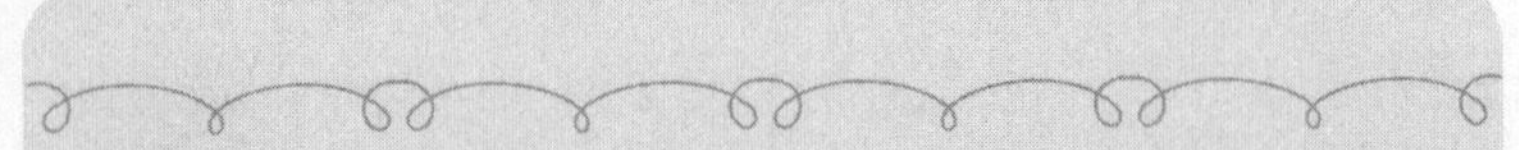

GIRL 5: We've got to think.

GIRL 3: But I'm not done with my story . . .

GIRL 4: (Pushing Girl 3 toward the cat clock) Watch the tail for a while, will you? We've got to get this figured out.

(Girl 3 becomes hypnotized by the cat clock.)

GIRL 1: Think. Think.

GIRL 2: The door won't open.

GIRL 4: There's no lock.

GIRL 5: This is like a really bad riddle.

GIRL 1: Think.

GIRL 2: Okay, this is LA. This apartment is state of the art. Maybe there's a switch over here or a button.

(She looks all around the door. When nothing happens, she begins banging on the door. The other girls join her.)

GIRL 4: Help.

GIRL 5: I don't even think anyone can hear us. This door is solid metal.

GIRL 1: We're going to die.

GIRL 2: If we're going to die, we need to die together. (She wakes Girl 3)

GIRL 3: So when we were trapped on that roller coaster . . .

GIRL 4: This is not how I want to go out.

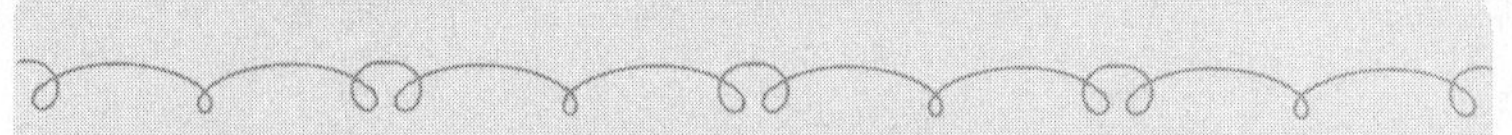

GIRL 5: What does it matter? Let her finish her story.

GIRL 3: We tried and tried to get that seat undone. But we couldn't. There weren't many people around, so the guy working there thought we wanted to ride again. So we kept riding and riding.

GIRL 1: So how'd you get out?

GIRL 3: The guy had a key. The seats were stuck, so he had to use his key to open them.

ALL GIRLS BUT #3: A key!

(They begin looking around.)

GIRL 3: We felt so dumb. And sick. I still can't go on roller coasters. Just thinking about them makes me feel dizzy. (She sways and puts her hand on the coffee table to balance herself) Hey, a key.

(Girl 3 walks to the door, puts the key in the lock, and walks out. The other girls stare at the door. It closes.)

GIRL 1: A key.

GIRL 2: I feel so ridiculous.

GIRL 4: Acting like we were going to die. Oh man. I hope no one finds out about that.

GIRL 5: All right, let's go. I need some fresh air after all that.

GIRL 1: (Looks on the table) Where's the key?

GIRL 2: No. Oh no.

GIRL 4: (Looking at the door) Don't tell me.

GIRL 5: She took it with her?

GIRL 4: I said don't tell me.

GIRL 1: What are we going to do?

(Girl 2 takes the other girls and walks them over to the clock. They all stare at it until they fall asleep.)

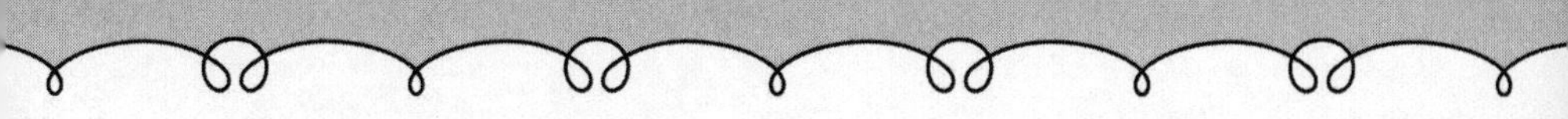

Chapter 28

"Sit down."

"Let me get you some ice."

"Would you like something to eat?"

Flora put her hand up, silencing the three Beacons. "I am merely here because Dr. Smith insisted at my follow-up visit that I spend my entire day off resting my ankle."

"And we are taking the entire day off to make sure that happens," Dad said.

"'The countenance is the portrait of the soul, and the eyes mark its intentions.' Cicero was certainly right. You mean well, and I love you for it. But, please, if you want to make me happy, sit and talk with me. The daily chatter of teenage girls has become a bit unnerving."

Mom sat on the leather couch beside Flora. "You have been doing a great job, Flora. Above and beyond what we asked. You really should have taken a day off before now."

"Nonsense. I'm staying at a house cooking and cleaning, things I would do if I were home on a day off."

"But at home, you're not cooking and cleaning for ten girls."

Flora waved her hand in the air.

Dad joined Mom on the couch and spoke slowly, with conviction. "Your ankle can't heal if you're working as a housemother for another two weeks."

"No." Flora shook her finger at Chad's parents. "I committed to this. I have prayed about this. I am invested in this. I might be damaged in body, but not in spirit. I will see this through."

"Flora." Chad knelt in front of her. "We can get someone else. You can still be praying. You can even be a consultant."

"Absolutely not," Flora said. "Chad, you have been my student and my helper. I have watched you since you were a baby. I can't say you're like a son to me, because I don't know if that is completely accurate. But I can say with confidence that you are like a very dear nephew."

Chad tried not to laugh. *Flora is so honest.*

"I agreed to this because of you, because I believe the girl we pick is going to be an important part of your life."

Chad nodded. "But it's just a show."

Flora shook her head, today colored a burnt orange. "It is your future. And I believe God has given me the job of helping to shape that future. No sprained ankle is going to keep me from that job."

Mom patted Flora's knee. "Could you make the decision now?"

Flora hung her head. "I am torn. I feel like Jane Austen's

Emma. There is a Frank Churchill and there is a Mr. Knightley. Frank is dashing and he says all the right things. He seems perfect for Emma."

Chad groaned. "Jane Austen again? And wasn't Knightley twenty years older than Emma?"

"Sixteen," Flora corrected. "And he could be insensitive at times, and pedantic. But he was right for Emma."

"Sixteen years? So you're looking at a one-year-old?" Chad laughed.

"Chad, you are being too literal," Flora said. "Metaphorically speaking, there are, in my mind, two serious contenders for your costar. A Frank Churchill and a Mr. Knightley."

"Knightley is the right one, isn't he?" Mom said. "I mean, she?"

"Yes, but my Knightley isn't quite ready," Flora said. "I need more time."

Dad leaned forward. "Is she the same one you talked about before?"

"She is."

"The one who isn't a Christian?" Mom asked.

"She isn't a Christian *yet*." Flora punctuated the last word with her hands. "There was a time, Maria, when you weren't a Christian yet. And you, Bill. And even you, Chad."

Dad rubbed his eyes. "The whole reason we're doing this is to find the girl God wants for this show. A Christian girl."

"And I want the same thing," Flora said.

"So, what about the 'Frank Churchill'?" Chad asked. "What's her story?"

Flora folded her hands in her lap. "She is very polite.

She is helpful. She doesn't fight with the other girls or get too wrapped up in the details of the show. She says she is a Christian."

"Wonderful." Mom clapped once. "She sounds like what we've been praying for."

Flora sighed. "I am uncomfortable saying that she is God's choice."

"Why?" Dad asked.

"I don't know."

"But what you've said about her is very positive," Mom said.

"Oh yes." Flora nodded. "Unfortunately, I find myself unable to put into words the reasons for my discomfort."

Chad looked at Flora. Her eyes were half closed, her lips tight. "We trusted Flora with this decision, Mom, Dad. I think we need to give her the extra time she's asking for."

Flora touched Chad's cheek with her small hand. "Thank you, Chadster."

"I don't know." Mom looked from her son to her friend. "What about your ankle?"

"I can take care of myself." Flora sat up straighter.

"We know that," Dad said. "But can you also take care of ten teenage girls?"

Flora pointed a finger in Dad's direction. "'No question is so difficult to answer as that to which the answer is obvious.'"

Chad wrinkled his brow. "Shakespeare?"

"No." Flora smiled. "But he is a British playwright: George Bernard Shaw."

"So you're going to stay on as housemother?" Chad asked.

"Of course."

"Two conditions." Dad walked around the coffee table so he was facing Flora. "If you go back, you must take it easy."

"I will," Flora said, as if the thought of not taking it easy had never occurred to her.

"And." Dad held up a second finger. "The girl you choose must be a Christian. I don't want you choosing by Jane Austen's standards. We have you in there to pick the one God has chosen."

"I know." Flora linked her fingers together in her lap.

"I don't want you thinking in terms of Knightley and Churchton."

"Churchill," Flora corrected.

Dad waved his hand. "It doesn't matter. The purpose for this whole audition process is so you can help us choose a godly young woman to work with Chad."

Mom cleared her throat. "I agree with Bill. Give this other girl a chance. I know you like your 'Knightley,' but even if she were to become a Christian, she would be young in the Lord. This other young woman is already a believer."

"We all love Chad." Flora looked at him and smiled. "He has been the center of all of our lives for the last seventeen years. And you both are superb parents . . ."

"But?" Dad asked.

"But perhaps this is not about Chad. Perhaps God orchestrated this whole thing—his fame, this show, these auditions—because he wanted to bring this one girl to himself."

Dad gave a heavy sigh.

Mom looked from her husband to her friend. "We still have two weeks. Let's just see what happens. We'll promise to keep an open mind if you do the same. All right?"

Flora straightened her leopard-print skirt. "Certainly."

Chad lifted his glass of cranberry juice. "Two more weeks."

The others did the same, glasses clinking in an unspoken prayer.

Chad excused himself and headed over to Will's house for a game of basketball, Flora's words still ringing in his ears. *God, am I being selfish? Thinking everything is about me, what I want, who I need? Flora might be right. This might all be about that girl: Flora's Mr. Knightley, who doesn't know God but needs to know him. And if that's what it's all about, help me to get out of your way. I don't want to be so self-absorbed I miss being part of your plan.*

So maybe this wasn't the Kara McKormick he was hoping for. But she was like her; she didn't know God. *Help me to be open to what you want. No matter what that means.*

Chapter 29

"I'm so glad you came to get me." Kara leaned back in the passenger seat of Addy's car, looking out at cow pastures on either side of I-4.

"Me too," Addy said. "But it's not going to be the most exciting day."

"I don't care." Kara clicked the seat back as far as it could go, making room for her long legs. "I just needed to get out of there for a little while."

"Are you sure you don't want to go to Disney with the others?"

"No," Kara said quickly. "Ashley said it was just for fun, no cameras or auditions. I'd rather wait and go with Ma and Pop."

"When are they coming?"

"As soon as Pop gets better," Kara said.

"He's still sick?"

"'Under the weather,' Ma says. But this has been going on since I got here. And he's so stubborn. Refuses to go see the doctor. He won't even let Ma bring the doc to him."

"But your mom is a nurse." Addy checked her rearview mirror before pulling into the next lane. "Can't she diagnose him?"

"Pop won't let Ma nurse him. He just wants to rest, says he'll be better in no time. He tried to get Ma to come down here without him."

"She refused, huh?"

"No, I did," Kara said. "She's not leaving Pop when he's sick. He needs to be her top priority. I have you. And the ugly stepsisters."

"It's not getting any better with the girls?"

Kara groaned. "It's not big stuff. Nobody is getting into fights or calling names or trying to sabotage anybody else. It's more subtle than that."

"Like what?"

"Like Haley always hogging the bathroom so I have no time to get ready. Or Anna Grace making little comments about my performance or my outfits."

"What kind of comments?" Addy asked.

"Right after our last audition, she came up and said that I was looking at the camera during the shooting."

"So?"

"So we're not supposed to look at the camera," Kara said. "And I wasn't. But she says stuff like that all the time, just to make me nervous."

"Maybe she was trying to help."

"Come on, Addy." Kara looked at her friend. "You know

Anna Grace. You saw how she was on *The Book of Love*: all sweet on the outside, but ruthless on the inside."

"What about the one girl you said was nice?"

"Oh, Jillian." Kara shrugged. "She is nice. And she really likes Flora. She's with her more than I am."

"She's a Christian, right?"

"She says she is."

"So they probably have a lot to talk about."

Kara looked out the window. "I guess."

"You're not really connecting with her either?"

"Not really." Kara looked at Addy again. "She just seems to say whatever Flora does. If she does say something different and Flora disagrees with her, Jillian changes her mind to agree with Flora. It's like she's trying to impress her."

"Maybe she's young in the faith and she sees Flora as a mentor."

"I just don't understand people who have no opinions of their own."

Addy laughed.

"I mean, is that what Christianity does to you, takes away your personality and your brain? You just think whatever people tell you to think?"

"Is that what you think of me?"

"No, of course not," Kara said.

"What about Flora? Is she like that?"

Kara grinned. "No way. Flora is one of the smartest people I've ever met. And she sure doesn't follow the crowd."

"Have you tried reading John?"

"Yeah. I've gotten to chapter five. It's pretty interesting."

"I told you." Addy grinned.

"I mean, I don't get all of it. Like this one part I read. It said Jesus healed a guy, and then he got in trouble for it. What was that about?"

"Only God can heal," Addy said. "The religious leaders knew that Jesus was claiming to be God, and they hated him for it. That's the reason he ended up being crucified."

"Because he claimed to be God? That's a lame reason to kill someone."

"Not to the Jews. They were looking for the Messiah."

"Don't you believe Jesus was the Messiah?"

"Yes, but they didn't. So they killed him because of it."

"Weird."

"Keep reading. The end of the story is the best."

"It's definitely not as bad as I thought. I still don't know if I can buy into all of it, though. But being a Christian doesn't seem as strange to me as it used to."

"That's good, because you're going to meet a whole lot more Christians today."

"I am?" Kara leaned forward. "Where are you taking me?"

"I told you I had plans." Addy smiled. "And you said you didn't care, that you were up for anything."

"Oh, great. Please tell me we're not picketing some senator or standing on the side of the road holding Jesus Loves You signs."

"No, nothing like that."

"Good." Kara leaned back into her seat. "Then what?"

"We're helping an inner-city mission restock their food pantry."

"Really?" Kara said. "Wow. Do you do this a lot?"

"Actually." Addy moved into the right lane to allow a sports car to pass her. "This will be my first time."

"You just woke up this morning and felt like restocking a homeless shelter's food pantry?"

"No." Addy laughed. "I was talking to Jonathon and he was telling me something he learned from Chad."

"Chad Beacon?" Kara turned to face Addy. "Do tell."

"You're still thinking about him?"

"All the time." Kara sighed.

Addy shot her a look before continuing. "Chad told Jonathon that he and his family have days when they go and serve others, doing lots of different things. They try to be Jesus to people. Jonathon loved that idea, so he went and helped a gardener at the White House one day."

"Jesus helps gardeners?"

"Jesus loved others and put their needs above his own," Addy said. "Listening to Jonathon talk about his day made me see that I don't do that enough. I'm so wrapped up in my own world."

"So you're doing this to feel better?"

Addy shook her head. "I want to be more like Jesus."

"So you'll get, like, brownie points or something?"

"No, we serve God because we love him," Addy said. "Not because we're trying to impress him."

Kara considered that as Addy pulled into the shelter.

The girls arrived at Tampa Cares just before noon. Over a hundred homeless men, women, and children were sitting in a cafeteria eating their lunch.

"They don't look like the homeless people on TV," Kara whispered to Addy as they entered.

"What do you mean?"

"You know. Gray sweaters and white beards."

"You watch way too much TV." Addy laughed.

Kara glanced at the sea of faces. There were teenagers and young adults, some in fairly fashionable clothes. There were a few of the "TV homeless" too, with their garbage bags clutched in their laps. But overall, these were just people.

"A guy who works here told me a lot of the people here are homeless because they lost their jobs and their homes and didn't have family or friends they could move in with," Addy said.

"That's terrible. I can't imagine."

Addy nudged her friend. "With the size of your family, you won't ever have to worry about that."

The girls found Ellen, the woman in charge of the food pantry, and got to work.

"I had no idea people sent so much junk to food pantries." Kara handed yet another can of expired cranberry sauce to Addy.

"Look at this." Addy held up a half-empty box of potato flakes.

The pantry was full of crates, some stacked with canned foods, others boxed foods, some with paper goods. Nothing looked very appetizing. As the girls sorted through the last crate for their shift, a woman just a few years older than them entered the building.

"Are you working the next shift?" Kara smiled at the woman.

"Not exactly." The woman smiled back, revealing

yellowed teeth. Upon closer inspection, Kara noted that the woman's T-shirt was worn and her jeans were a size too big and about a decade out of date. "I was wondering if I could get some food." The woman's eyes watered, and Kara looked at Addy.

"I'm sorry." The woman hung her head. "I don't want to bother you. It's just that I didn't know where to go. And I'm so hungry. A friend told me I could come here." The woman began crying, and Kara held her breath.

Addy walked over to the woman and touched her shoulder. "Of course you can get some food. But let's go into the cafeteria. They're between lunch and dinner, but I'm sure we can find something good for you there."

"I'm Jalina." The woman held her hand out to Addy. "Thank you."

"My name is Addy." She grasped Jalina's hand and held it in both of hers. "I'm happy to be able to help."

Addy guided Jalina to the cafeteria, where she was able to get her a hot meal. Addy and Kara sat with Jalina and watched as she ate her meal quickly, barely stopping to take a drink.

"Are you from Tampa, Jalina?" Addy asked.

Jalina looked up from her plate. "No. I'm kind of from all over, you know? I was born in Pensacola, moved all around the panhandle. I haven't always been . . ." She paused. "I had a home and a family."

"What happened?" Addy leaned in, her voice kind.

"Drugs." The woman shrugged. "I started when I was fourteen. My parents told me I couldn't come home if I didn't get clean." Jalina fought tears. "So I didn't go home.

Spent ten years doing everything I could to make money so I could buy more drugs. Made one stupid choice after another."

"And your family?" Kara asked, finally speaking.

Tears fell down Jalina's face. She couldn't speak.

"You haven't spoken to them?" Addy's voice was soft.

Jalina shook her head, wiping her tears with a napkin.

"Would you like to?" Addy asked.

"No, I can't," Jalina said. "You don't understand. When I left, they told me I can't ever come back."

Addy scooted her chair closer to Jalina. "Have you ever read any of the Bible?"

"Not really," Jalina said.

"Jesus once told a story about a young man who asked for his inheritance early, then went out and spent it on all kinds of things. Worthless things. He wasted all the money his parents gave him."

"Mmm-hmm," Jalina said. "That's me, right? I know."

Kara looked at Addy. *What is she doing? Trying to make the poor girl feel worse?*

"This guy got so low he was eating food the farmer threw out to the pigs."

Jalina looked at the food on her plate and all three girls laughed.

"So what happened? Did the guy die out there with the pigs?"

"No." Addy smiled at Jalina. "He finally got up the courage to go home."

Jalina pushed her empty plate toward the center of the table. "I bet he got told what's what."

"Actually," Addy said, "his father had been waiting for him every day, hoping he'd come home."

"What?"

"Yes." Addy's smile was brighter. "He was prepared to beg for his father's forgiveness. The man was going to ask his father if he could be a family servant. But when he got to his house, his father hugged him and called to the others to prepare a feast to celebrate his coming home."

Jalina bit her lip. "That's a true story?"

"It's a parable that Jesus told."

"A parable?"

"It's a story that teaches a lesson," Addy said.

"But what if I don't have a dad like that?"

"You do." Addy gazed deep into Jalina's eyes.

"You mean God?"

"That was the point of that story, Jalina. To teach us that God is waiting for his children, and he will welcome us no matter what we've done."

Jalina reached for a napkin. "God can't love me. I've done too many terrible things."

"God doesn't love you because you are lovable," Addy said. "He loves you because he is love."

"Really?" Jalina's eyes watered. "God really loves me?"

"He does. And he's waiting for you."

Ellen walked over. "Well, ladies, how's the meal?"

"It's not pig slop," Jalina said.

Kara laughed, a deep belly laugh. Jalina and Addy joined her and Ellen looked on, her face blank.

"Sorry." Kara took a deep breath. "No offense. Addy was just telling Jalina a story about a guy who ate pig slop."

"The prodigal son?" Ellen asked.

"Yes." Addy nodded.

"I love that story," Ellen said. "I was just like him."

Kara saw Jalina look at Ellen, taking in her white smile and shiny black hair. "You?"

"I sure was." Ellen sat down. "I'd be happy to tell you about it."

Kara knew that was their signal to leave. She said goodbye to Jalina, hugging her lightly, then looked back as she left the cafeteria. The young woman was listening to Ellen, nodding and crying as they walked out to Addy's car.

"I have never seen you be so quiet." Addy buckled her seat belt and looked at Kara.

"I didn't know what to say. But you were like a little preacher girl. That missionary DNA keeps on coming up, doesn't it?"

Addy laughed. "It isn't a genetic disease."

"No, it was good." Kara stared out the window. "You gave that woman hope."

"God gave her hope. But he allowed me to be part of it. That was great."

"That was pretty great." Kara looked at Addy. "And the prodigal son. I've heard people talk about that story, but I didn't know it was about God."

Addy didn't speak.

"The Bible really says God loves people like that?"

"He really does love people like that," Addy said. "All people. Drug addicts. Homeless people. Even people who don't believe in him."

"Oh, I see." Kara leaned her head against the window. "I'm lumped in with the drug addicts."

"And homeless people." Addy grinned.

"Actually, that's not such bad company." Kara thought about Jalina, the hope in her eyes when Addy talked about God's love. "Can we do that again?"

"We sure can."

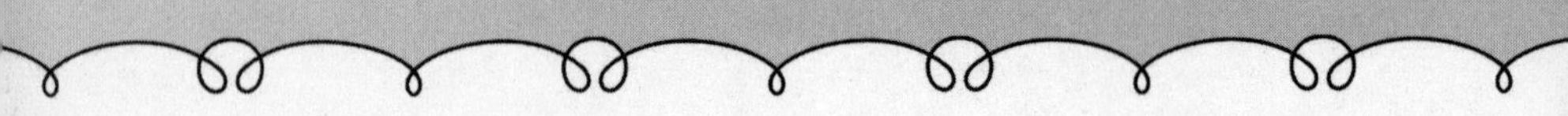

Chapter 30

"A live audience." Kara clapped her hands. "Awesome."

"You'd better be careful not to look at the people in the audience like you look at those cameras." Anna Grace smiled venom in Kara's direction.

"Still not working, Anna Grace." Kara walked past the blonde. "When will you learn that I am immune to your southern intimidation?"

"I'm not trying to intimidate you." Anna Grace's smile faded. "I'm trying to help you out. Every time I watch you, you're looking right at the cameras. It looks very unprofessional."

"And Kylie plays with her hands. Zoey blinks too much. Jillian's voice is high pitched," Kara said. "You have a criticism for everybody here."

"I notice things, okay?" Anna Grace placed her hands on her slender hips. "And Ashley agrees with me. So maybe you'd better listen too."

Ava joined Anna Grace and Kara. "Ashley nodded once

when you said something about me needing to pull my hair back. Don't go try to turn that into you being her favorite."

"You're taking her side now?" Anna Grace waved a hand in Kara's direction.

"No." Ava walked from the living room into the kitchen. "I'm on my side. I'll have time for friendships after this audition is over. Until then, it's war."

Flora walked into the kitchen just in time to hear Ava's last comment.

"May I offer a piece of advice, Ava?" Flora asked.

"Hmm, let me think." Ava looked at Flora, taking in her floor-length mustard yellow sarong, her blue-black hair, and her crutches, covered at the ends with mismatched scraps of fabric. "No. Don't think I want any advice from you."

Ava walked off toward her room. Anna Grace waited a few seconds and then walked down the same hallway to her room.

Kara sat on a stool at the bar. "I'll hear the advice, Flora."

"Thank you, dear." Flora leaned her crutches against the kitchen wall and hobbled over to the table. "I was going to tell her a quote by C. S. Lewis. He says, 'Friendship is unnecessary.'"

"What?" Kara sat up.

Flora held up a small hand. "'Like philosophy, like art . . . It has no survival value; rather it is one of those things that gives value to survival.'"

"Okay." Kara exhaled. "I get it. Friendship brings beauty to life."

"Well said." Flora smiled. "The right kind of friendship, that is."

"I don't think there's any kind of friendship going on here."

"Unfortunately, I have to agree with that assessment. And it seems that behavior like this is to be expected if you are in the entertainment industry."

"I've been thinking about that too. I love acting, Flora. More than anything. But I don't know if I'm cut out to be around all these attitudes all the time. I like my drama onstage. Not off."

"Are you second-guessing your career choice?" Flora motioned for Kara to join her at the table.

Kara sat next to Flora and sighed. "I don't know. I've never doubted that this is what I wanted. And when I'm performing . . . it's great. I'm so happy. But then I'm done and the girls are all catty or critical. I'm worried this is what it'll be like. I don't know who else is on this show we're auditioning for. What if the other actors are like Ava and Anna Grace?"

Flora nodded. "Those are good questions to be asking."

Kara stared at the table. "If I get this part, I'll be working most of the school year. My schoolwork will be supervised by a teacher on set. My costar will be my classmate. I'll be spending most of my time with him."

"That's true," Flora said.

"It could be miserable."

"Have you asked God what he thinks about this situation?"

Kara looked at Flora. "I don't even think I believe in him. How can I ask him what to do?"

"You don't *think* you believe in him?"

"I don't know." Kara leaned back in the kitchen chair. "I'm beginning to wonder."

"Good."

"Are you a psychiatrist pretending to be a housemother?" Kara laughed.

"Certainly not." Flora sat up and shook her blue-black head.

"A preacher?"

Flora laughed loudly. "Oh, my dear. I'm just a woman who wants to see you live life to the fullest."

"That's why I'm here." Kara smiled.

"'There are more things in heaven and earth, Horatio, than are dreamt of in your philosophy.'"

"I know that one." Kara closed her eyes. "*Hamlet*, right?"

"Very good." Flora smiled.

"You think I'm missing something?"

"I think you're missing some*one*."

"You know what?" Kara thought back to her day at the homeless shelter with Addy. "You might be right."

"Might be," Flora said. "We're getting closer, aren't we?"

"Between you and Addy, I can't get away from all this God-talk."

"He is pursuing you, Kara."

"That sounds like he's a detective or some boy with a crush."

"He seeks you out like a detective." Flora cocked her head to the side. "And he loves you more passionately than any boy ever will. But he is neither of those things. God is God."

"But if he really is who you guys say he is—and I'm not saying I'm ready to believe that—then why would he even be interested in me? Why pursue me? I'm just some puny human in this massive universe. Why does he care?"

Flora folded her hands on the table. "That, my dear, is

one of the great mysteries. Thankfully, we don't have to understand God's great love. We just have to accept it."

"Just accept it?" Kara shook her head. "But there's more than just accepting he loves me. What about all those 'Thou shalt not's'?"

"To which are you referring? 'Thou shalt not steal'? 'Thou shalt not murder'?"

Kara smiled. "You know what I mean. You Christians have all kinds of things you can't do and places you can't go."

"Everyone has a set of rules he follows."

Kara raised her eyebrows. "I'm from New York. I can promise you not everyone lives by a set of rules."

"I didn't say everyone follows *God's* rules."

"What about gangs? They don't follow any rules at all."

Flora leaned back in her seat. "I have a good friend who used to be in a gang in Miami. He says the rules he used to follow were myriad, from what he could and could not wear to whom he could and could not speak to. To maintain his position in the gang, my friend had to follow the orders of his superior. Those orders were often dangerous and illegal. But he had to follow them or face dire consequences."

"And did he?"

"He did until the police captured him carrying out one of those orders—the murder of a rival gang member."

Kara's eyes widened.

"He is in jail now, and I correspond with him."

"You're pen pals with a murderer?"

"I correspond with several murderers." Flora shrugged.

"I never thought of doing that," Kara said. "Can anyone just send letters to guys in prison?"

"You are still young, Kara." Flora laced her fingers together. "I wouldn't recommend putting yourself in that situation just yet. Some men, unfortunately, like to take advantage of beautiful young girls."

"So how did you get started? Weren't you nervous they'd take advantage of you?"

"I mail the letters to a man I know who runs a prison ministry. He takes them out of my envelope and puts them in a plain one, so the inmates don't have my street address. We must balance our love with wisdom."

"But how'd you get started? You just woke up one day and said, 'I feel like writing a murderer'?"

"A very good friend of mine told me about it. She used to write inmates. But when she was diagnosed with multiple sclerosis, she lost that ability. So I felt God calling me to take it up."

"What do you write about?"

"I let them know God loves them and offers forgiveness. Many of the men and women I write to have become Christians. They tell me that following Jesus offers much more freedom than following the ways of the world. They have hope and purpose."

"But they took lives. How can you tell them God loves them?"

"Because he does," Flora said. "God doesn't love us because of what we can do for him. He loves us because we are his."

Kara inhaled deeply. "But I'm a good person. I'm not a murderer or a gang member."

"You are a sinner."

"What?"

"The Bible tells us that all have sinned."

"Sure, maybe I've told a lie here and there or lost my temper, but nothing major."

"Sin is sin. And sin keeps us from having a relationship with God."

"So I can't know God because I've told some little white lies? That doesn't seem fair."

Flora held out her cup of carrot juice. "What if someone put a drop of cyanide in this cup? Just a drop?"

"You'd die?"

"And what if someone put a whole spoonful of cyanide in this cup?"

"You'd die faster," Kara said.

"Very true." Flora took a sip of her carrot juice. "Sin is like poison. We are all infected, and it is always fatal. However, Jesus offered a cure."

"That's why he died?"

Flora nodded. "Because he was the only one to ever walk this earth and live a sinless life."

"Because you believe he's God?"

"Because he said he was God, and Scripture affirms that."

"So he's like the antidote to sin?"

"Exactly."

"And other religions?"

"They are taking the wrong antidote, to continue your analogy," Flora said. "If I were to ingest cyanide, and someone gave me aspirin, would I live?"

"No."

"Is that fair?" Flora grinned.

"I get what you're saying. But what if there is no sin? What if you're wrong?"

"When God gets ahold of your heart, he shows himself to you in so many ways that you will know he is real. Ask him to do that for you."

Kara sighed. "You keep saying that."

"Because knowing God isn't about the intellect, Kara. I can answer your questions, and I don't mind doing that. But true, saving faith involves all of you: heart, mind, and soul. Only God can speak to your soul."

"I'm going to keep thinking about it, okay? I'm still not sure, though. It's a little scary."

"I am praying for you, Kara."

She looked at her phone. "Oh no! Pray I memorize my lines really quickly. I totally forgot about the live show. We're going on in just a few hours. I better go."

Kara stood to leave the kitchen and turned back to face Flora. "I'm glad you're here."

Flora's smile was broad and her laugh deep. "Oh, Kara. I feel the same way."

Kara walked back to her room. *All right, God. Maybe you are real. And maybe you're trying to help me see that. You sure aren't letting me forget about you. So let me see you. Somehow. If you're out there and you really love me, like Flora and Addy say, show me. How about letting me get the part on this show, God?* Kara smiled as she picked up her script. *That would definitely make me believe.*

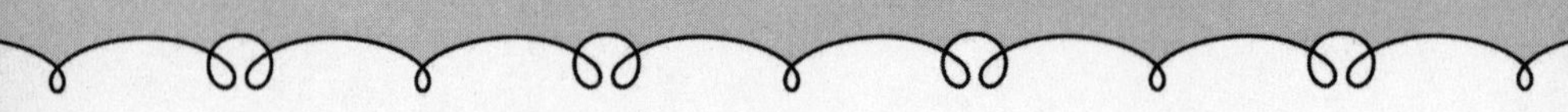

Chapter 31

"I'm going to need somebody to move this couch." Anna Grace walked around the set. "When we rehearsed, it was over there."

One of the crew stepped forward. "This is where we were told to place it. I'm sorry."

"You sure are sorry." Anna Grace snapped her fingers in the man's face. "Now move it back."

The man picked up his phone and pressed a number. "One of the girls wants us to move the couch . . ." He held the phone out to Anna Grace.

"Hello? This is Anna Grace. Who is this? . . . Ashley. Oh, well, I was just telling this man that the couch wasn't here when we rehearsed . . . Of course I'm flexible, but— Yes, yes, I can manage changes, but— No, don't do that. It's fine . . . All right." Anna Grace handed the phone back to the man and glared at Kara.

"What are you looking at? You know you were thinking

the same thing. You just didn't have the guts to say anything. At least Ashley knows I'll stand up for myself."

Kara rolled her script in her hands. "Can we practice now?"

"Yes," Jillian said. "I had a little trouble remembering my lines in the middle. I'd like to run it a couple more times before the audience gets here."

Anna Grace walked to Jillian. "You had a little trouble? Puh-lease, you were mumbling and stammering all over the place. Good thing I know enough about acting to save your sorry behind. Fine. Let's go. But I want some lights, folks. Too many shadows here."

I could strangle that girl. Kara fought down frustration at Anna Grace. *At least I know if I do, Flora will write to me in prison.*

"Jillian, move," Anna Grace yelled. Jillian got into place and Kara followed. The scene was rough. The girls were supposed to be playing best friends, but it was hard when there was so much tension. Anna Grace stopped every few minutes to give directions and Kara bit her tongue to keep from lashing out.

"Kara, you need more energy." Anna Grace stopped the rehearsal—again. "Ashley should have given *me* that part instead of making me play Shelby. I would have killed it. You're killing it too, but in the 'laying dead on the floor' kind of way."

"Are you going to do this when the audience is here?" Kara motioned toward the rows of empty seats.

"Are you going to show some talent when they come? 'Cause I sure don't see anything now."

Jillian stepped between the girls. "Come on now. Let's

channel our energy into this scene, not each other." She looked up to wave at Flora, sitting in the back row.

"Whatever." Anna Grace walked away. "The worse you two act, the better I'll look."

After a second run-through, Anna Grace announced she had to go find some solitude so she could get into character. "Not that you two would know anything about that," she added on her way out.

Jillian mumbled a curse word under her breath and Kara turned to her.

"Oh." Jillian glanced toward Flora's seat. The woman was gone. "Sorry. She just makes me so mad."

"I think she does it on purpose. To try and psych us out." Kara's phone rang and Addy's picture popped up. "Addy!"

"Kara, I'm out front. Where are you?"

"You made it!"

"Of course. I wouldn't miss a chance to see you perform live. Can you come out for a minute? They won't let me inside."

"I'd love to get out of here." Kara waved good-bye to Jillian. "Be right there."

Kara found the stage manager and informed him she'd be out for a few minutes, then she headed for the back door.

"Addy?" Kara peeked her head around the corner of the building and whispered. A long line of teens was in front of the building, and Kara didn't want to have to talk to anyone but Addy just then.

Addy ran toward Kara and hugged her. "Your hair looks great!"

"I know." Kara shook her long auburn hair. "I let the

stylist work her magic. Pretty impressive, isn't it?" Hair parted in the middle, with soft curls framing her face, Kara felt like a supermodel ready for a photo shoot.

"It is." Addy touched one of Kara's curls. "I've always loved your hair, but this is extra spectacular."

"I need all the help I can get." Kara smirked. "I'm on with Jillian and Anna Grace."

"Oh." Addy followed Kara to a shady spot under the awning of the building's back entrance. "This isn't a beauty contest, though."

"Thanks."

"You know what I mean." Addy laughed. "You're all beautiful."

"But those girls are perfect. I know." Both of the blond bombshells could be on the cover of *Glamour* magazine.

"So, are you ready for tonight?"

"I guess." Kara fanned herself to try to keep her makeup from melting in the Florida heat. "It's weird. I've done theater, so audiences don't scare me. But in theater, you have to be bigger, you know? You've got people in the back, so you have to speak louder and make your movements big enough so everyone can see and hear you. But on TV, the camera is right in your face, so you don't have to do all that. It's subtler. So I'm not sure what to do with the audience. Play to them or play to the camera?"

"Don't you have a director telling you what to do?" Addy pulled a water bottle from her backpack and handed it to Kara.

"My prepared friend." Kara took the water and gulped half of it down. "Thank you. Yeah, we have a director—Anna Grace."

"What?"

"Ashley wants to see how we'll do on our own. So other than some basic help, we've had to block and rehearse this by ourselves. We're all doing the same scene. Three groups. One group has four people in it, so I guess they have another character. But we're basically competing against the other groups."

"That's got to be tough," Addy said.

"Yeah, it is. And one of the things Ashley said she's looking for is 'chemistry.'"

"And you and Anna Grace are like gasoline and a lighted match."

"You've got that right."

"What about Jillian?"

Kara took another sip of water. "She doesn't cause problems. But she doesn't really give much to work with either."

"What do you mean?"

"I don't know." Kara stretched her long arms. "She just doesn't seem to try all that much. I don't get her."

"I'm sure you'll be great."

"I hope so." Kara looked at her phone. "I've got to get in there. I'm so glad you came. Can you stay after?"

"Of course, if the star can make time for a little nobody like me." Addy laughed.

"I don't have time for just *any* nobody, but for you . . . always!" Kara took a quick bow before running back to the set for her performance.

Contrary to Anna Grace's opinion, Kara did take time to get into character. This time, to Kara's relief, she got the fun part. She enjoyed adding some of her own personality and spunk to the part she was playing—Ashley. *Ironic, since the Ashley I'm playing is so different from Ashley the casting director.* Kara thought through her part again and walked onto the set in character, going past the "misplaced" couch to the door she'd enter from.

Anna Grace, ignoring Kara's "hello," got into place and screamed for Jillian. They froze in place as the doors opened and a hundred girls and their parents filed in. The network tweeted that they were doing "market research" on a possible new show. A total lie, but they did what they thought was necessary. The executives wanted the girls to perform in front of an audience, but they didn't want to give away the premise behind the new show.

The stage manager walked on to tell the audience to please respond—laughing and clapping were acceptable, even encouraged. Flash photography was strictly forbidden, as was videotaping of any sort. After a final request that everyone turn their cell phones off, the stage manager exited and the lights came on. The red flashing light on the camera in front of Anna Grace meant that it was time to begin the performance.

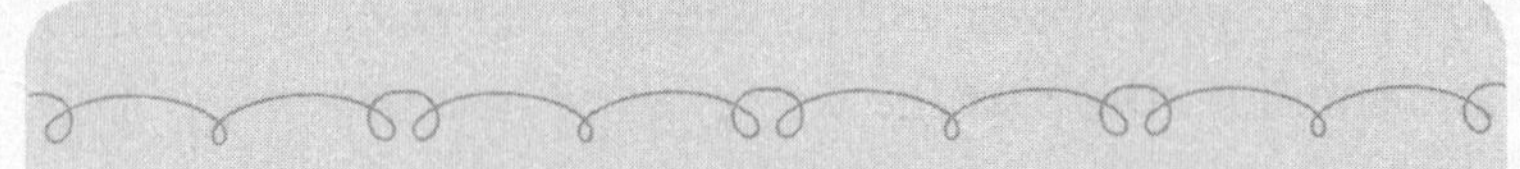

Intervention

(A living room: couch, chair, and coffee table. Shelby and Olivia are sitting.)

SHELBY: We've got to do something.

OLIVIA: I know.

SHELBY: This is serious.

OLIVIA: I know it's serious. But we have to be careful.

SHELBY: You're right. This is a delicate situation.

OLIVIA: And it's been going on for so long.

SHELBY: I kept thinking it was just a phase, you know? Like when she was ten and the only color she would wear was purple.

OLIVIA: Or when she was fourteen and she forced us to call her Mademoiselle.

SHELBY: But this is so much . . . different.

OLIVIA: I know!

SHELBY: What do we do?

OLIVIA: We've been best friends since third grade. It's our job to confront her.

SHELBY: Like an intervention?

OLIVIA: Exactly.

SHELBY: But what if she doesn't listen? What if she won't speak to us anymore?

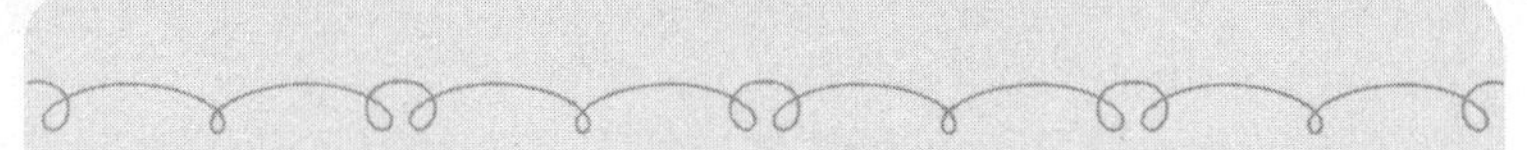

OLIVIA: Shelby, this Ashley isn't our Ashley. We're trying to get *our* Ashley back. This is the only way.

SHELBY: You're sure?

OLIVIA: No, I'm not sure. But can you think of anything else?

SHELBY: No. How do we do it?

OLIVIA: We sit her down and tell her that she isn't living in reality.

SHELBY: But we've tried that.

OLIVIA: This time will be different. We'll write her letters in advance and we'll read them to her.

SHELBY: But what if she doesn't believe us? She thinks she really is—

OLIVIA: No! Don't say it. (Getting upset) She can't keep living like this. I can't handle it. She has to listen to us.

SHELBY: All right, Olivia. Calm down. Look, let's write our letters and wait. She'll be coming over in a little while.

(A voice-over—with a French accent—"Thirty minutes later.")

SHELBY: (Looking out the window) You ready?

OLIVIA: I guess. I'm nervous.

SHELBY: Deep breaths. Here she comes!

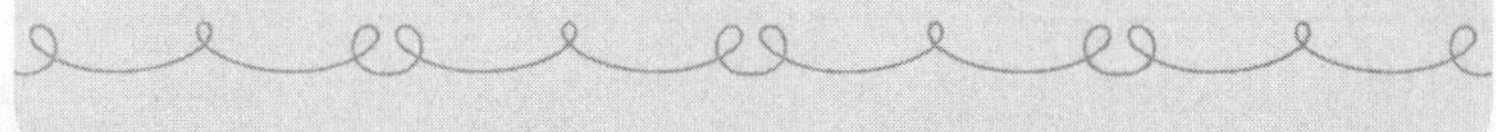

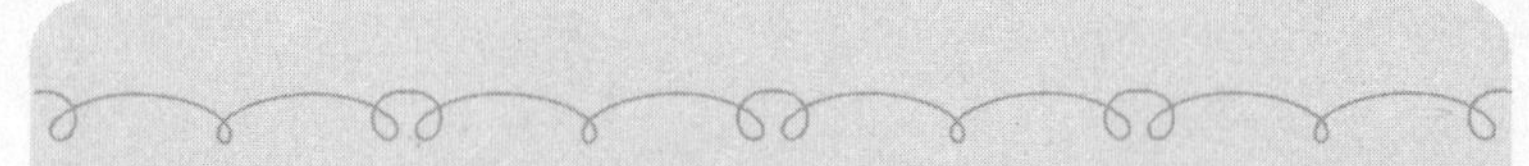

(Ashley enters wearing goggles and flippers and looking through binoculars.)

ASHLEY: Oh, please don't hide. Come out. I'm your friend. I'm here to help you.

OLIVIA: (To Shelby) Oh no, it's the "Mermaid" episode.

SHELBY: The one where she—

ASHLEY: (Singing very loudly and off-key) *OoOoOoOo-AaAaAaAaA. Mermaids hear my song—come out and sing along. OoOoOoOo-AaAaAaAaA*

OLIVIA AND SHELBY: Stop!

ASHLEY: What? I'm calling the mermaids. I have been swimming all day, looking for them.

OLIVIA: Past the giant octopus's cave.

SHELBY: Beyond the underwater volcano, ready to erupt.

ASHLEY: Yes, yes! How did you know?

OLIVIA: Ashley, sit down.

ASHLEY: Ashley? Who is Ashley? My name is Laguna.

SHELBY: Please, sit. We need to talk to you.

ASHLEY: I can only sit for a minute. The mermaids must be found. I have to deliver them back to their home. Their poor father is so worried about them. There's a party tonight and—

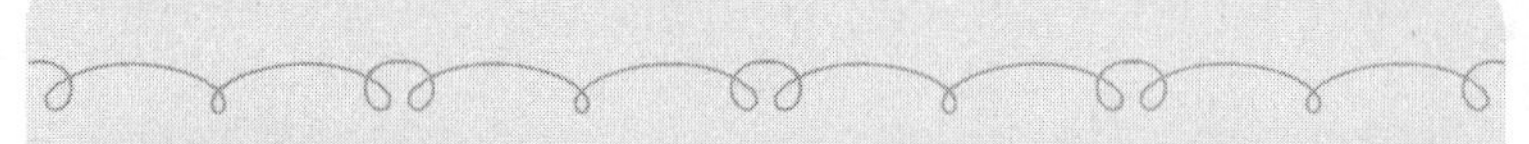

SHELBY: And if they don't arrive on time, the party can't start.

ASHLEY: Yes, yes, that's right! Very good!

OLIVIA: Thanks!

SHELBY: Olivia. Focus!

OLIVIA: Right, sorry. Okay, Ash—Laguna. Shelby and I have something to say to you.

ASHLEY: Listening is very important, so my ears are all yours.

OLIVIA: Right. Thanks. Okay. Um, how about you go first, Shelby?

SHELBY: Me?

OLIVIA: Yes.

ASHLEY: That's very kind. It's good to be kind.

SHELBY: (Takes out her paper) Fine. Me first. "Dear Ashley . . ."

ASHLEY: Oh dear. You weren't listening, were you? My name is Laguna, remember?

SHELBY: No! Your name is not Laguna. (She crumples her paper) *Laguna the Spy* is a television show. For four-year-olds.

ASHLEY: Don't be silly. TV isn't good for your brain. You need to use your imagination. I believe in

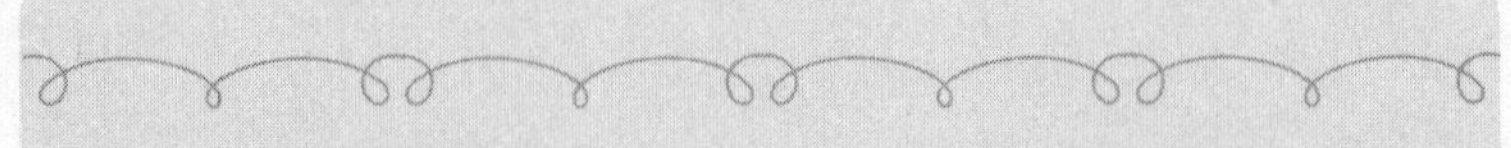

brainpower! That's how I know the mermaids are here. I used my brain.

SHELBY: Look around. This isn't the ocean. It's my living room. You're breathing air, not water. And there are no mermaids.

ASHLEY: I know this isn't the ocean.

OLIVIA: Good!

ASHLEY: The mermaids came here to hide. They can grow legs when they're on land. And they can breathe air. Just like us! But they've had enough time here. (Raising her voice) Their party is tonight, and they can't be late. So come out, mermaids. Come out!

SHELBY: This isn't working.

OLIVIA: We can't give up.

ASHLEY: Of course not. Never give up trying. You can do anything you set your mind to. Just like me. I'll find those mermaids, just like I promised. I made it past the giant octopus's cave and beyond the underwater volcano, ready to erupt. I'll find those mermaids and get them home. I won't give up!

OLIVIA: (Taking Ashley's binoculars) You are not Laguna. Your name is Ashley Chambers.

ASHLEY: My special binoculars! You can't take those. I need them.

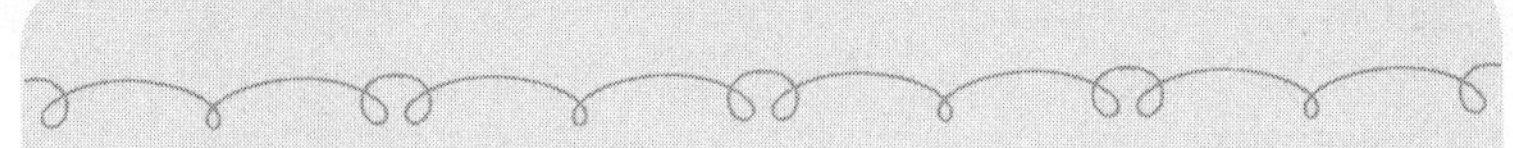

OLIVIA: No, you don't.

ASHLEY: I know who you are. You are working with that sneaky old Grabber Crab. Well, I know what to do with you.

SHELBY: Oh no.

ASHLEY: (Sings) *Grabber, Grabber, Crab. You try to steal and nab. But that's not right and that's not fair. Now off you go to the time-out chair!*

SHELBY: (To Olivia) Say it.

OLIVIA: No way!

SHELBY: Say it, or she's going to sing it again.

OLIVIA: Aw, guppies.

(Olivia walks to the time-out chair.)

ASHLEY: That's right. Off you go, you Grabber. And give me those binoculars. How am I ever going to find those mermaids without my special binoculars?

SHELBY: Hey, Laguna. I have an idea where the mermaids might be.

OLIVIA: (From the time-out chair) What are you doing?

SHELBY: (Winks at Olivia) I think they might be hiding in the television.

ASHLEY: The television? Oh dear.

SHELBY: (Picks up the remote) I know. Let me see.

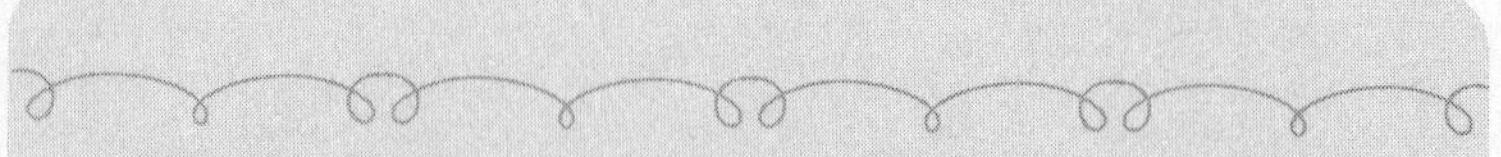

ASHLEY: (Leans in and watches. The *Laguna the Spy* theme music plays) What's this?

SHELBY: This is a television show.

OLIVIA: (Walking over) The *Laguna the Spy* show.

ASHLEY: But I'm Laguna the Spy.

SHELBY: No, you're not. You're Ashley Chambers. You're sixteen years old.

ASHLEY: No!

OLIVIA: You spent a weekend babysitting twin girls. When you came back, you were Laguna. We think it was an overload of TV.

ASHLEY: Too much TV is bad.

SHELBY: Too much *Laguna the Spy* is very bad.

ASHLEY: But that can't be. I've been swimming all day. Looking for the mermaids.

SHELBY: (Presses the remote) Listen . . .

TV: "We have to go past the giant octopus's cave, beyond the underwater volcano, ready to erupt, then we'll find the mermaids!"

ASHLEY: (Coming to her senses) Wait. Wait. I—I'm not Laguna.

OLIVIA: No, you're not.

ASHLEY: I'm Ashley Chambers.

OLIVIA: Yes!

ASHLEY: What's going on?

SHELBY: Oh, Ashley. You watched too much *Laguna the Spy*. For the past few days, you've been walking around saying you're her.

ASHLEY: (Removes the goggles and flippers) I'm so embarrassed. It was those twins, wasn't it?

OLIVIA: Yep.

ASHLEY: Thanks for saving me!

SHELBY: That's what best friends are for.

ASHLEY: But let's make a deal, all right?

OLIVIA: What's that?

ASHLEY: I'm taking my mom's advice and getting a job at the mall. Babysitting is definitely hazardous to my health!

Kara stepped to the front of the stage at the end of the performance. The crowd was on its feet, clapping and cheering. *Oh yes.* Kara took it all in. *This is exactly where I belong.*

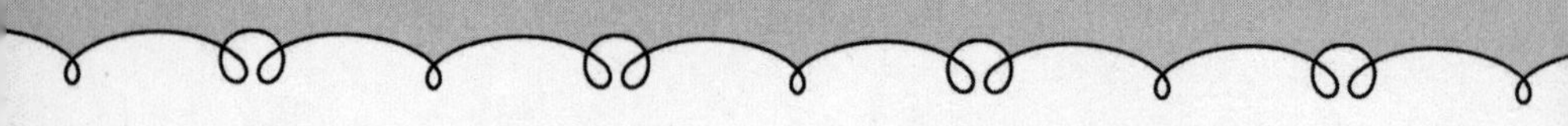

Chapter 32

"You were great!" Addy rushed backstage after the show finished.

"What about the other groups?" Kara led Addy to a corner.

"What other groups?" Addy smiled. "Seriously, you were so funny! Everyone was laughing so hard at you. I had tears in my eyes."

"Thanks, Addy." Kara hugged her friend. "It was so much fun. You have no idea."

"I could tell. Was there a big fight over who'd get to play the Laguna part?"

"Oh no." Kara's eyes widened. "From the beginning, we've been given a script with our parts highlighted. I don't know who picks the roles, but we do not get to question which ones they are. We memorize the part we're given. A couple of the girls have complained about that, but Ashley nips it right away."

Kara watched as Anna Grace grabbed Ashley for a one-on-one conversation. "I wonder what that's about?"

Addy looked over. "That's the casting director, right?"

"Yes." Kara tried to interpret Ashley's body language. "She's pretty no-nonsense. She just tells us what to do and that's it."

"So?"

"So she's having a conversation with Anna Grace." Kara watched as Anna Grace pulled out her cell phone and showed it to Ashley. "She doesn't have conversations with us."

Addy grabbed Kara's face with both her hands. "Stop spying. You're being paranoid."

"I'm just a couple auditions away from the decision." Kara took a deep breath. "How can I not be paranoid?"

"You did a great job tonight."

"But so did Anna Grace." Kara looked back at Anna Grace and Ashley. "And I'm sure the other girls did too. Kylie is an acting machine. And Ava—"

"Kara, relax." Addy pulled her from their corner to the door leading outside. "Let's go out here."

"Fine."

The girls exited the building and Kara tried to calm her knotted stomach.

"So, what's it like to perform in front of a live audience?"

"Oh, Addy." Kara beamed. "It's so amazing. I know I was worried about an audience and cameras being there, but it just worked. I can't even explain it."

"You looked very natural out there."

"Do you really think so?"

"No." Addy smirked. "Of course. You're really good. I'd never be able to do that."

"Sure you could."

"No way." Addy crossed her arms. "You couldn't pay me enough to act in front of a bunch of people. Or remember lines. How do you do that?"

Kara shrugged. "I don't know. I just do it. It's fun."

"I'm praying it works out. I've enjoyed having you in the same state."

"And I'm still waiting for you to take me waterskiing."

"I can arrange that," Addy said.

The door opened and Anna Grace stuck her head out. "There you are. I've been looking for you."

"You found me." Kara leaned against the wall as Anna Grace came outside.

"Addy Davidson." Anna Grace's eyes narrowed. "Still trying to find that fifteen minutes of fame?"

"Addy is here to support me, her friend. Not that you'd know anything about friendships."

"Who needs friends when you've got talent?" Anna Grace glared at Kara. "I just got word I've been offered a role in a new movie. Starring Devlin Tyne, no less."

"Really?" Addy said. "That's so exciting."

"I bet you think it is," Anna Grace said. "Get me out of the way so your little friend can get this role? Well, too bad. I just talked to Ashley. I can do both."

"And you came out here because . . . ?" Kara asked.

"Because it's all over, missy. Pack up your toys and go on home."

"The audition isn't over."

Anna Grace opened the door, walked through, then turned back. "Oh yes it is."

The door shut and Kara rolled her eyes. "Could she be any more dramatic?"

"Don't worry."

"Don't worry that she's being offered a part in a movie? Or don't worry that Ashley told her she could do both? Or don't worry that with a part in a movie, she'll get a leg up on all the rest of us? What should I not worry about, Addy?"

"Breathe, Kara. You're getting way too nervous. Don't worry about tomorrow because tomorrow will worry about itself."

"What?"

"It's a Bible verse," Addy said. "It means that worrying about the future is pointless. Just focus on getting through today."

"Easy for you to say."

Addy opened the door. "You can do it. Are you all done with the show?"

"It sure looks like it."

"Kara, I meant are you done with today's show?"

Kara sighed. "Yes."

"Do you have to go straight back to the house?"

"I don't know."

Addy walked behind the set. "Let's find Flora. I'll ask her if I can take you home. We can stop at that yogurt place you liked."

"Yogurt sounds good." Kara exhaled loudly.

"There you go." Addy patted Kara on the back. "Keep breathing."

Kara pointed to Flora, standing by the fake door to the set, talking with Jillian. "Flora, can I ask you a question?"

"'Who questions much, shall learn much, and retain much.'"

Kara wrinkled her eyebrows. "Another Bible verse?"

Flora shook her head. "Oh no. Francis Bacon, the philosopher."

"Of course." Kara smiled.

"So what was your question, my dear?"

"What *was* my question, Addy?"

"Yogurt."

"Yes." Kara clapped her hands together. "I would like to get yogurt with Addy so I don't get an ulcer from worrying."

"Yogurt is quite healthy," Flora said. "Its cultures do help the digestion, but I don't know if it can prevent an ulcer."

Kara looked at Addy and laughed.

Flora smiled. "Of course you may go. And thank you for asking. But be sure to return by eleven."

"No problem," Kara said.

Kara went to the green room, grabbed her purse, and met Addy at her car.

I want this part so much, but I'm not going to get it. Anna Grace has it in the bag. She knows it. I know it. The show's producers would be crazy not to pick her. She's going to be in a movie. Kara slammed the door harder than necessary. *I knew I should have stayed in New York and auditioned for* Broadway Bound.

Looking out the window, Kara watched the soundstage fade away in the distance. *Just like my dreams.*

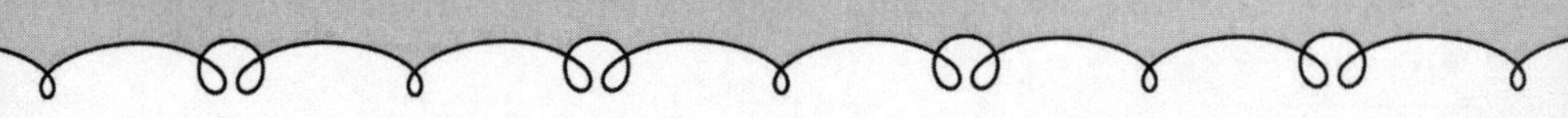

Chapter 33

"You totally defeated the whole purpose of getting frozen yogurt." Kara eyed Addy heaping chocolate chips and peanut butter candies on her dessert.

"The candy balances out the yogurt." Addy sprayed a mountain of whipped cream on top of her frozen yogurt.

"I don't know how you stay so thin."

"I don't know how you eat so healthy."

"Only when I'm away from home." Kara paid for her dessert. "There's no healthy eating in the McKormick household."

"So this is your rebellion?" Addy pointed to the mango yogurt with coconut shavings on top.

Kara laughed. "Yes. When Ma and Pop aren't looking, I eat yogurt and drink smoothies."

The girls looked around the yogurt shop, walls painted cotton-candy pink and decorated with hand-drawn ice-cream cones and circles in all sizes and colors. Each table was unique, all hand painted, and the counter extended the length of the far wall, every kind of frozen yogurt and topping imaginable under the refrigerated glass.

"Ooh." Kara pointed to a "Hollywood" table, with paintings of some of the city's famous landmarks in miniature all over the rectangular surface. "Let's sit here!"

"I'm glad to see you laughing again."

"I'm just so nervous."

"I know."

"But it's so fun."

"So I've heard."

Kara mixed the coconut into her yogurt. "But it is. I mean, I've been in plays since I was little. And I love doing that. But this . . . this is the big leagues. It's so professional and exciting. Did I tell you what we get to do next?"

"No, what?"

Kara's eyes danced. "We get our very own variety show!"

"Isn't that what the actual show is going to be?"

"Exactly!" Kara leaned forward. "But we get to be the stars. We get our own group of actors and writers, and we get to help plan the whole thing. It's so exciting."

Kara's voice had grown louder as she explained, and the other customers in the shop looked on, annoyed.

Addy placed her hand over her eyes. "Everybody's staring at you."

"I know." Kara smiled and waved. "Isn't it great?"

"So a whole show, huh?" Addy asked, once the other customers returned to their desserts.

"And I'm the star."

"They're filming ten of those?"

"Yes." Kara took another bite of her yogurt. "We each

get our own. No more working with the other girls. At least that part of the competition is over. Of course, if what Anna Grace said is true, it's all over."

"Kara, don't say that. Who cares if she got a part in a movie?"

"I care."

"I can't wait to see you in your own show. How much will they show on TV?"

"I don't know." Kara took another bite of her yogurt. "They haven't really given us many details about that."

"Can I come watch?"

"I don't think this one is live." Kara frowned. "But I can see if I can get you backstage. Or in it. That would be great. You could be in some of the sketches with me."

"Whoa, there." Addy threw her hands up. "I don't want to be anywhere near a camera. Remember?"

"That's so hard for me to comprehend." Kara smiled. "To not want attention. What's that like?"

"It's not as tough as it seems." Addy dug into her yogurt for a peanut butter candy. "I much prefer working behind the scenes. Way behind the scenes."

"Speaking of being behind the scenes, I had a really interesting discussion with Flora the other day."

"Really? About what?"

"God and sin and cyanide."

"Wow." Addy laughed. "Sounds like quite a talk."

"Do you know she writes to murderers in prison and tells them God loves them and will forgive them?"

"My uncle is involved in prison ministry," Addy said. "He loves it."

"Hmm, Uncle Mike and Flora." Kara rubbed her hands together. "I can see it. Straitlaced ex-army with intellectual hippy. How fun would that be?"

Addy shook her head. "I doubt either of them wants a matchmaker."

"That would make a good sketch." Kara pulled a piece of paper from her purse and began writing. "An Internet dating site that messes up the matches. I could be Flora and we could have one of the guys be Mike. Yes! I love it. Maybe they could bring in Chad Beacon to play Mike."

"You're still thinking about Chad?"

"Do you still think about Jonathon?"

Addy's face turned red. "But we're . . . we talk and . . ."

"Mmm-hmm." Kara arched an eyebrow. "Chad and I are just taking things slowly."

"So slowly that he doesn't know anything is going on?"

"He knows." Kara smiled. "We have a connection. Like ESP. He senses my thoughts and returns them. It's just a matter of time before he starts calling."

"How did we even get on this subject?" Addy laughed.

"Let's see." Kara focused on a purple circle above Addy's head. "Chad, TV show, Uncle Mike and Flora, murderers, cyanide, sin. That's it. From sin to Chad. That's about right."

"Kara." Addy rolled her eyes. "So what did you think about your talk with Flora?"

"Actually, she told me I should ask God to reveal himself to me."

"And . . . ?"

"And I have been." Kara shrugged. "But I'm not really sure what I'm supposed to be looking for."

"The fact that you're even asking is huge."

"Why?"

"Because you wouldn't even acknowledge the existence of a God when I first met you. Now you're willing to consider he might be real."

"But that's because of you and Flora."

"Who just happened to be in your life."

Kara looked at Addy. "Huh?"

"Think about it. What are the chances we just 'happened' to be thrown together on *The Book of Love*?"

"Pretty slim, I guess."

"Slim? Only a hundred schools were chosen." Addy ticked off the reasons with her fingers. "We were one of a hundred girls chosen from those hundred schools. We were then put in the same room. Then we both made it into the top five, giving us time to get to know each other. Time we would never have had in any other circumstance. And Flora . . ."

Kara held up a hand. "I get it. So God put you guys in my life so I would hear about him."

"Does that really seem so strange?"

Kara thought for a moment. "Not as strange as it used to seem."

Kara's phone interrupted the girls' conversation. Kara began to dig through her purse. "I bet it's Flora. Are we out past curfew?"

"No." Addy looked at her phone. "It's just ten fifteen."

"It's my brother." Kara pressed the Talk button. "So you finally get around to calling baby sister, huh, Joey?"

"Kara." His voice sounded distant. "I'm sorry. I thought

I was dialing Ma's number. I must have hit the wrong name."

"Why are you calling Ma at ten o'clock at night? You know she's not up."

Joey didn't say anything. Soft music played in the background.

"Joey, are you on the phone in the car? You never call from the car. What's going on?"

"Nothin', sis. Don't worry about it. I'll call you later."

"*Joey.*" Kara's heart began to race. Something was going on. Something bad. "Tell me what's happening."

He exhaled loudly into the phone. "It's Pop."

"Oh no." Kara gripped the table and Addy looked on, her eyes wide. "What happened?"

"I don't know. I'm on the way to the hospital."

"The hospital?"

"Don't worry," Joey said. "It might not be anything."

"What happened?" Kara's voice caused the crowd in the yogurt shop to look at her again.

"Ma came downstairs about half an hour ago and found Pop in his chair. She couldn't wake him up."

"Oh no." Tears formed in Kara's eyes. Addy grabbed Kara and pulled her outside. "Was he breathing?"

"I don't know." Joey's voice was cracking. "Valerie, next door, saw the ambulance and came outside. She's the one who called me. The driver told her what Ma had said on the call, that Pop was unconscious. Val said the EMTs had Pop on a stretcher with an oxygen mask on his face. Ma was right with him. She hasn't called anybody."

"Oh no." Tears were streaming down Kara's face. She grabbed Addy's hand and squeezed. "I'm coming home."

"No, Kara. Ma hasn't even made any calls yet. She would call us if she thought we needed to be there."

"Pop's in the hospital," Kara said. "Of course we need to be there. Ma needs us to be there."

"Which is why I'm going, and I've called the others."

"But not me? You were going to leave me in the dark?"

"No, Kar." Joey took a ragged breath. "We just didn't want to worry you. Not until we knew something specific. You're in Florida."

"I can go to the airport right now."

"But the auditions . . ."

"Auditions aren't as important as family."

"At least wait until we get to the hospital, okay?"

Kara wiped the tears from her face. "Fine. But call me as soon as you get there."

"I will."

"I love you, Joey."

Joey sniffed. "I love you too, sis. Don't worry. Pop's strong. He'll be fine."

Kara pressed End and looked at Addy, her eyes firm. "I don't care what Joey says. I don't care if I lose my shot at the show. I'm going home. Now."

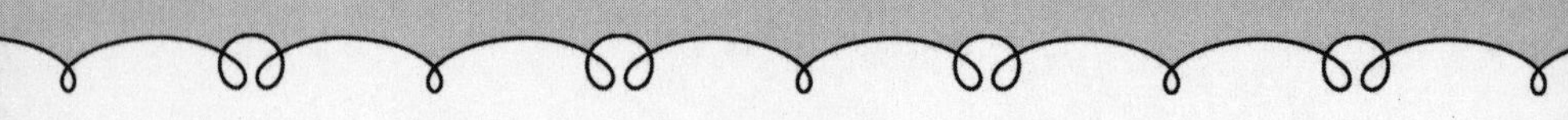

Chapter 34

"Hey, man." Jonathon reached out to give Chad a bear hug. "I'm glad you came. You sure you're up to singing? How's the rib?"

"It's been almost two weeks. I'm doing much better. Besides, when the president calls, you come, right?" Chad put his suitcase down in the spacious bedroom. "But I'm thinking I should get a title: Official White House Singer."

"How about Pop Star Laureate?" Jonathon slapped Chad on the back. "The prime minister's daughters are apparently your biggest fans."

"Hey, I do what I can to help my country. Even sing for eight-year-olds."

"You're the best." Jonathon carried Chad's suitcase to the closet.

Chad walked to the window. The night sky was filled with clouds and rain pelted the glass. "So, how's Addy doing? It was really nice of her and Kara to come see me."

Jonathon blushed. "She's really good. I'm trying to get

her to come up and visit again in a couple weeks, before I have to head up to school."

"Is Kara coming with her?" Chad moved to sit on the bed.

"Wow." Jonathon shook his head. "You really like her, don't you?"

"I'd really like to get to know her." Chad sat back and put his arms behind his head. "She's so fun. And she treats me like a normal guy. That's a nice change."

"I know what you mean." Jonathon sat in a wing-backed chair beside the window. "But she lives in New York, and you're in Florida."

"You're in DC—soon to be New Jersey—and Addy's in Florida."

"That's different."

"Why?"

Jonathon folded his arms. "Because . . . we already had time to get to know each other."

"Do you know God has had me pray for Kara every day since I met her?" Chad sighed. "That's one of the reasons I can't stop thinking about her."

"What do you mean, God has had you pray for her?"

"Haven't you ever gotten a thought in your mind about someone or something, and you just know it's God?"

"Don't think so."

"I bet you have; you just didn't know it. Random thoughts about your friends or family."

Jonathon shrugged. "Yeah, I guess so."

Chad smiled. "That's God."

"I never thought of it that way." Jonathon leaned forward. "So what else are you praying for?"

Chad shifted in his seat. "Actually, I was praying that you'd ask me that."

"What?"

"Can you keep a secret?"

Jonathon smiled. "You have no idea."

"Of course, what was I thinking?" *I keep forgetting this guy is the president's son.* "Okay. My next project is going to be a TV sketch comedy. Kind of like *Saturday Night Live*, but clean, and for teens. It's going to be awesome. I'll get to sing and help write the scripts and be part of a brand-new network."

Chad watched Jonathon's face register surprise, then something else. Was he holding back a grin? "This is funny?"

"No, no." Jonathon cleared his throat. "Go on."

"I'll be the main star, along with a girl, and every week different teen actors will be guest starring."

"Who's the girl?"

"That's the secret." Chad lowered his voice. "My parents want my costar to be a Christian, so they worked out a deal with the executives."

"A deal?"

"Yes. The execs chose ten girls, and my parents will choose from those ten."

Jonathon's eyes got large. "And those girls think they're auditioning for the show?"

Chad sat up. "How did you know?"

"I'm very smart." Jonathon shrugged. "But how will your parents choose?"

"Flora is living with the girls as their housemother."

"Flora!" Jonathon clapped once. "Of course."

"You know about this?"

Jonathon looked at the ceiling. "I'm just listening. So Flora is going to choose your costar."

"Right."

"And she's looking for a Christian?"

Chad nodded. "Right."

"Has she made her choice?"

Chad stood and walked to the window. "She's made her choice, but the girl isn't a Christian. Yet."

"Yet?"

"That's what Flora says. But my parents aren't thrilled with that. They really want me working with a Christian."

"Why?"

"Because we'll be spending so much time together." Chad leaned against the windowsill.

Jonathon's grin widened.

"You sure are excited about this."

"Of course I am," Jonathon said. "My buddy, a TV star."

"I wish everyone were that excited about it."

"What do you mean?"

"The producer of my recording studio is really upset with me." Chad sighed. "He thinks I'm throwing away my career. No one goes from being a big singing star to hosting a TV show."

"So you're a pioneer."

Chad folded his arms. "Very funny."

"You think this girl may end up being more than just a costar?"

"I was thinking that, but then Flora said something."

"What?"

"She said maybe this whole audition process—maybe even my becoming famous—was orchestrated so this girl would be able to hear about Jesus."

Jonathon stood still. "I can see that."

"I know, right?"

"Maybe it's that *and* you'll end up dating her." Jonathon flashed a knowing smile.

"I don't know about that. I'm just praying she's fun and creative. If I have to spend eight hours a day with a girl, I want her to be a friend."

"Well, I think I know exactly how to pray, then."

"If you want to know the truth, I really wish Kara was the girl Flora was talking about."

"Wouldn't that be something?" Jonathon said.

"What am I thinking, though? Kara was visiting Addy when I was in the hospital. And that was after the auditions started. So there's no way."

"You're probably right." Jonathon folded his arms. "Forget her."

"Hey, what kind of friend are you?"

"I was agreeing with you."

"Well, don't."

"What do you want me to say?"

"I want you to say, 'Maybe she didn't say anything because the subject didn't come up. Maybe Kara is on the show, and she is the one Flora is talking about.'"

"Okay, so maybe she is on the show." Jonathon smiled.

"Don't mock me." Chad shook his head. "Why can't I just meet some nice Christian girl like you did? Why does the one girl I can't get my mind off have to be off-limits?"

"Why not just give her a call? Couldn't you just be friends?"

Chad stood. "I don't want to be just friends with Kara."

"So you just keep thinking about her and not doing anything about it?"

"That seems to be the safest thing." Chad shrugged. "Is that your phone?" Chad pointed to Jonathon's pocket, where a faint ring was emanating.

"I didn't even hear it." Jonathon pulled out his phone and looked at the screen. "I've missed eight texts. From Addy." He scrolled down the screen and handed the phone to Chad. "Kara's dad is in the hospital?"

Chad began texting a reply. "I told her we'll be praying for him."

"Let's do it, then."

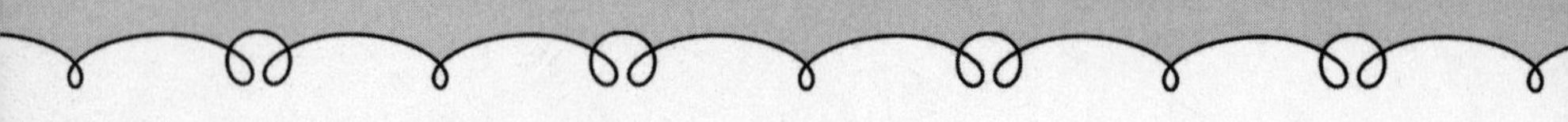

Chapter 35

"What do you mean you don't have any flights tonight?" Kara leaned over the ticket counter at the Tampa International Airport.

"It's eleven o'clock, miss." The woman took a step back. "The next flight is at six tomorrow morning. That's just a few hours away."

"I can't wait a few hours," Kara yelled.

A security guard touched Kara's arm. "Is there a problem?"

"Yes, Officer." Kara's voice grew louder. "My pop is in the hospital, and this woman won't get me a flight out of here to go see him."

Addy stepped in and looked at the ticket agent behind the counter. "Are there any flights tonight? Anywhere? Maybe she could fly somewhere else and connect to Islip?"

The woman's fingers flew over the keys. She stared at her monitor, then looked at Kara. "The Islip airport doesn't have incoming flights until tomorrow morning. Even if you did fly out of here, you'd just be stuck at another airport. I can get a direct flight tomorrow at 6:14 a.m."

Kara ran her fingers through her hair. "What if we rented a car and drove?"

Addy pulled Kara away from the ticket counter. "Kara, it takes twenty hours to get to New York from here. Let's just buy the tickets for tomorrow and wait at the gate."

"But what if we're too late?" Kara wiped the tears streaming from her face.

"Joey said your dad is stable." Addy handed Kara a tissue.

"But they don't even know what's wrong yet."

"Exactly." Addy led Kara to a bench and the pair sat. "They're waiting, just like you are."

"I should have been there. I never should have tried out for this show. I should have stayed in New York. Why didn't I just go on *Broadway Bound*? Then I'd be there right now instead of having to wait until tomorrow."

"There's nothing you can do there that you can't do here."

"There's nothing I can do, period."

"We can pray."

Kara shook her head. "I can't come running to God now. Not after I've ignored him for seventeen years."

"Of course you can."

"Addy, I'm not having this conversation right now, okay?" Kara took a deep breath, trying to keep herself from completely falling apart.

"Look, why don't you go over there and get something to drink?" Addy pointed to the Airport News store. "I'll go back and reserve the flight."

Kara tried to stand, but her legs felt too weak. "I can't even move. What's wrong with me?"

"You're worried about your pop." Addy smoothed Kara's hair. "I'll get you something to drink, okay? Orange juice?"

"Sure." Kara put her head in her hands and cried.

Pop is lying in a hospital a thousand miles away. What am I doing here? What was I thinking? If something happens to Pop and I'm here . . . I'll never forgive myself. If Pop dies . . . The thought was too painful. Kara tried to focus on something else. Anything else.

God? I know I shouldn't come to you now, when I'm in trouble, when I've barely spoken to you before. But this is my dad. He's a good man. Please don't take him. Please, God, I'll do anything you want. I'll never act again. I'll stay home and take care of Ma and Pop both. Anything. Just please, please, let Pop be all right.

"I got you a granola bar to go with your orange juice." Addy handed the brown bag to Kara and opened her own. "I got a Coke and a Snickers bar."

Kara laughed, in spite of her tears. "You're hopeless, you know that? Pop eats bad too. I always tell him to eat better. But he won't listen . . ."

Addy hugged her and Kara leaned in and cried on Addy's shoulder. "I texted Jonathon. He's praying for your pop."

"Tell him thanks." Kara wiped her eyes and sat up.

"Already did." Addy handed her another tissue. "I'm going to go get the plane tickets now."

Kara's eyes widened. "How am I going to pay for them?"

Addy patted Kara's head. "I called Uncle Mike. He told me I could use his credit card. I have it in my wallet for emergencies. And he said I could come with you."

"Thanks."

"Now, you need to eat, okay?"

Kara sniffed. "Yes, Mom."

"Good girl." Addy smiled and walked toward the ticket counter.

Kara's phone chirped and she picked it up on the first ring. "Joey? What's going on?"

"It was a heart attack." Kara could hear the hospital intercom in the background as Joey continued. "They're taking him into surgery."

"Surgery?"

"He's going to need a triple bypass."

"What does that mean?"

"Three of his arteries are clogged and need to be opened."

"Is he going to be all right?"

He sighed.

"Joey, tell me the truth. What are the doctors telling you?"

"You know he smoked for thirty years."

Kara swallowed hard. "But he quit when I was a kid."

"I know, but all that smoking may have weakened his heart."

"Can't the doctors do something?"

"They're doing all they can, Kar. But they don't know how he'll do with the surgery."

Kara absorbed this news. *Pop could die. He could die and I didn't get to say good-bye. I've barely been able to talk to him the last few weeks.* "Joey, I can't get out of Tampa until after six o'clock."

"It's all right." Joey's voice was soft. "There's nothing

you can do here. Pop is going into surgery now. By the time you get here, he'll be in ICU. Only Ma is allowed in there the first few hours."

"But what if he . . . ?"

"Don't, Kar. He's got a lot to live for."

Addy returned, handing Kara the boarding pass. "I'll be in at 9:05."

"I'll be there."

"Addy is coming with me."

"I'm glad. She's with you now?"

"She is." Kara reached for Addy's hand.

"Listen, sis, try to get some sleep. We love you."

"I love you too. Tell Ma I love her."

"She knows."

A sleepless night, turbulent flight, and ten hours later, Kara ran off the plane into her brother's arms. "How is he, Joey?"

"The same." Joey had circles under his eyes. He held Kara for several seconds. "Still in ICU. He hasn't woken up yet."

"I've been praying for him, Joey. He's gonna be all right. He has to be."

"Ma is furious at me for calling you." Joey walked beside Kara toward the exit. Addy followed behind.

"Too bad." Kara walked faster, knowing she was finally within a few miles of her father. "I'm not a baby."

"Don't tell Ma that." Joey stepped on the black mat and the automatic doors opened. The overcast sky and slight breeze greeted Kara and she breathed deeply.

The trio power walked to Joey's Mercedes. Neither girl had stopped to bring a suitcase, so they were able to jump in the car and leave the airport parking lot quickly, arriving at the hospital in less than half an hour.

Kara opened the car door before Joey had come to a complete stop. Kara bounded out of the vehicle and ran to the front double doors before she realized she didn't know which floor her father was on. She turned back to Joey, who shouted "six," then ran on, pushing the elevator button a dozen times.

"Come on."

Joey and Addy came through the doors, stopping at the information desk to receive visitor's stickers. Kara remained, pressing the Up button.

"Why is this taking so long?" Kara asked as Joey handed her a bright orange sticker.

"One of the elevators is broken." Joey pointed to the unlit arrows above the third elevator.

A loud bell announced that one of the remaining elevators had finally made it to the ground floor.

An orderly pushing an elderly woman slowly made his way out of the elevator.

You're killing me here. Kara waited for the young man to turn the wheelchair, fix the leg braces, and ease the woman into the lobby. Kara rushed into the elevator as soon as the pair was out, pressing the number six button over and over.

"Kara, relax." Joey pulled her hand away from the button. "Pop's still in ICU."

"I don't care. I just want to be up there."

The elevator seemed to go in slow motion, stopping twice for people on the fourth and fifth floors before finally opening to the sixth. McKormicks filled the small waiting area. Kara rushed through them to her mother, sitting on a blue plastic couch with a Styrofoam cup in her hand.

"Ma!" Kara grabbed her mother and held her for several moments. When she pulled away, both women were crying. "I'm sorry, Ma. I should have been here. I should have known when Pop wasn't feeling good that it was something more. I'm so sorry."

Her mother wrapped an arm around Kara and eased her next to her on the couch. "You couldn't have known. I'm a nurse, and I didn't know. And you shouldn't have come. The show . . ."

"Ma." Kara took the tissue her mother offered and wiped her eyes. "Forget the show. It's done. How can I be down in Orlando when you need me here?"

"Kara, don't talk like that. Your pop wouldn't want you to give up your dream."

"You're not talking me out of it." Kara shook her head. "Besides, I don't think I would have won anyway."

"Of course you would."

"This is where I belong, Ma. Right here. I can't believe I even thought about leaving you guys."

Kara looked up to see Addy standing in the corner of the waiting room. "Addy, come here."

Ma rose to greet Addy, pulling her into a hug. "Thank you for helping my Kara. You're a good friend."

"I'm praying for Mr. McKormick. And for you. This must be so hard."

"I appreciate your prayers, Addy." Ma rubbed her back.

"Any updates? Have you seen Pop? How does he look?" Kara asked.

"He's recovering." Ma sat back down and took a sip of coffee. "The doctors said that the next forty-eight hours are crucial."

"Is he awake?"

A tear slid down Ma's cheek. "Not yet. I don't know how long he was unconscious. He was in his recliner, watching the news. I was upstairs watching my show. I wasn't with him when it happened. He may have been out for a while . . ."

"Ma, no." Kara looked at her mother. "You couldn't have known. He'll be fine. I'm sure."

"I just want him to wake up, to be okay."

"Me too, Ma."

Every head in the waiting room turned as a doctor in green scrubs entered through the heavy door leading to the ICU.

"Mrs. McKormick?" he said, panning the sea of faces. "I need to speak to Mrs. McKormick immediately."

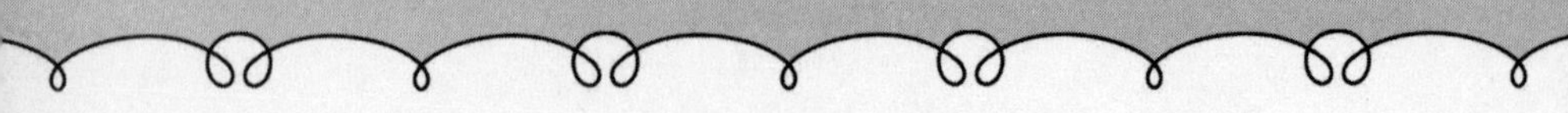

Chapter 36

"Mom, you in there?" Chad knocked on the door to the room where his parents were staying in the White House.

The heavy door opened and Mom ushered Chad in. The spacious room was decorated in deep reds and browns, with two huge windows on either side of the large bed. The curtains were tied back, and the sun shone brightly into the room.

"Need help with your tie?" Mom smiled as Chad handed the black bow tie to her.

"I hate these things." Chad sighed. "And this is a luncheon. Couldn't we be a little more casual at lunch?"

"This is the White House." Mom looped the tie around Chad's neck.

"I know, but seriously. A tuxedo at eleven in the morning?"

"Yes, dear, you have such a difficult life." She winked as she finished tying the bow. "There you go."

Chad sat on the bed. "Where's Dad?"

"Working with the soundmen. Do you need him?"

"No." Chad lay down on the feather pillows, his mind drifting to Orlando. "The auditions will be over this week."

"Are you nervous about that?"

"A little."

"About the show, or about your costar?"

"Both." Chad put his arms behind his head. "Do you think I'm doing the right thing? Giving up my singing career for this show?"

"Still thinking about what Jim said?"

Chad nodded. "I'd forgotten what it was all like before I won the show. But when I was at the auditions with all those kids waiting for their chance . . . I don't know. Am I throwing that away? Is that right?"

"You haven't enjoyed being a pop star, Chad." She sat next to him. "I don't think any of us ever thought about how difficult all this would be."

"But what if I don't like being on the show either? I don't want to be ungrateful or discontent."

"I know, son." Mom held his hand. "Your dad and I have asked the same questions. But this show allows you to use all of your talents, not just your voice. And you can settle in Orlando again, at home. You don't have to travel all around."

"As much."

Mom smiled. "But we've always traveled some."

Chad thought of the family's yearly vacations. They had traveled the continental United States in their RV, seeing the Grand Canyon, Mount Rushmore, most of the state capitals. "I just want to be a little more normal. I know life won't go back to what it was before. But I just don't want it to be as crazy as it has been."

"Then I think you're making the right choice." Mom squeezed his hand. "Or you could just drop everything and go to work for your dad."

Chad laughed. "I don't want to be *that* normal."

The bedroom door opened and Dad walked in.

"Hey, Dad. Are we all set for lunch?"

"Boy, are we." He walked to the adjoining bathroom and washed his hands. "I still can't get over how much state-of-the-art equipment they have here."

"You look like a little boy in a toy store," Mom said.

"That's about right. I had a lot of fun with those guys. Got some ideas to run past our folks down at the recording studio."

Mom's cell phone rang, and she walked over to the night-stand to answer it. "It's Flora. I'll put her on speakerphone."

"I'm sorry to bother you." Chad listened as Flora's voice crackled over their speakerphone. "I know you're at the White House, and I wouldn't have called if it wasn't an emergency."

"Flora." Dad laid his palms on the nightstand. "What's wrong? Is it your ankle? Are you hurt?"

"No, I'm fine." Flora's emphasis on the word *I'm* made Chad nervous.

"Who is it, then?" Chad asked.

"One of the girls here. Her father had a heart attack. She flew home last night. This is the girl I've been telling you about. The one I think is *the* one."

"I'm so sorry," Mom said. "Is there something we can do?"

"I'd like to fly up and be with her." Flora spoke so quickly that Chad had to stand next to the phone to catch everything she said. "She has a large family. But her family doesn't know Christ. And this young woman doesn't either. But I think God will use this circumstance to draw her to him. I want to be there to help her see that. I know I'm needed here at the house, but this is so much more important."

"You don't need to explain," Dad said. "You feel like you need to be there, then go. We'll pay for the ticket."

"What about the other girls?"

"We'll have someone else come in and stay with them," Mom said. "There's just one more audition, right?"

"Yes," Flora said. "But I still think we should cancel it. This girl is it. I'm positive. I've prayed about the others, and I have spent time trying to speak with each of them. This young woman is the one for Chad."

Mom looked at Dad, her expression clouded.

"Let's not worry about that right now," Dad said. "The girls have rehearsed, and they deserve a chance to film the show. We'll look at the footage and sit down with you when we come home this weekend. Until then, you go be with this young woman. We'll take care of everything else."

Dad ended the phone call and looked at his wife. "If we don't pick this girl, I think we'll have a mutiny on our hands."

"But she's not a Christian." Mom shook her head.

"I know," Dad said. "But Flora is determined."

"So am I."

Chad's mind was spinning. *Is it possible? No, what am I thinking? Kara was visiting Addy when I was in the hospital. It can't be Kara. Can it? God, what are you doing to me? I'm trying to forget Kara. You're not making it easy.*

Chad left his parents' room, praying for Kara's dad, and for . . . Kara's dad? He tried not to hope these girls were one and the same. Either way, lives hung in the balance. *Whoever this girl is, heal her father. And Kara, God, I know how close she is to her folks. Help her right now.*

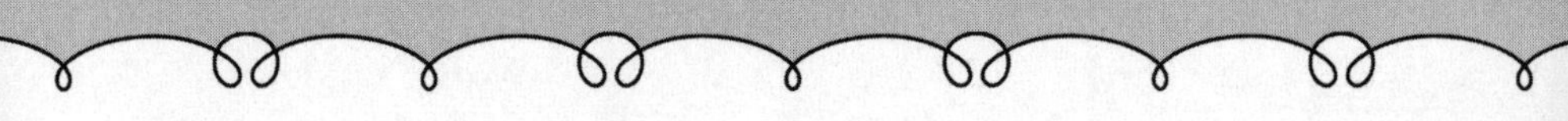

Chapter 37

Kara joined the crowd of McKormicks surrounding the doctor. The waiting room was silent. Kara gripped two of her brothers' hands while her mother looked expectantly at the doctor.

"Your husband is awake, Ruthie." The entire room heaved a collective sigh. "But he's not fully aware of where he is. Because we don't know how long his brain was deprived of oxygen, we can't determine yet whether or not he's experienced any brain damage. We need you to try to get him to talk. Ask him about specific dates, like your anniversary or his birthday. Try to get him to recall as much information as you can."

Ma nodded, her eyes wide.

The doctor pulled a small steno notebook from his jacket pocket. "I'll be in there, taking notes."

"Can we come with her?"

The doctor looked at the room full of people. "I'm afraid that wouldn't be a good idea. Just one or two at a time, until we know for sure what we're dealing with."

"Please, Ma." Kara spoke quietly into her mother's ear. "Let me come with you."

She looked at her children, all of whom nodded their agreement. "Okay, Kara. You gotta help me, though. I don't want Ralph to think I'm scared."

"I'll do my best."

Kara walked beside her mother as the doctor used his ID badge to open the doors leading to the ICU. The hallway smelled like stale bleach and plastic. It was cold too, and the temperature combined with her nervousness made Kara shiver. She peered into rooms with patients sleeping in beds, monitors beeping, and IV bags dripping. The nurses greeted Ma.

"Good to see you, Ruthie."

"We're taking good care of him."

Their smiles were genuine, but Kara could see the concern behind their eyes. Kara swallowed hard. *Please, God, let Pop be okay.*

The doctor pointed to the last room on the right, and Kara entered behind her mother. Pop was pale and an oxygen tube was in his nose. IVs led from his hands to two different bags at the head of his bed. The green hospital gown hung below his collarbone, revealing a neat row of stitches from the top of his chest below the neck of his gown.

He looks so helpless. Kara watched her father's eyes ease open and focus on her and her mother.

"Ruthie." He smiled.

Kara's heart beat faster. *He knows us!*

"Ralph." Ma took his fingers in her hand. "I'm so glad you're okay."

"What happened?"

"You had a heart attack. Triple bypass surgery."

Pop winced. "Explains why I feel like I got an elephant sitting on top of me."

"I need to ask you some questions." Ma wiped the tears from her eyes. "Dr. Busti wants to make sure your brain is all right."

Pop let out a weak smile. "Too late for that."

"Do you remember our anniversary?"

Pop closed his eyes. "I remember seeing you in your dress. You were beautiful."

"But do you remember the date?"

Pop sighed. "No. Did I used to remember it?"

Ma looked at Kara.

"What about my birthday, Pop? Do you remember that?"

The blood pressure machine beside the hospital bed came to life, causing both women to jump. Ma's expert gaze watched as her husband's temperature, pulse, and blood pressure reading appeared on the screen.

"My birthday, Pop? Remember?"

He took a deep breath. "I'm tired. I can't think right now. I'm sorry."

Kara looked at the doctor.

"That's all right, Mr. McKormick. You get your rest. Your wife and daughter can come back later."

The doctor motioned for Kara and Ma to leave the room.

"Can't we stay?" Kara asked the doctor.

"He'll be asleep for a while. I'll send a nurse for you as soon as he wakes up again."

"He couldn't remember dates," Kara said.

The doctor walked beside Ma. "That doesn't necessarily

mean he won't remember them. I'm encouraged that he knew both of you and that his speech wasn't impaired. Both of those are good signs."

"Good." Kara nodded. "So he's going to be all right?"

Ma held Kara's arm. "The first couple days will tell us whether or not he'll recover."

"B-but he's awake and t-talking," Kara stammered.

"I know, sweetie, but that doesn't mean he's out of the woods."

Dr. Busti touched Ma's shoulder. "Sometimes being too knowledgeable about medicine is a bad thing."

"What do you mean?" Kara asked.

"Your mom has seen a lot of cases. Not all have ended well. But your father is strong."

"You have to say that," Ma said. "But we both know Ralph's heart is weak. And a triple bypass . . ."

"Positive thoughts, Ruthie," Dr. Busti said before walking down another hallway.

Positive thoughts? What do those do? Pop needs more than positive thoughts. He needs a miracle. Positive thoughts don't bring miracles.

The double doors opened, and Kara and her mother were assaulted by family. Kara couldn't stand the thought of hearing her father's condition repeated, so she pulled Addy out and into the elevator.

"That was quick."

"Pop's tired." Kara tried to force herself not to cry. "But he knew us."

"That's good."

"Ma says he's still not out of the woods."

The girls were silent as the elevator stopped at the

fourth floor and a woman stepped on. Kara remained silent as the elevator inched its way to the bottom floor. When the doors opened, she made her way outside, to the small garden someone from the hospital had donated in memory of a loved one who had died.

"What if he dies?" Kara picked a purple flower from a bush.

"Don't think like that."

"It's possible, Addy." Kara looked at her friend, tears in her eyes. "I have to prepare myself. Thinking there's no God and nothing after life is fine when everyone you love is healthy. Things change when your pop is lying in ICU, fighting for his life."

Addy sat on a bench. Kara joined her.

"Both your parents died." Kara remembered the story of how Addy's parents had been killed in Colombia, South America, when Addy was just six. "How did you deal with it?"

"It was awful. I was so young, I don't remember what I thought about it. Just that I missed them."

"But you believe you'll see them again, right?"

"I do." Addy breathed deeply.

"But if my pop doesn't believe? Then what? He's a good person. God wouldn't send him to hell, would he?"

"The Bible makes it clear that there's just one way to heaven." Addy's smile was sad.

"Yes, but this is my pop." Kara's tears streamed down her face and she felt like her lungs would explode. "He can't—What kind of loving God would send a man like my pop to hell, just because he didn't believe in him?"

Addy held Kara's hand. "Kara, God loves your father more than you can imagine."

"Then why did this happen?"

"I don't know. Why did my parents get killed for doing what was right? Why do innocent children die in Africa because of diseases we have cures for? Terrible things happen here on earth."

"So what good is God, then? Why doesn't he fix all this?"

Addy sighed. "I heard a quote once that said our lives here on earth are like a one-night stay in a really bad hotel."

"What?"

"Eternity is forever." Addy motioned to the sky with her hands. "Compared to that, this time here on earth is short. It's not perfect, but God never promised it would be. He even told his followers that they would experience difficulties."

"So what's the point of following him?"

"Because those who follow Jesus have him to help us through those difficulties. And we have the hope of being with him in heaven forever."

Kara thought about that. "But Jesus healed people, right? In John, he healed tons of people."

"He did." Addy nodded.

"So he can heal my dad."

"He can."

"So what do we have to do to make him heal Pop?"

"We can pray, but God isn't a genie."

"So we can pray and he can still let Pop die?"

"He could."

"What good is your faith, then?"

"My faith isn't in God healing me here on earth," Addy said. "My faith is in him helping me through life and then allowing me to spend eternity with him in heaven."

"But I want Pop to live."

"I know, and I'm praying he will." Addy rubbed Kara's back. "But even if he does survive, he'll eventually die."

"Thanks."

"We all will. We die of old age, or we die from heart attacks, or we die at the hands of others. But we all die."

"God could stop that."

"He could, but heaven is so wonderful that for those of us who believe, death isn't something to fear."

Kara turned to Addy. "How can you not be afraid of death?"

"Because even the greatest joy we can experience here is nothing compared to the joy we'll have in heaven. There will be no tears, no pain, no loss, no sin. Just pure joy. My parents are experiencing that right now. I'll get to be there with them someday. I'm not wishing for death, but I'm not afraid of it."

"I want that, Addy." Kara pulled her knees to her chest.

Tears fell from Addy's eyes as she spoke to Kara. "Then tell Jesus. Tell him you want him to save you."

"How?"

"Talk to him, like a friend."

"Out loud?"

"If you want. Or you can pray silently. He'll hear you either way."

Kara laid her head on her knees. "God, I'm sorry. I'm sorry I ignored you. I'm sorry for refusing to believe in you before. I do believe you love me. I believe you can forgive my sins."

Kara's tears fell onto her jeans. "I want to know you, God. Help me know you. And, please, let my pop be all right. I know you don't have to. But please make him better. Give him some more time so he can know you too."

Kara couldn't speak. Cleansing tears poured from her cheeks and she let them flow, feeling a sense of peace like she had never known before. God *was* real! He was right here with her. She knew it in a way she couldn't explain. But she knew it. He would be with her no matter what happened. He would help her. She wanted everyone she knew to know this feeling.

"I have to tell Ma and Pop." Kara jumped up. "I have to tell everyone."

As the girls walked toward the elevator, they saw a tiny woman with electric blue hair, dressed in a tie-dyed shirtdress, at the visitor's desk.

"Flora?" Kara ran to her and lifted Flora in a huge hug, her crutches falling loudly to the floor.

"Is your father all right?"

"I don't know." Kara put Flora back on the ground. "But I'm all right. Better than all right."

Flora looked at Kara's face, then at Addy. "My sister!"

"What?"

Flora held Kara's hand. "When you become a Christian, you join the body of Christ. So you are now my sister. I knew God was after you. I told you that."

"You were right." Kara hugged Flora again.

The elevator opened to allow the three women on.

"Wait, Flora . . . How can you be here? What about the auditions?"

"Oh, Kara." Flora smiled. "The auditions are over. Most definitely over."

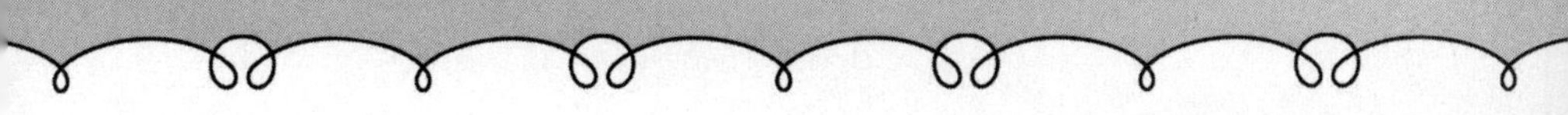

Chapter 38

"I don't understand." Kara tried to take in what Flora was saying. "Those weren't really auditions?"

"Oh no." Flora's hands waved. "They were most certainly auditions. But we were auditioning your character, not your talent."

"We?"

"Yes, I represent the family of the young man who is going to star in the show."

"Who is he?"

Flora shook her finger. "We want you to meet in person. As friends and costars. We don't want you intimidated by his popularity."

"He's famous?" Kara said.

"He's a wonderful young man with whom I believe you will share a beautiful friendship—both on- and offscreen."

The elevator's bell announced that the trio had arrived at the sixth floor.

"I can't . . ." Kara looked at her family in the waiting room as the elevator doors opened. "I have to stay here."

Addy tried to stop Kara, but she ran into the waiting room, speaking as loudly as she thought the hospital would allow. "McKormick family." Kara held out her arms, and the twenty people sitting and standing in the room looked up at her. Bloodshot eyes and wadded tissues attested to the heartache they were all feeling.

"Listen up. I need to tell you something. God is real. He is real and he wants to help us, and he wants to speak to us. We can't make this better, but he can. He can help us through this."

Kara's family was frozen. Kara wasn't sure if their looks were skeptical, patronizing, or genuine. But she didn't care. "I know we're not really church people. And I know we're good people. Ma, you and Pop are the best people I know. But there's more than being good. Addy here and Flora have been teaching me that, and I finally got it. I got it! And it's amazing. And Pop has to wake up and get better so I can tell him."

Kara felt light-headed, and she realized she hadn't taken a breath at all during that speech.

Ma stood to hug her. "We need all the help we can get right now, Kara."

Flora put a hand on Kara's shoulder. "I have some good news too, Mrs. McKormick. Your daughter has been chosen to costar in Teens Rock's newest show!"

The family, who had been eerily silent during Kara's speech, suddenly erupted in shouts of "Hooray!" Kara felt herself being lifted off the ground as her brothers hugged her.

"That's terrific!"

"My sister, the star."

"Aunt Kara, can I have your autograph?"

Kara cleared her throat and asked her brothers to let her down. She turned to Flora. "I'm sorry, but I can't."

The room erupted as Kara's family shouted, "What are you talking about?" "Don't be ridiculous!" "She's emotional—don't listen to her."

"No!" Kara shouted. "Pop had a heart attack and I wasn't here. If I had been home, I'd have found him. We always talk at night, after Ma goes to bed." Kara began crying. "I need to be here. I belong with you guys. TV can wait. Family is more important."

Ma waved the crowd aside and pulled Kara to the corner of the room. "Sweetie, I know this has been difficult, with your pop sick and everything. But this is your dream. I've never seen you so excited. Don't give this up. Your pop wouldn't want that."

Flora hobbled over. "I appreciate the devotion you have to your family. My parents have been gone for two decades now, and I'd give anything to have one more day with them."

"So you understand." Kara looked from Flora to her mother.

"Of course I do." Flora nodded. "But you can have your family and the show. You can fly home every weekend when you're filming, and you can live at home when you're not filming."

Kara considered that possibility. But then she remembered all the articles she had read about celebrities in the teen magazines. "But what about special appearances and tours and things like that? Teens Rock isn't going to just want me to film and that's it. They're going to want more."

"Then you go," Ma said. "Your pop and I will be your biggest fans."

"No, Ma." Kara shook her head. "I won't leave you and Pop. I can't."

"But why?"

"I don't know," Kara said. "I can't explain it. But it just doesn't feel right."

"But your dream . . . ," Ma said.

"I'll just have to find a new dream."

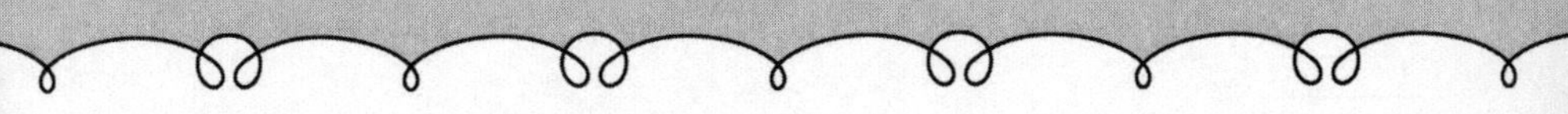

Chapter 39

Addy held Kara's hand as Flora stepped into the cab that would take her back to Orlando, back to the network. Most likely, Jillian would be chosen as the star of the new show. When Flora explained that the star's parents wanted a Christian in the show with their son, Kara knew there was only one choice.

"Kara?" Addy watched the taxi pull away from the curb. "Are you all right?"

Kara sighed. "I will be. I think I'm going to jog upstairs, though, just to clear my head."

"You're going to jog up six flights of stairs?"

"Sure! It'll feel great."

"Is this more of your teenage rebellion?"

"Yes, that's exactly what it is." Kara smirked. "And when I'm done, I might even eat a granola bar."

"You won't be offended if I take the elevator, will you?" Addy asked, laughing.

"No, I'm good. God and I have some stuff to talk about, anyway."

Addy pressed the up arrow, and Kara looked around the lobby for the door leading to the stairs. Finding it hidden beside the door leading to the finance office, Kara hit the door and began running, taking two steps at a time as she prayed for help with the decision she had made.

All right, God. So what do I do now? How do I convince my family that you're real? How do I go back to my boring old high school after being so close to having my own TV show? How do I find a church and Christian friends? How do I help Ma take care of Pop? Because you know he's gonna be the biggest baby that ever had open-heart surgery.

Kara prayed with each step, not really knowing the answers but feeling calmer just voicing her concerns to one she knew was listening and would answer. She was surprised to look up and realize she was already at the seventh floor. She turned around and made her way down a flight of steps, slowing so her breathing returned to normal. Wiping the sweat from her forehead, Kara pressed the metal bar on the door leading to the ICU's waiting room.

"Kara." Addy ran to her. The room was much emptier than before.

"Where is everybody? Is Pop all right? Did something happen?"

"He's all right." Addy walked with Kara to the nurses' station. "But the doctor wanted to meet with your mom and brothers and sisters."

"Excuse me." Kara leaned over the counter to speak to

the nurse who was typing at her computer, oblivious to the fact Kara was even there. "Ma'am?"

The woman, who appeared annoyed at having been interrupted, turned to Kara. "Yes?"

"My pop is Ralph McKormick. The doc is meeting with my family. Can I go in?"

The woman turned back to her computer, pressed a button on the wall, and continued typing. The doors opened and Kara rushed through. Seeing her oldest sister's turquoise shirt, Kara ran for the door at the end of the hallway and poked her head between Mary and Joey.

"I know this will be difficult and a major adjustment," the doctor said. "But that's my recommendation. I'll go get the paperwork I was telling you about."

Dr. Busti squeezed Ma's arm and left the room. Kara moved aside to let him leave, then pushed through to get to her mother.

"Ma, what is it?" Kara held on to Ma's arm. "What's going on? What did the doctor say?"

Ma had a strange smile on her face, an unusual sight after seeing her face etched with worry the last few hours. "Everybody leave," she announced. "Me and Kara have got some things to discuss."

Kara looked around and saw that everyone was smiling. Joey winked at her as he went out.

The whole family has cracked under the pressure.

"Sit down, sweetie." Ma patted the plastic seat next to her. "Are you all right?"

"Am I all right?" Kara remained standing. "Are you

kidding me? What's going on? Is Pop gonna be okay? What did the doctor say?"

Her mother pulled Kara down. "He said Pop is recovering nicely, but he'll have to make some major changes."

"I'm already planning his menus," Kara said. "And an exercise routine. I'll be Pop's personal trainer."

Ma patted Kara's leg. "That's great. He does need to change his eating habits. We both do." Ma looked down at her full figure.

"No problem," Kara said. "I'll have you both ready for bathing suit season."

"I don't know about that." Ma laughed. "But a size twelve would be pretty exciting."

"What else did the doctor say?"

"Your pop isn't a young man."

"Sixty-four isn't *that* old." Kara was beginning to get worried.

"He'll be sixty-five next month."

"With good eating habits and exercise, he can live another twenty years."

"I hope so." Ma's eyes watered. "But he's got to slow down. Teaching math to middle schoolers is demanding. Very stressful."

"He can retire, right?"

"I've been trying to talk him into that for a while," Ma said. "He's been eligible to draw his pension for the last five years. But he hates the idea of not doing anything."

"So his new job is to get better. Taking long walks with his favorite daughter and learning to appreciate vegetables."

"Dr. Busti said the recovery will be pretty extensive,"

Ma said. "More than just a change in his diet and exercise. He's going to need to be part of a rehabilitation center."

"What?"

"He doesn't have to live there, but he does need to be near one because he'll be going three times a week for the first few months, then regularly for checkups after that."

"There you go." Kara shrugged. "Something to do."

"I have a lot of respect for Dr. Busti. He knows his stuff. And he says that Pop has a better chance to recover somewhere else. Off the Island. Somewhere warmer, so he can get outside every day and walk. The doc says staying indoors too much isn't good for him. He could get depressed, which would make recovery more difficult."

Kara sucked in her breath. "Dr. Busti wants us to move? But this is home. You guys have lived here my whole life."

"The house is more than we need. But Mary could use it, what with her family growing bigger every day."

"But where would we go?"

"You know how you said you believe in God now?"

"Yeah, I remember." Kara tried to understand why the conversation had suddenly switched.

"Do you believe God can do miracles?"

"Sure. Look at Pop. Look at me. Are you saying you believe too, Ma?"

"I'm saying I just saw something happen that sure seems like God was involved."

"What happened, Ma?"

"The rehabilitation center. The one Dr. Busti recommended, the one he says is the best in the country . . . ?"

"Yes?"

"It's in Orlando." Ma smiled. "So I'm afraid, like it or not, we're moving down there."

"What?" Kara jumped up. "We're moving to Orlando?"

"Yes, we are." Ma stood and hugged Kara. "Doctor's orders."

"So I can do the show?"

"You'd better."

"And I can live at home!"

"And make Pop all the healthy meals you want, and make him exercise, and . . ."

"Flora!" Kara ran toward the door, tearing through the hallway. The double doors were opening to allow a nurse out, and Kara dodged the woman, ran to the elevator, and waited for it to stop at her floor. Addy stood beside her.

"Orlando. Flora. I can do it. We can do it." Kara's thoughts were so jumbled she couldn't compose a complete sentence.

"No idea what you just said." Addy turned Kara to face her. "But Flora left awhile ago. You can't catch her. Do you have her cell number?"

"Cell number. Yes! I'll call her. What if she already called Jillian? Oh no. I have to let her know I can do it."

"What are you talking about?" Addy asked.

Kara dug through her purse and found her phone. She scrolled through her phone book and punched Call as soon as she came to Flora's name. The call went straight to voice mail.

"No, no, no." Kara began texting. "If she calls Jillian, it's over. She can't take it back. God, please, please, let me get through."

The elevator doors opened and Flora stepped out.

"I was trying to call you." Kara ran to Flora and grabbed the woman's shoulders. "We're moving to Orlando. I can do the show!"

Kara enveloped Flora in a hug and spun her around.

"I appreciate your enthusiasm," Flora said. "But I am prone to vertigo, and circuitous motion is detrimental."

"I think she wants you to put her down." Addy grabbed Kara's shoulders, forcing her to stop.

"Oh, sorry." Kara set Flora down and the smaller woman held on to a chair for support. Addy scrambled to pick up the crutches that had, once again, fallen to the floor.

"I just got off the phone with Jillian."

Kara's heart sank. "Oh no. It's too late. I'm too late. I'm going to be living in Orlando, watching Jillian play my part."

"Have a seat." Flora motioned to the couch where Kara and her mother had been sitting earlier. "Remember when we were at the recording studio?"

Kara looked at Flora. What in the world did this have to do with Jillian being cast? Was it because Kara's voice wasn't as good as the other girls'?

"I noticed something odd that day," Flora said. "Jim, the manager, seemed to recognize Jillian."

Kara remembered that. "So they knew each other. Does that matter?"

"Yes. Jim stood to lose some business as a result of this show. He has been against it from the start."

"Then why did he help with the recording?"

"Jim is a businessman," Flora said, "and this show paid top dollar for that day at the studio. So I did a little sleuthing. Unbeknownst to Jim or Jillian, or even my bosses."

"And . . . ?" Kara was getting the feeling that this would end well. For her. She liked that feeling.

"It turns out that our Miss Jillian wasn't exactly who she claimed to be."

"Really?"

"Right after I got into the taxi, I received a call from a friend. I had asked him to look into Jillian and see if there was any connection to Jim."

"And there was."

"Jim is good friends with Jillian's agent."

The pieces were falling into place. Kara's eyes lit up. "She knew what this show was really about."

"She did."

"So she pretended to be a Christian so she'd get the part."

"Sadly, that is true." Flora shook her head.

"But how does Jim benefit from that?"

"That's what I called Jillian to find out," Flora said.

"What did she say?"

"She was very upset that I had found out." Flora cocked her head to the side. "But in the spirit of self-preservation, she confessed the whole story. She was to be cast in the role. After a couple weeks of rehearsals, she was to admit she wasn't a Christian. Jim hoped that would force the family to remove their son from the show."

"So he'd go back to making money in Jim's recording studio?"

"Precisely."

"But what does Jillian get from it all?"

"Her agent assured her that the network would let the boy leave the show and then she would be the star."

"Wow, that's pretty low," Kara said. "I can't believe she'd do that. She acted so nice."

"She was a superb actress. It is a shame she used those skills to deceive."

"So the show needs a Christian in this part, huh?" Kara sat up straight and cleared her throat.

"That it does."

"So that means . . . ?" Kara raised her eyebrows.

"You are the one." Flora smiled. "I knew it from the first day. I prayed God would show me his choice, and he did."

Kara stood and screamed, jumping around in circles. Nurses came rushing out of the heavy doors.

"Is she all right?"

Addy held Kara down. "She will be."

Kara kept jumping but managed to bring her voice down a few decibels. "Thankyouthankyouthankyou!"

"Don't thank me," Flora said. "God orchestrated all of this. And not just for this show. For you. Because he loves you."

Kara stopped jumping and bent down to look Flora in the eye. "So now can you tell me about my costar?"

"I can do one better." Flora wrapped an arm around Kara's waist. "I can take you to meet him."

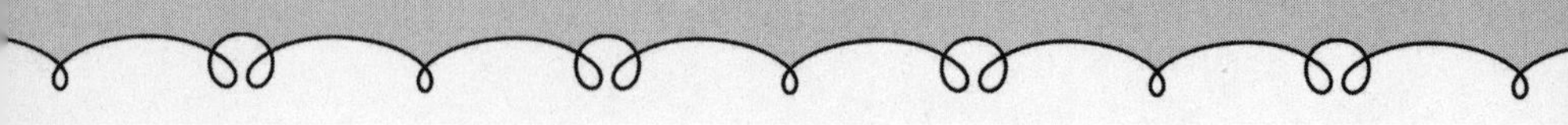

Chapter 40

"Are you sure it's okay, Ma?" Kara asked. Again.

She hugged her daughter. "Pop is recovering nicely. He'll be going home in another day or two."

"But I don't have to go now." Kara looked around her living room. She couldn't believe how much had happened in one short week. "You need help packing."

"I didn't have six kids for nothing." Ma smoothed Kara's hair. "I'll be putting them all to work. And you too. You and Flora gotta find us a house down there in Orlando."

"I can't believe this is really happening." Kara hugged her mother. "We're moving to Orlando!"

"And you better make sure our new house has at least four bedrooms. Your nieces and nephews are gonna take turns coming down in the summers. And the whole family is coming out for Christmas."

"Will four bedrooms be enough?"

"Well now." Ma patted Kara's hand. "We don't want them getting *too* comfortable, do we?"

Kara laughed. "Four bedrooms it is."

"A pool would be nice."

"Nice?" Kara put her hands on her mother's shoulders. "Oh, Ma. A pool is necessary for Pop's recovery. And a hot tub too. Definitely a hot tub. For Pop."

"Sure, for Pop." Ma winked.

"All right, then." Kara walked down the hallway. "Next time I'm here, this'll be Mary's house."

Ma walked behind Kara. "This is a wonderful house to raise a family in."

Kara looked at the pictures on the wall. Her parents and grandparents, brothers, sisters, nieces, and nephews all smiled back. A lifetime of memories.

"She's probably going to turn it all modern." Kara continued walking, looking in each of the bedrooms. "Rip up the carpet, replace it with hardwood. Ikea furniture."

"Your sister has different tastes than me." Ma smiled. "But it's her house. She can do whatever she wants with it."

"As long as she doesn't take down my tree house." Kara walked into her bedroom and looked through the window.

"We kept the ER busy with that tree house." Ma laughed. "Remember when you tried to play Tarzan?"

Kara laughed with her. "Sure do. I was just telling Flora about that a little while ago."

"Scared me to death, seeing you lying on the ground, your head all bloody."

"But you were so calm." Kara gazed at her mother. "Sam was screaming like crazy, running around the yard, yelling for an ambulance. I remember that."

Ma smiled, a tear falling down her cheek. "He loved his

baby sister. Thought it was his fault you fell—said he dared you to do it."

"He did? I thought it was my idea."

"It probably was." Ma sniffed. "But he still felt guilty."

"Oh, Ma. I'm going to miss this house."

"Me too."

Kara peered into her parents' bedroom. Memories of nights spent cuddled between the two of them flooded her mind. Kara began to cry, excited about the future but sad that a piece of her past was changing.

"I've been praying, Kara, like you said." Ma walked beside Kara to the kitchen.

"You have?"

"I never really thought much about God. My life was so good."

"But God makes your life even better."

"So I've heard." Ma smiled. "I want us to find a church there in Orlando. Maybe we can all get to know God together, as a family."

"That sounds great."

A horn sounded in the front yard. Kara opened the door to see a huge Hummer limo in front of her house. Her entire family—all her brothers and sisters, their spouses, and her nieces and nephews piled out. Kara couldn't stop the tears as they fell down her cheeks.

"You didn't think we'd let our big star just sneak off, did you?" Joey said. "Go inside for a minute. We've got more stuff for you to bring."

Kara hadn't noticed until then that every person had a gift. "My suitcase is full already, Joey."

"Don't worry." Sam smiled. "These won't take up too much space."

Kara was led into the living room by her family and given the seat of honor, her father's recliner.

"Pop insisted on coming." Mary reached into a briefcase and pulled out her laptop. "Hang on." Mary pressed a few keys and her father's face popped up on the screen.

"Kara, my girl." Pop sat up in his hospital bed. "I wouldn't miss your send-off for anything. Not even for a heart attack."

Kara wiped more tears from her eyes as little Ethan handed her his gift. Kara opened the bag and found a boarding pass inside.

"I'm coming in two weeks." Ethan smiled up at Kara. "And Mommy said you'll take me to meet Buzz Lightyear."

Kara hugged her nephew. "You bet I will, buddy."

Emily was next and her gift also contained a boarding pass. Gift after gift contained the same thing. Plane tickets to Orlando. The only differences were the dates. Someone from her family was coming every month for the next six months.

"You guys are the best." Kara hugged each one in the room.

"Enough of that." Pop spoke up. "You're making me jealous. Now get my girl to the airport. She's got big plans today."

"Thanks, Pop." Kara walked to the computer. "I love you."

"I love you too, Kara. Now get going. And I expect a call tonight. I want to hear about this mystery boy."

The rest of Kara's family joined in, each wanting a call.

"He's just my costar," Kara said. "No big deal."

The room erupted in laughter. "Right, Kar. No big deal. Like we believe that," Joey said.

"Stop, you're embarrassing me." Kara ducked past her family and exited the front door. "Now, come on, you slow pokes. I call the sunroof!"

Kara entered the monstrous limousine and stuck her head out of the top. "Good-bye, New York. Good-bye, house. Hello, Orlando!"

Chapter 41

Come on, Flora, please?" Chad begged. Again.

"You have waited over a month." Flora adjusted the straps on her neon green jumpsuit. "You can wait a few minutes more."

Chad had never felt so nervous. Not when he was on *America's Next Star*, not when he was standing in front of crowds of people in a concert. This unknown girl was far more frightening.

"What if we don't get along? The executives said chemistry between the stars is important. What if we have none? What if we went through all this for nothing?"

"That is certainly a possibility." Flora nodded. "But even if that's the case, this young woman became a Christian as a result. Isn't that more important than a TV show?"

"Of course." But the more Chad had thought about the show, the more excited he was. Ideas were flying through his head, sketches he wanted to write, parodies of songs he would sing. The possibilities were limitless. As long as his costar felt the same way.

Chad's mother walked down the stairs. "Chad, stop standing by the front door. Come sit down. Have some tea."

"He's excited." Dad walked behind his wife. "Understandable. He's been waiting awhile for this girl."

"Maybe I will get some tea," Chad said, needing to move. He walked into the kitchen and opened the refrigerator. "No, I don't want tea. The last thing I want is to meet the girl and then have to excuse myself to go to the bathroom. That would make a great first impression."

I wish this wasn't the first impression, Chad thought, not for the first time. *I still can't stop thinking about Kara. Especially now that I know she's a Christian. But there's no way it's her.* She was still in New York. And Jonathon made Chad promise not to call her. Addy said Kara was still processing everything—her dad's heart attack, her conversion. Jonathon said Chad would be a distraction. *I understand that, but, God, come on. Kara McKormick is available, and I'm going to be working every day with some other girl. This isn't fair.*

"Chad," Mom called out. "There's a car pulling up."

He ran into the living room and pulled back the curtain. He didn't understand what he was seeing. "But that's Addy Davidson's car. What is she doing here? She's not . . . Is she?" Chad racked his brain, trying to determine whether or not it was possible for Addy to have been auditioning for the show.

The front door opened and Jonathon walked in.

"Jonathon? What are you doing here?"

Jonathon smiled and pointed toward the back of the house. "Good to see you too. And I'm here because there's no way I would miss this. Not for anything."

"But how'd you get here?"

"Addy."

"What about the Secret Service?"

"Bull's right behind us." Jonathon opened the back door and pointed Chad toward the orange groves. "With someone special."

"My costar is with Bull? Is it Addy?"

"Nope." Jonathon kept walking.

"Don't tell me it's your sister."

"Alexandra?" Jonathon laughed. "She's twenty-two. And not at all interested in a television career. No, not Alexandra."

Chad stopped. "What is going on?"

"Look, before I tell you that, I need to tell you something else."

"Seriously, we're going to have a heart-to-heart *now*? Are you trying to kill me?"

"No." Jonathon leaned against a tree. "I wanted to thank you."

"Thank me?"

"I talked to my dad. You were right—he wasn't upset that I didn't want to go into politics."

"That's great."

"I know," Jonathon said. "When I told him I'd like to pursue film editing, he was actually excited for me. He said his parents encouraged him to follow his dreams, and he did. He wants to do the same for Alexandra and me. He said if that's what I want to do, then I should go for it. As long as I get my college degree, of course."

"Of course." Chad smiled.

"I did some research. You know what college has an amazing film program?"

"No idea." Chad noted that his friend had never been more animated—except, maybe, when he was talking about Addy.

"Hartson University."

"Here in Orlando?" Chad's eyes lit up. "That's awesome."

"But I need a favor." Jonathon folded his arms. "I need actual practice editing. Since you have your own show and all . . ."

"You want to help edit my show?"

"Is that an offer?"

"Are you kidding? I'll talk to the producers tomorrow. How soon can you start?"

"I have to see if I can get into Hartson first," Jonathon said. "I've heard it's pretty tough."

"I think between your family and mine, we might be able to pull a few strings there." Chad laughed.

"Good." Jonathon pulled his phone out of his back pocket. "They're ready."

Chad tried to look around the house, but Jonathon had brought him to a spot in the orange groves that made seeing the front of the house impossible.

"So you've seen her?" Chad asked.

"Yep."

"And?"

"And what?" Jonathon feigned innocence and Chad held up a fist.

"Don't make me use this."

"She's beautiful. And funny. And tall."

"Redheaded?" Chad asked hopefully.

"See for yourself."

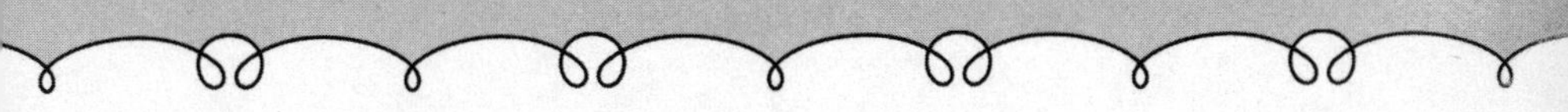

Chapter 42

"I'm so confused." Kara sat in the black SUV. "You know I love you, Bull, but why are you picking me up? Oh my goodness. Is Jonathon the star? Of course. That makes sense. Why it needs to be secret, why the parents are concerned about the costar. But he's so quiet. I had no idea he was into acting."

"It's not Jonathon." Bull looked at Kara in the rearview mirror.

"Then who?"

"And ruin the suspense? No way. Not this guy. Just enjoy the ride."

"It is beautiful." Kara looked out the window. Bull had pulled off on a dirt road leading right through an orange grove. "The trees are so pretty. But what does this have to do with the show? Is the studio out here?"

"Nope."

"Is the star out here?"

"Maybe."

"Come on, Bull." Kara leaned forward. "We're buddies, right? You can tell me."

Kara's pleas were silenced as Bull turned a corner and Kara saw the house.

"Now *this* is what I've been looking for." She surveyed the multilevel home, just like the ones in pictures of Florida she had looked up on the Internet. The exterior was white with red shutters and a quaint red door. The front porch wrapped all around the house. Each window had a box of flowers in front of it, and the front porch had white swings facing each other. "Is this for sale? Ma would love this house."

"Nope, sorry. That's not why you're here." Bull put the SUV in park, stepped out of the vehicle, and opened her door.

The front door of the house opened and a very excited Addy came running out.

"Kara!" Addy hugged her friend and Kara returned the embrace halfheartedly. "Aren't you glad to see me?"

"Of course, but why are you here? I'm supposed to meet the costar. And Bull said it wasn't Jonathon. So why else would you and Bull be here?"

"Jonathon's here too." Addy wrapped her arm through Kara's and led her to the backyard.

"But why?"

"I can't believe you haven't figured it out." Addy looked at Kara. "Me and Jonathon, you and . . ."

"Don't toy with me." Kara pulled away from her friend. The possibility that Chad Beacon could actually be the boy she'd be working with caused her heart to race. "If you're joking and some less-than-Greek-god boy is waiting for me, I don't know if I could forgive you."

"He's waiting for you in the orange groves."

"Is it Chad? Please say it's Chad."

"I'm not saying anything."

"You're not saying it's not Chad," Kara said, her heart racing even faster. "If it wasn't, you'd tell me, right?"

"Maybe there's another guy just as great as Chad who you don't know but Jonathon and I do."

"Addy, I don't like this side of you." Kara looked at the groves but could only see trees. No boy who may or may not be Chad Beacon peeking through the leaves.

Jonathon stepped out of the groves.

"It *is* you." Kara's heart dropped.

Jonathon smiled and walked toward Kara. "Are you disappointed?"

"No, of course not." Kara tried to sound convincing.

"You're excited to be in a show with me?" Jonathon kept walking.

"Sure I am." Kara glanced at Addy, who was shooting Jonathon a disapproving look.

"Too bad, then." Jonathon reached Addy and placed an arm around her shoulders. "Because I'm just working behind the scenes."

This time it was Addy's turn to look surprised. "What?"

"Tell you in a minute." Jonathon held Addy tighter. "Right now, Miss McKormick, you have someone waiting for you. Second row of trees, about forty paces back."

Kara looked at Addy and Jonathon, who were looking at each other.

"Second row of trees, huh?" Kara found the second row and began walking. "Forty paces. What is this, some kind of treasure hunt?"

"You could say that," a very familiar voice said.

Chad Beacon stepped out from behind a tree. He walked up to Kara and looked at her, his hazel eyes dancing. "I was really hoping you were the one."

Kara swallowed hard. The Greek god was looking at her. And she wasn't turning to stone. *I might melt into a puddle, though.* "Me too. I thought it was Jonathon."

"He and Addy have had way too much fun planning this. He had me thinking Addy was the costar."

"You're not disappointed?" Kara asked, glancing from Chad's eyes to his tan face in time to see his perfect smile.

"Are you kidding? I haven't been able to get you off my mind since that day at the White House."

"Really?" Kara inhaled Chad's cologne and willed herself to remain standing. "'Cause I've barely given you a second thought."

"Oh yeah?" Chad pulled a leaf from a branch above his head. "That's not what Jonathon said."

"Jonathon is a politician's son." Kara folded her arms, enjoying the game. "Don't you know anything? Politicians lie."

"Too bad, then, 'cause you're stuck with me."

"Only if the show does well," Kara said. "We have to have chemistry. That might be tough."

"I'm willing to work on it if you are." Chad walked toward Kara and placed his arms around her neck.

Kara wrapped her arms around Chad's waist, and it felt

natural. Perfect. Meant to be. "It won't be easy, working with you every day."

"Your family hanging around my family."

"Jonathon and Addy will probably be there too." Kara smiled.

"Probably."

"And I'm sure the network will make us do stuff together."

Chad stepped forward, his face just inches from Kara's. "We might have to act like we like each other. You know, for the good of the show."

"I'm willing to do that." Kara gazed into Chad's eyes. "For the show."

Chad took a step back, his hands on Kara's shoulders. "Did I say I hoped it would be you?"

"I think so." Kara smiled, her hands still on Chad's waist. "But you can say it again."

"I really hoped it would be you."

"God sure did some work to get me here."

"I was praying for you, you know. A lot." Chad picked up a piece of Kara's hair and held it in his hands. "I'm probably the reason you're here."

"So I voted you into *America's Next Star* and you prayed me into heaven."

Chad laughed and turned to walk back, his hand reaching for Kara's. "I definitely win."

"I wouldn't say that." Kara loved the feel of Chad's fingers in hers. "If you hadn't won *America's Next Star*, then you wouldn't be on this show. So, technically, it was all me."

"Oh really?"

"Well, it was all God. Then me."

"Then me?"

"Maybe you after Addy."

"So I'm third on this list?"

"Third sounds good." Kara squeezed his hand. "I don't want you getting a big head. You know how those big stars can get."

"Sure of themselves? Always thinking they're right?"

"Exactly." Kara nudged her shoulder into Chad's arm. "I'll protect you from that."

"Thanks. Glad to know you have my back."

"I definitely do."

Reading Group Guide

1. This story is loosely based on the story of Isaac and Rebekah in Genesis 24. What similarities did you see between that story and *Starring Me*?
2. Chad's parents were accused of being "overprotective." Do you agree with that assessment? Would you like to have parents like the Beacons? Why or why not?
3. Kara wanted, more than anything, to be an actress. Do you know someone who wants to be an actor/actress? Is that person like Kara?
4. Chad has never dated because he believes the purpose of dating is to get married. Early in the story, however, Kara argues that it's important to date lots of guys so you know which is your type. With whom do you agree? Why?
5. Kara was kind to Flora right from the start. Why do you think that is?
6. Did you suspect Jillian wasn't really a Christian? If so, why?
7. Chad and his family served the Miller family by helping them relocate. Addy took Kara to help at a homeless shelter. Have you and your friends or family ever been involved in any service projects? What were they? How did you benefit from helping others?

8. Chad struggled with being famous because he couldn't go many places without being noticed or mobbed. How would you feel if you were in his shoes?
9. Kara got serious about God when she realized her father might die. Have you ever been in a tough situation that forced you to think more seriously about what happens after we die? Have you had the opportunity to talk to someone in a situation like that?
10. How do you think the story would have ended if the doctor hadn't recommended the McKormicks move to Orlando?

Acknowledgments

I could not have finished this book without my amazing in-laws. That's right, *amazing* and *in-laws* in the same sentence. It happens. And I'm so grateful it happened to me! Like Chad, I prayed for my future spouse since I was thirteen, and boy, did God answer. Not only did I get a terrific, incredibly handsome husband, but he came with a terrific family as well. Twice a year, the whole gang comes down here to Tampa. It's kind of like the McKormick clan—lots of noise, lots of fun, and lots of food. This year, when the gang was down for spring break, I handed my kids off to their grandparents/aunts/uncles and waved good-bye. I had a deadline coming up and a lot of blank pages to fill. My in-laws, in true McGee fashion, kept my kids so entertained, they had no idea Mom was holed up in her room, immersed in Kara and Chad's story. The kids had a blast, and I was able to meet my deadline.

As always, a huge "shout-out" goes to my students at Citrus Park Christian School. The only thing I hate about my job is that every single year, students graduate and say good-bye. The good ones, though, always come back to visit (hint, hint).

This book wouldn't be in your hands without the immensely talented Thomas Nelson fiction team. From editing to marketing to the fabulous cover, these men and women are godly, professional, and lots of fun. I am honored to be part of this amazing team.

Julee Schwarzburg takes my mess of words and cleans them up, always with tact, grace, and smiley faces. Her input is invaluable.

My husband, Dave, and my three kids, Emma, Ellie, and Thomas, are the greatest gifts on earth. I thank God every day for the privilege of getting to go through life with them.

But as great as all these people are—and they are great—the real reason I write, that I live and breathe and do anything, is because of Jesus Christ. My prayer for you, my reader, is that you grow to know him better, to experience his love and grace and power in your life, and to know that our story is HIS story and that everything he writes is perfect.

"Anyone who enjoys reality television and a well-told story shouldn't hesitate to read this great book."

—*Romantic Times* review of *First Date*

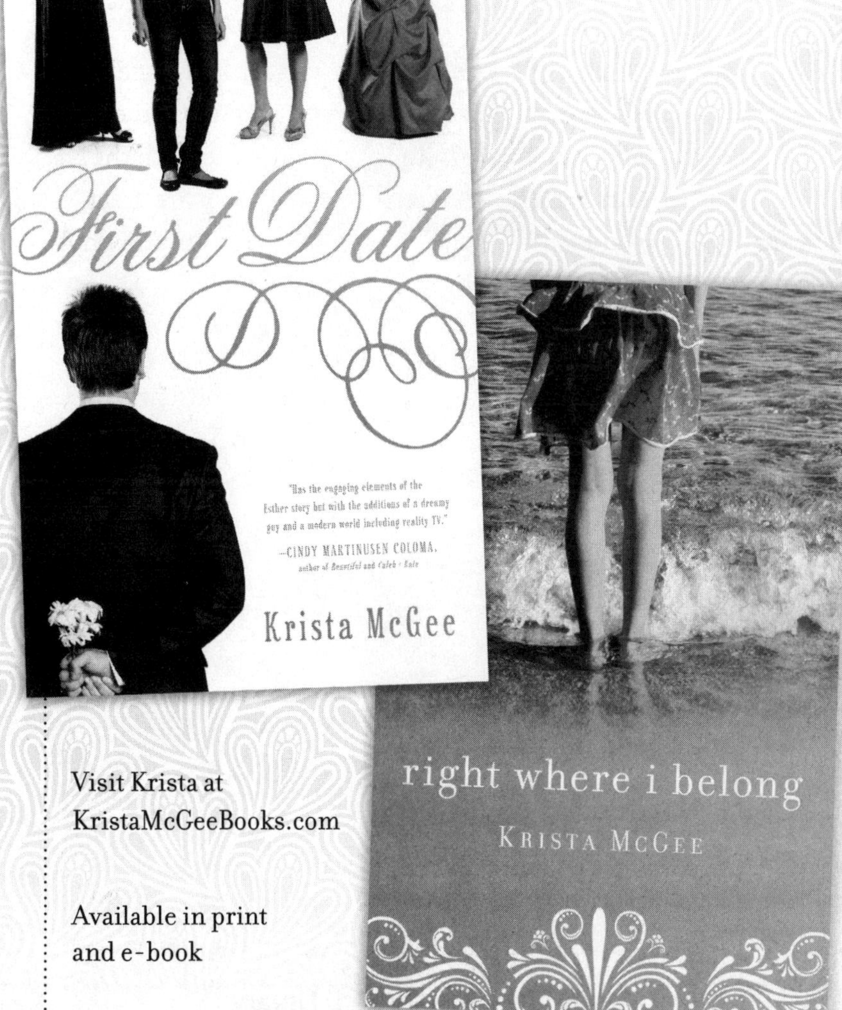

Visit Krista at
KristaMcGeeBooks.com

Available in print
and e-book

Available December 2012

9781401684891-A

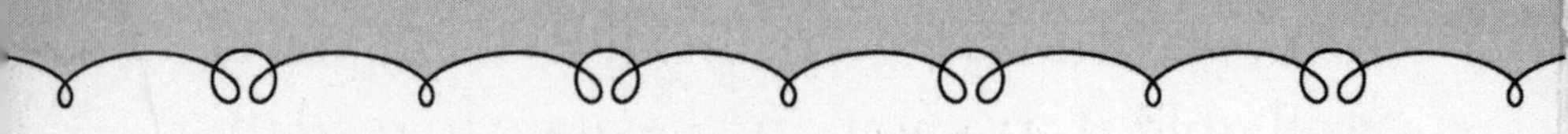

About the Author

Author photo by Amanda Allotta

KRISTA MCGEE writes for teens, teaches teens, and, more often than not, acts like a teen. Along with her husband and three kids, Krista has lived and ministered in Texas, Costa Rica, and Spain.